Jason Rohan

THE SWORD OF KUROMORI

EGMONT

EGMONT
We bring stories to life

First published in Great Britain in 2014 by Egmont UK Limited
The Yellow Building, 1 Nicholas Road, London W11 4AN

Text Copyright © 2014 Jason Rohan
The moral rights of the author have been asserted

ISBN 978 1 4052 7060 1

56953/1

www.egmont.co.uk

A CIP catalogue record for this title is available from the British Library

Printed and bound in Great Britain by the CPI Group

Stay safe online. Any website addresses listed in this book are correct at the time of going to print.
However, Egmont is not responsible for content hosted by third parties. Please be aware that
online content can be subject to change and websites can contain content that is unsuitable
for children. We advise that all children are supervised when using the internet.

MIX
Paper
FSC   FSC® C018306

EGMONT

Our story began over a century ago, when seventeen-year-old
Egmont Harald Petersen found a coin in the street. He was on
his way to buy a flyswatter, a small hand-operated printing
machine that he then set up in his tiny apartment.

The coin brought him such good luck that today Egmont has
offices in over 30 countries around the world. And that lucky
coin is still kept at the company's head offices in Denmark.

THE SWORD OF KUROMORI

For Christine, the treasure I went to Japan to find.

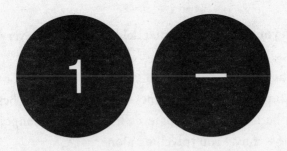

Kenny's fingers dug into the armrests of the aeroplane seat so tightly that his knuckles ached. The first time he had flown in a plane it had been an exciting adventure. Now, though, it was more of a chore.

The 747 lurched again and he felt his stomach float upwards before his weight settled back into the seat. It was like being on a slowed-down roller coaster, only a lot less fun.

Relax, Kenny told himself, *it's safer than driving. Try not to think about being strapped into a pressurised metal tube that weighs a thousand tonnes, is eleven kilometres above the ground and travelling at a thousand kilometres an hour. All perfectly safe.*

The airline steward, whose name badge read *Daniel Mayer*, rested on one knee in the aisle beside him and patted the boy's tensed arm. 'Nervous about flying?' he asked, with a practised smile.

Kenny shook his head, which wasn't easy with a stiffened neck. 'No,' he said through clenched teeth. 'Only about crashing. Why is it there's only turbulence when you serve food? Is that deliberate, to spill everyone's drinks?'

Dan smiled. 'Don't worry. I've flown this Seattle–Tokyo route a hundred times and I'm still here. Besides, we'll be there soon.' His eyes flicked to the empty seat beside Kenny. 'You travelling alone?'

Kenny nodded. 'Yeah, I'm meeting my dad. He works out there. I'm staying for the summer.'

'You don't sound too happy about it.'

Kenny shrugged. 'Well . . . it's complicated.'

Dan patted Kenny's arm again and rose to his feet. 'Is this your first time in Japan?'

The boy nodded.

'You're going to love it. It's an amazing place. Super high-tech on the one hand and super traditional on the other.'

'Kenny Blackwood?' said a female voice.

Kenny and the steward both looked up to see a Japanese flight attendant standing in the aisle, an envelope in her white-gloved hands. Her badge said *Naoko Iwamoto*.

'Seat 57C? Kenny Blackwood? Is that you?' she said again.

Kenny nodded.

'I was asked to give you this, before we land,' Naoko said and handed him the envelope.

Dan raised an eyebrow. 'Since when do we play mailman?' he muttered.

Naoko smiled at him and moved on.

Kenny turned the envelope over in his hands; it was blank, sealed, but he could feel the edges of a folded sheet of paper inside and a small cylindrical object, about the size and shape of a lipstick.

Weird, he thought. *Who'd be sending me a letter on a plane? More to the point, who would even know where to find me?*

He slit open the envelope using the plastic knife from his meal tray and took out a single typed page, which he began to read:

To my dearest grandson, Kenneth,

Yes, I know you hate being called 'Kenneth' but it could have been worse – your grandmother wanted to name you 'Aloysius'.

If all is well, you will be reading this upon an aero plane high above the Pacific Ocean, making your final approach to Japan, where I have arranged for you to spend the summer with your father.

I remember what it was like for me, travelling alone to a strange and unfamiliar place, but, once I adjusted to the local customs, I found it a place of magical wonder. I suspect that you too may be embarking on a similar journey of self-discovery.

If I have any advice for you, it is this: believe in yourself; trust your feelings; do what is right, especially when it is most difficult; and always carry a cucumber near fresh water.

With all my love,

Your grandfather, Lawrence

Kenny scowled at the paper. His grandfather was in his nineties, a former Professor of Oriental Studies, now retired and living in Buckinghamshire. He was also famously eccentric, but this was bizarre, by anyone's standards.

After turning the paper over, Kenny looked in the envelope again. Inside was a small square of translucent paper, about the size of a large postage stamp, and a small wooden whistle.

He took the paper out first and held it up to the overhead light. Some more writing was on it, which read:

Make a copy of the letter. Use the whistle only in emergencies. Now eat this note.

Kenny had to smile. His grandfather had always

been fond of mysteries, puzzles and codes. In fact, the previous summer, he had insisted Kenny fly out from the States to join him on an elaborate treasure hunt.

This was obviously another sophisticated game he was playing. Kenny shrugged to himself, picked up his phone and took a photograph of the letter. He then nibbled one end of the pearly paper. It dissolved on his tongue like a wafer. *Rice paper*, he thought, before popping the rest into his mouth.

That left the whistle. It was a short length of bamboo, with a slot to blow through, a square hole on the top and a drilled hole at the end. Underneath was a carving:

狸

Kenny poked his nose up over the headrest to check that no one was looking and then gave a gentle blow on the pipe. *Pfft.* No sound came out. Kenny tried again, this time blowing harder. *Pffftt.* As before, all he could hear was his own breath rushing through the tube. Thinking it must be a trick, he gave it one final blow, with all the force his lungs could muster. *Pfffff–*

He stopped, mid-puff, as a furious knocking came from the overhead storage compartment. Kenny froze, the whistle to his lips, and listened. The knocking stopped, to be replaced by a scratching noise from the same place. *That is totally freaky.* He felt goosebumps rising on his arms as he sat there, unsure of what to do.

The cabin address system pinged, making Kenny jump, and the purser said, 'We are now commencing our final approach to Narita International Airport.'

As passengers took this cue to move around, making last visits to the bathroom, stowing bags in the overhead bins and under seats, stretching and yawning, Kenny stood and stared at the door to the locker above his seat. He wanted to open it, to look inside, but he was afraid of what he might find. Instead, he rapped twice on the door. Instantly, a *tap-tap* came in reply. He took a deep breath, opened the door slightly and peered in.

Staring back at him were two round, liquid eyes. Kenny yelled in surprise and fell backwards, landing on an extremely large lady who was munching on a packet of peanuts.

'Watch what you're doing!' the woman said, as peanuts sprayed across the cabin.

'I'm very sorry, ma'am,' Kenny mumbled, backing away from her, but keeping his distance from the half-opened locker.

Dan, the steward, reappeared. 'Can I help anyone?' he said.

Kenny pointed at the overhead bin. 'There's a . . . There's a . . . thing, in there,' he said.

'A thing? What sort of thing? Has something happened to your bag?'

'No, some kind of . . . animal,' Kenny said, his voice small.

'Isn't it a bit late for pranks? Listen, I know you've had a long flight, but we're almost there now and you'll soon be off the plane,' Dan said.

'I'm telling the truth,' Kenny said, his voice shaking. 'There's an animal in there. Really. I saw it.'

'Animals aren't allowed on flights,' the peanut lady said. 'Everyone knows that. I've never heard such garbage in my life.'

'OK, OK,' Dan said, reaching up for the handle. 'Let's have a look in here and see what all the fuss is about.'

Kenny stood behind the steward, peering round him. The door swung upwards and there, sprawled in the wide bay, leaning against Kenny's backpack with legs crossed, was a fat, furry animal, about the size of a badger. Its face was foxlike, with a long narrow nose, and its thick hair was reddish-brown. Its legs were black and the dark fur ran up its chest and around the snout to circle the eyes.

'There,' Dan said, 'nothing in there, just your bag.'

Kenny's mouth fell open. 'Are you . . .? But-but can't you see . . .?'

The creature, whatever it was, waved a paw at Kenny and placed a finger over its pursed lips. It then yawned and farted. Kenny stared before whipping his head round to see his fellow passengers all watching him.

'Does . . . does anyone else . . . see *that*?' he asked, struggling to form the words and pointing at the furry creature.

'Kid, there's nothing in there,' said the peanut lady,

measuring each word.

'Poor thing, he must be really tired if he's hallucinating,' someone said.

'Probably on drugs,' another voice added. 'Kids these days, eh?'

'Oh, come *on*. Is this some kind of joke?' Kenny said, his voice rising and eyes searching face after face. 'Are you really all telling me that you can't see that . . . thing in there?'

Rows of blank faces answered Kenny's question before the passengers lost interest and returned to their pre-landing activities.

'Look, young man, I think it's time you returned to your seat and got ready for landing,' Dan said, his voice gentle but firm. 'You've had your fun, but now the joke's getting a bit old, OK?'

Kenny nodded, numbly, and took one last look at the furry creature snuggling against his backpack. It blew him a kiss before Dan closed the door on it. He slumped back into his seat, his head spinning, and fastened his seat belt.

Naoko, the Japanese attendant, came along the aisle. She reached over to take his rubbish and said quietly, 'That thing you saw. Was it large and hairy, with black eyes like a raccoon?'

Kenny nodded. 'Yeah, how did you . . .?'

Naoko smiled. 'I didn't see it, either.' She winked at him.

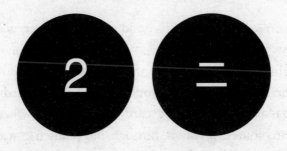

Kenny slumped back in his seat, his arms crossed, and ignored the curious looks directed his way. This was not what he was expecting at all. It was bad enough that his grandfather had sent him to Japan of all places, but to spend the next twelve weeks with his dad was worse. And now, to top it all, some weird animal was stalking him.

He closed his eyes, picturing his room back in the Oregon International School. His room-mate Chad would be home by now in Boston. He would be off soon to Namibia for a safari with his family, the lucky git. Kenny sighed. How nice it must be to have a family.

The remainder of the flight passed uneventfully and when Kenny went to collect his backpack from the overhead storage, the animal, whatever it was, had gone; he must have imagined it after all.

He made his way down the walkway into the spacious, ultra-modern terminal building and on towards immigration control. He was feeling much happier to be back on solid ground. His good mood, however, was not to last.

When his turn came, the uniformed immigration officer beckoned Kenny forward and he handed over his passport and landing card. The official swiped the claret-coloured passport through the biometric scanner, stopped, examined the computer screen intently and then swiped the document again. He waved for his supervisor and the two men spoke briefly. Kenny shifted his weight and thrust his hands into his pockets.

The supervisor inspected the passport photo and compared it to Kenny's face.

'What is your name, please?' the officer said.

'It's Kenny, sir. Kenneth Blackwood.'

'How old are you?'

'I'm fifteen.'

'You are travelling alone?'

Kenny nodded, wondering where the questions were leading.

The official tapped a finger on the landing card. 'You have British passport, but this address is in America. Is that right?'

'Yes. I was born in England, but I moved to the States when I was eight. My mum was American, so I have dual nationality. Is that a problem?'

'This address is not a house,' the officer said, reading the card.

Kenny sighed. 'No, it's a boarding school. It's where I live.'

The official raised an eyebrow. 'Boarding school? Like Harry Po–'

'No. Nothing like him. He loves his school.'

The senior officer studied Kenny, as if seeking the source of the boy's sudden anger. 'What is the purpose of your visit to Japan?' he asked.

'My dad's a professor at Tokyo University. I'm spending the summer with him.'

The officer nodded at each answer. 'I'm afraid we have more questions for you,' he said. 'Please, come with me.'

'Is this going to take long?' Kenny couldn't help saying. 'It's just that my dad's waiting for me and –'

'Come. Please.'

The officials ushered Kenny past his gawking fellow passengers, including the peanut lady.

'See? I knew he was on drugs,' she said smugly.

Kenny followed the officials to a small office.

'Please, sit,' the senior official said, gesturing towards one of two hard chairs.

Kenny sat and drummed his fingers on the table while the two men departed. The door opened and another man entered. He wore a dark suit, sunglasses and his raven hair was slicked back.

'Mr Blackwood,' the newcomer said, extending his hand to shake. 'My name is Sato.' He slid a business card across the table and sat opposite Kenny. 'I am here to help you. You can trust me.'

'My counsellor says I have trust issues.' Kenny chewed his lip. 'What's this all about, Mr Sato? I thought I didn't need a visa to visit Japan.'

'You are Ken Blackwood, yes? Son of Charles Blackwood and grandson of Lawrence Blackwood?'

'Yes, that's right,' Kenny said, unable to hide his surprise. 'How do you . . .?'

'Your grandfather is a great man. A hero to some Japanese people. Did you know that?'

Kenny blinked. 'Uh, no, sir. Not really.'

Sato leaned back and steepled his fingers. 'I am not sure how much of this I should tell you, if any, but I shall try to help you and you will help me, yes?'

From the corner of his eye, Kenny glimpsed a huge shadow looming over the frosted-glass door.

'Your *ojiisan*, your grandfather, came to Japan after World War Two, yes?'

Kenny's eyes flicked back to Sato. 'He did tell me that, yeah.'

'And he told you he was here to help the Japanese people recover, after the war?'

'Something like that.'

Sato smiled. 'Your grandfather, I'm sorry to say, was a liar, as well as a thief.'

Before Kenny could respond, there was a light knock at the door.

'Enter,' Sato said.

The door swung open and in came another official, followed by an enormous figure, who had to stoop to enter the office. Although the thing was wearing a tailored suit, it was easily three metres tall and heavily muscled. This was alarming in itself, but what really troubled Kenny was the brick-red skin, the tusks growing up from the lower jaw and the two horns on its head. He jumped up, grabbed his chair to wield as a weapon and cowered against the wall.

'Taro! *Ike*!' barked Sato, pointing to the door. The ogre-like creature bowed and hurried out.

'Mr Blackwood, please be seated. You are safe,' Sato said, coming over to help Kenny to his feet.

'What . . . was that . . . thing?' Kenny asked, his voice hoarse and shaky.

'Tell me what you saw.'

'Oh, not again! Don't tell me you didn't see it.' Kenny's heart was still thumping against his ribs.

Sato tapped his sunglasses. 'No, I saw it. I just want to be sure you saw the same thing.'

'What, that big red horned thing? Like a cross between Shrek and Hellboy.'

Sato arched an eyebrow. 'So, you have the Gift of Sight? Interesting. I thought *gaijin* cannot see *oni*.'

'*Oni*? Is that what it's called?'

'I call him Taro, but yes, he is *oni*.'

'And what's a guy-jean?'

13

'You. An outsider, a foreigner.' Sato sat down again. 'Mr Blackwood, what you have just seen is something that most people never see. You have looked behind the curtain and peeped at the hidden world beyond.'

Kenny rubbed his face with his hands. 'I don't understand.'

'You do not have to. Your grandfather has sent you here to finish his work. Of that, I am sure. I am here to help you.'

'Finish his work? What work? I'm just here to see my dad. Can't I just go now?'

'Empty your pockets, please. Do you have anything from your grandfather? Anything at all?'

'Wait. You brought that *oni* thing in here. Why?'

'Call it a test. The fact that you can see Taro tells me everything I need to know. Now, empty your pockets, please.'

'And what if I don't?'

'Then Taro will empty them for you.' Sato inspected his manicured fingernails. 'I can wait.'

Swearing under his breath, Kenny placed the contents of his pockets on to the table: a set of keys attached to a Newcastle United key ring, some loose change, a half-empty packet of chewing gum, his phone, a pack of trading cards secured with a rubber band, and the wooden whistle.

'Is that everything?' Sato asked, rising to his feet again.

Kenny nodded and then stiffened as Sato approached

him. Something about the man set Kenny's teeth on edge, something not quite right, but he couldn't decide what.

'Stand up, raise your arms,' Sato said and patted Kenny down. Paper rustled as his hand pressed against the boy's ribcage. Sato reached into Kenny's jacket and removed the envelope from the aeroplane. 'Something you forgot?' he said, taking out the letter, his eyes skimming over the writing.

'Hey!' Kenny protested. 'That's private. You can't read other people's –'

Sato's free hand drew a shape in the air and Kenny's voice vanished as suddenly as if an off button had been pressed. Bewildered, Kenny continued to protest; his mouth moved, he felt air pass over his vocal cords, but no sound came out. He tried screaming, but he was like a character in a silent movie.

Sato read the letter a third time and then addressed Kenny, a puzzled frown on his face. 'This is a strange letter. Not very informative. I am going to make a copy of it. Please stay here, for your own safety. Do not try to leave as Taro will be guarding the door.' He smiled, without warmth. 'You can shout for help if you want.'

Sato tossed the envelope on to the table and left the room. The hulking shadow of the *oni* moved in front of the door.

Kenny's mind was racing. None of this made any sense. Barely twelve hours ago, he was a kid looking forward to a trip to the Far East. Now he was stuck in some kind of waking nightmare, complete with monsters that most people couldn't see.

He reached for his phone and swore silently when he saw that there was no signal. Slipping it back into his pocket, he gathered up the rest of his belongings. The last item he picked up was the envelope and, when he did, something rolled out from underneath it: the whistle.

What was it that Grandad had said? *Use the whistle only in emergencies*. Ridiculous, but then again, if this wasn't an emergency, what was?

Kenny blew on the whistle as hard as he could. As before, no sound came out. He was about to blow again when he heard a scuffling sound overhead. He looked up and saw the corner of a ceiling tile lift up. A snout poked through, followed by two sparkling eyes.

Kenny took an involuntary step back at the sight of the fat, furry creature from the aeroplane. It was real and it was watching him. Kenny stared as it lowered its hindquarters through the gap, dangled by its arms and then plopped awkwardly on to the table. It stood up on its back legs and reached its arms out, as if asking for a hug.

Not knowing what else to do, Kenny picked it up. The creature's quick paws loosened four buttons on his shirt and it slithered under his clothing.

'Hey!' Kenny mouthed silently. He was about to wrestle the thing loose when it shifted and seemed to melt, flowing round his abdomen and flattening out like a pancake. In seconds, it was wrapped round Kenny in a wide furry band. Hearing footsteps approaching, he quickly redid the buttons, just as Taro stepped aside and Sato came back in.

'There has been a change of plan,' Sato said. 'You are now under arrest and will be taken to Tokyo for further questioning.'

'But I haven't done anything!' Kenny tried to yell, his lips shaping the silent words.

Two policemen entered the room and, moments later, Kenny found himself being escorted through the terminal, handcuffed to an officer.

They stopped outside Narita Airport Terminal One, where two police cars and a pair of motorcycle cops were waiting. Sato climbed into the first car and Kenny was bundled into the second. Sirens wailing, the cars pulled out and headed towards Tokyo, the city lights glittering in the distance.

Kenny looked back at the receding terminal. His father would be in there, waiting for him, not knowing what had happened. This was crazy. He'd only just arrived and already he was Public Enemy Number One. There had to be a simple explanation for this. There had to be.

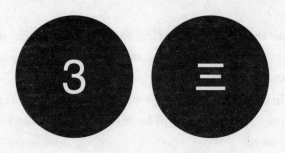

The police convoy pulled out on to the short connecting highway which led away from the airport, before joining the six-lane Higashi-Kanto Expressway. Low humpbacked hills slunk in the distance and the setting sun seared the sky a hot neon-pink.

Kenny stared out of the window, his mind a whirl. He knew his grandfather had once lived and worked in Japan, but that was over half a century ago. How could anything that had happened then be affecting his grandson now? What did Sato mean when he had said that Grandad had sent Kenny to finish his work? And what had happened to his voice? How could Sato just turn off someone's speech?

Kenny was reminded of the animal hiding under his shirt as it shifted its grip, digging its claws into his ribs and making him wince.

The driver muttered something in a low warning tone and the police officer handcuffed to Kenny whirled round in his seat to examine the view from the back window. Sensing something was wrong, Kenny looked back too.

'*Honto, da!*' the police officer said, pointing.

Kenny watched, seeing nothing unusual, until a black object swung out from behind a heavy truck and sped towards the police car. It was a motorcycle, black, shiny and sleek, moving so fast that it had shot silently past them on the inside lane before Kenny had registered it. Pressing himself against the window, Kenny watched as the motorbike swept past Sato's car and hurtled towards the two police motorcycles in front.

The driver snatched up his police radio and started speaking quickly into it. The police officer beside Kenny leaned forward, nose twitching, and pressed against the front seat in his eagerness to see what was happening.

The motorcyclist was clad in black leathers and was wearing a helmet with a mirrored visor. He slowed momentarily as he passed the police riders and then sped out in front of them again. Reaching into a side pannier, he took out a handful of small objects and scattered them on the road behind him.

There was a bang, then another, and Kenny realised the sound was tyres blowing out on one of the police motorcycles. It flipped on to its nose and somersaulted across the road. The other motorbike swerved to avoid it. Sato's car, close behind, braked hard and skidded as the stricken bike slewed towards it in a cascade of sparks.

The driver of Kenny's car cried out and wrenched the steering wheel as Sato's car loomed instantly larger before them. The nose of the police car veered to the left and clipped the back of the squad car in front, shattering the brake lights, but the swerve brought it straight on a collision course with the wreck of the police motorcycle.

Kenny barely had time to grab the seat in front before the car hit the motorbike with a bone-jarring crunch, the front wheels lifting and the underside of the vehicle screeching over the mangled remains. With a jolt, the car scraped over the bike and its four wheels hit asphalt again.

Cars behind slammed on their brakes and, looking back, Kenny saw bits of broken metal and glass glinting across the highway, rapidly fading into the distance. In front, Sato's car sped up to catch the motorbikes. Kenny's driver floored the accelerator too, shouting into his radio mike while he did so.

The remaining police motorcycle raced after the rider in black, weaving in and out of cars and trucks. Kenny craned his neck to follow the chase. The black motorbike slowed and waited for the police bike to draw alongside. The rider then jumped up, keeping both hands on the handlebars, and lashed out with an outstretched boot, catching the police rider on his helmet. His balance thrown off, the bike slipped from underneath the officer, and both vehicle and rider clattered to the hard shoulder.

Sato, riding in the car in front, sprang into action. He punched open the glove compartment and snatched up a short stubby sub-machine gun. He smashed the passenger window with the stock and, wrapping his hand round the seat belt as an anchor, he sat up on the side. He levelled the gun and fired off several short sharp bursts at the black motorcycle in front.

The black rider saw the tarmac explode into a bouquet of tiny craters around him and swung in front of an eighteen-wheeler truck for cover. Kenny watched in growing disbelief as Sato urged the police car forward, to overtake the truck, and fired off several more rounds of bullets in the direction of the black bike. The rider pressed himself flat against the motorcycle, squeezed the brakes and jerked the handlebars. The bike swooped close to the ground and slipped under the moving truck and out the other side.

Sato's car slowed down, waited for the truck to roar past and once again accelerated to catch up with the rider in black. The motorcycle swung out to the right; the rider reached for something on his back and then slammed on his brakes.

Kenny saw a long black smear of fishtailing tyres, a puff of rubber dust and the flash of a sword as the police car zoomed past the motorbike. The barrel of Sato's gun fell in two and the rider thrust the curved blade back into the scabbard on his back before picking up speed once more.

Sato, still perched on the car door, drew something in the air with his free hand. The motorcycle swerved and swung from side to side, as if dodging unseen obstacles. Sato then drew a larger pattern and a huge wall of flame, some six metres high, erupted across the width of the road. The motorcyclist gunned the engine and shot through the flames, unharmed.

Kenny's driver yelled and stamped on the brake. Nothing happened. He pumped his foot again as they advanced towards the wall of fire. Kenny threw an arm over his eyes and screamed silently. The police officer handcuffed at his side prodded him and giggled in relief which made Kenny look up. The flames had completely vanished and they were still speeding after Sato's car and the mysterious rider in black.

Sato reached up again to draw in the air, but a flash of metal landed on his outstretched arm: a grappling hook, attached to a thin line – and the other end was in the firm grip of the black rider. Standing up on the footrests, the rider pulled with all his strength. Sato just had time to scream before he was yanked out of the speeding police car and bounced along the road.

The rider let go of the line, looked back once and then raced to catch up with the police car. Kenny saw Sato rise to his feet, unhurt, and throw his tattered jacket on the ground in disgust.

The driver again stamped on the brake pedal, but it was loose. He looked at Kenny in the rear-view mirror and shrugged apologetically. '*Dameh da,*' he said.

Up ahead, the black rider pulled alongside Sato's police car. He lobbed a small canister in through the passenger window and moved clear. There was a flash and white smoke filled the car. The driver immediately braked, pulling the car on to the hard shoulder so that he and the other police officers inside could burst free from the choking fumes and fall to their knees, retching.

Kenny's mouth was dry, his pulse was racing and his chest was tight. Here he was, trapped in a police car without a voice, careening along at eighty kilometres per hour with no brakes. And, to top it all, it seemed like he was being hunted by a mad ninja on a motorbike who had just totalled three police vehicles and was coming to finish the job.

The driver pumped the brake pedal one last time before giving up. 'No brakes,' he shouted to Kenny. 'You must jump before crash. *Gambatte, ne?*' And with that, his features melted away and his empty uniform sagged on to the seat.

Kenny stared in mute shock. A striped, furry nose poked from the trouser waistband and a brown badger shrugged out of the clothes, clawed open the door and dived out on to the road, clear of the speeding car.

'*Okubyomono!*' shouted the police officer next to Kenny. He jumped forward to hold the steering wheel steady with his free hand; the other tugged at the handcuff anchoring him to Kenny, until his wrist stretched like putty and the hand slipped out.

Kenny had completely forgotten about the creature wrapped round his middle until he felt it now loosen its hold and begin to grow thicker as it unflattened itself. It oozed out from under his shirt and dropped to the floor of the squad car, just as the black motorcycle drew up alongside, its speed matching the car's, and took up position by Kenny's door. The rider drew a symbol in the air and Kenny felt a twitch in his throat. Before he could wonder about this, he saw that the rider had unsheathed the sword again and was taking aim at him through the window.

Kenny yelled and hurled himself across the back seat as the sword came down. There was a *clang* and the door fell away completely, cut from its hinges. It cartwheeled down the road behind them.

'Not good!' shouted the police officer steering the car.

Kenny looked up and saw a bright row of lights across the road in front: toll gates. In about twenty seconds, the car was going to smash into the waiting traffic ahead. He had to get out quickly.

The furry animal evidently had the same idea as it was now jumping up and down, tugging Kenny's collar and pointing in the direction of the black motorcycle. Kenny glanced up and saw that the rider was holding out a hand, gloved fingers beckoning him to take hold.

'No way!' he cried and then realised that his voice had filled the car. His voice! It was back, and that meant the rider had– There was no time for that.

'Trust me!' the rider said, his voice filtered through a speaker.

Kenny saw the line of parked cars looming closer. There were mere seconds left. He grabbed his backpack lying on the seat beside him, scrambled across the car and tried not to look at the gritty blur of speeding tarmac below. He reached for the outstretched hand. The bike wobbled, moving out of reach. Kenny slipped and almost fell. He steadied himself and reached out again. The rider's strong grip closed round his and Kenny was about to jump when he felt a sharp tug on his jacket. The police officer was holding on tightly and pulling him back.

'You, prisoner!' the officer yelled. 'Under arrest!'

'No! Let go!' Kenny shouted.

The line of tollbooths grew larger and a truck was parked directly in front.

Kenny saw a flash of red-brown fur and the police officer shrieked as the animal sank its teeth into his arm. His grip loosened, Kenny jumped and the motorcyclist swung him on to the pillion. The bike peeled away from the police car which ploughed into the back of the truck and exploded.

Kenny stared numbly as the flames licked the back of the trailer, shocked at how close he had come to a fiery end. A blur of movement drew his eye and he saw the furry creature bounding after him. The bike slowed and the animal scampered aboard, its fur smoking, and tucked itself between Kenny and the rider.

The motorcycle slipped through a toll gate and moved silently towards Tokyo.

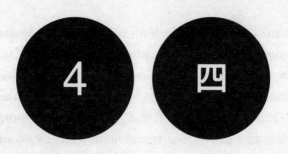

Kenny kept his arms around the leather-clad rider, with the furry animal pressed warm against his belly. He was tired, but his mind was abuzz with too many questions – and there was something weird about the motorbike, but he was too sleepy to pinpoint what it was. Still, he was fairly sure that neither the odd creature nor the rider meant him any harm, not yet at least, so that was something.

From time to time, he opened his heavy eyes to see road signs flash overhead in Japanese and English, plus bright, shining skyscrapers in the near distance; once, he even thought he glimpsed an orange and white painted Eiffel Tower lit up against the darkening sky. The only thing he was sure about was that the bike was keeping to the back roads.

At one point, the rider stopped and pulled over at the sound of approaching sirens, but when it became clear that the police cars weren't stopping, they resumed their journey.

After what seemed to Kenny like more than an hour, the

motorcycle slowed and circled a large plot of land protected by a high stone wall. Satisfied that the way was clear, the bike approached the iron gates, which were ornamented with two fighting dragons, claws raking at one another. A man in a dark suit watched the bike draw closer and signalled to another to open the gates. Sliding silently on well-oiled runners, the dragons withdrew from their brawl.

The bike glided in and eased up the long driveway towards the magnificent house at the centre of the plot. Kenny stirred himself enough to see gracefully curved gable roofs, black wooden beams, slate-coloured tiles and soft light filtering out through the windows.

Parking the bike to one side, the rider dismounted and strode towards the main doors.

'Hey! Wait up,' Kenny called. 'Where am I? Who are you?'

The rider disappeared into the house.

'Great. My turn to be invisible,' Kenny muttered.

The furry creature slithered from the bike and waddled after the rider. Kenny climbed off the seat, winced, and squatted to loosen the stiffness in his legs and the numbness in his backside. With both hands on his lower back, he flexed his hips. Feeling something tugging at his leg, he looked down to see the small animal impatiently pointing towards the house.

'OK, I get the idea. Let's go see what this is all about,' Kenny said, and he followed the creature through the open front door.

The hallway inside was softly lit by recessed lighting. The walls were papered in sage green and on one hung a scroll with large Chinese characters written upon it. There was no sign of the biker, but a huge Japanese man stood in the entrance, holding out a pair of white slippers in his plate-sized hands.

Looking down, Kenny saw that he was standing in a kind of shallow pit. The biker had left his boots there, neatly placed side by side, the toes pointing to the door. *Small feet*, Kenny thought, before he shrugged, kicked off his trainers and took the slippers from the giant of a man.

'Thank you,' Kenny said. 'I don't suppose you're going to tell me what –'

The big man turned and gestured for Kenny to follow.

'I guess not,' Kenny finished. He pulled on the slippers, stepped up on to the wooden floor and followed the huge servant into the house.

His guide led him to a screen door and slid it open. Beyond was a spacious room furnished only with a low table and a cushion on the floor in front of it. The man ushered Kenny inside and then left him.

The first thing Kenny did was take out his phone. He was about to call his father when he noticed that the signal reading was again at zero. *How can there be no signal in the middle of Tokyo?* he thought, scowling at the screen. *For a smartphone, this thing's pretty stupid.*

He plonked himself down on the edge of the table and rubbed his burning eyes. This was not exactly the welcome to Japan he'd been expecting. After a long flight, all he wanted was a hot shower, a proper meal and maybe even a chat with his dad. Instead, he'd been arrested, interrogated, confronted by a horned monster, caught up in a high-speed car chase, almost killed and now kidnapped by a maniac ninja. And that was just in the past two hours.

His fingers idly danced over the touchscreen, calling up images of home – his new home in Oregon and his real home, back in London. It was funny; even after seven years in America, he still thought of England as home. His room-mate Chad would tease him about this, both for his accent and his manners. 'Stop living in the past, Kenneth old bean,' he would say. 'Let it go, dude. Today is a gift, that's why it's called the present.'

Kenny stopped when an old photo filled the screen. He hadn't been thinking about it; it was just that he always seemed to find this picture when he was feeling low, which was every other day lately.

A five-year-old Kenny grinned back at him, a squidge of pink tongue poking out through the gap in his bottom teeth. Kneeling beside him, with a protective arm around his waist, was his mother, Sarah. She was still beautiful, despite the hollowed-out cheeks and missing eyebrows brought on by all the radiotherapy she'd been having at the time. His father, standing behind, was cropped from the photo, left only as a pair of trouser legs.

The door slid open again and the big man came in,

holding a lacquered tray. With surprising grace, he set the tray on the table and withdrew once more.

Kenny hadn't realised how hungry he was until the tempting smell of fried food drifted towards him. He jumped on the cushion and knelt to inspect the meal. On the tray, carefully arranged, was a bewildering variety of small plates, bowls and dishes. Some were round, some oval, some hexagonal; some were plain, others floral; a few were striped. Inside each was a tiny portion – no more than a single bite – of a different food. Kenny recognised something fried in batter, but that was all he could make out. In one bowl was a clear soup with some leaves swimming in it and a thick layer of sediment on the bottom. Another held what looked like an omelette squashed into a cube. On a plate was something resembling a pink and white eraser. A leaf folded into a samosa-like triangle sat beside a bowl of sticky, slimy blobs.

Kenny's appetite wavered, but he finally settled on a deep-fried battered prawn. It was delicious – firm, sweet and crispy – and he could easily have devoured a dozen more, but there was only the one. He sipped a steaming, bitter-tasting, dirt-coloured drink in a cup and sat back to wonder where he was and what was happening to him.

His thoughts were interrupted by a scratching sound at the door. Cautiously, Kenny opened it a crack to peep out. A furry paw inserted itself into the gap and slid the door open wide enough for a fat little body to squeeze through. The now familiar creature waddled over to the tray, picked up a pair of chopsticks and began to tuck in.

'You have got to be kidding,' Kenny said to the animal. 'Of all the weird stuff I've seen today . . . Did someone train you to do that?'

He sat and watched, amazed at the easy manner in which the creature transferred food from plate to mouth. When it had finished, it belched loudly and pushed the tray away.

The door slid open again and the huge man motioned for Kenny to follow him. He led the way down a short passage and knelt before another sliding door, which he opened. Kenny went inside and stopped dead in his tracks.

The far wall opposite was a bank of flat television screens, easily ten deep and twenty across. Each was tuned to a different channel and Kenny could see international news bulletins, stock-market updates, documentaries, quiz shows and sporting events among the competing images.

Standing in front of the screens, with hands clasped behind his back, and his shape silhouetted by the ever-changing light, was a Japanese man wearing a white suit. He watched the chaotic medley of programmes for a few more minutes before abruptly snapping his fingers. All of the pictures went dark at once and a large screen slid into position to cover the televisions completely.

The man turned towards Kenny and nodded once to acknowledge him. 'Kuromori-*san*,' he said, 'welcome to my humble home.'

For a moment, Kenny wondered who the man was addressing. He looked around, but he was on his own. 'Um, my name is Kenny . . . sir. Kenny Blackwood. I live in Portland, Oregon –'

'Please, sit.' The man gestured towards an elegant mahogany table with high-backed chairs. 'I apologise for the . . . unpleasantness of your arrival to our shores. I had hoped to meet you under more hospitable circumstances, but events overtook me. I am Harashima.'

'I need to call my dad,' Kenny said, taking out his phone.

'In 1942, your grandfather, Lawrence Blackwood, was recruited into British Intelligence because of his skills in the Japanese language.'

'Say what?' Kenny's eyes narrowed. 'You're the second person to mention my grandad since . . . And that Sato guy called him a thief. And did you just say "British Intelligence"? Are you saying . . . he was a spy?'

'No, his role was translation and code-breaking, to begin with. In 1945, at the request of the United States government, your grandfather came to Japan to assist the Americans during the period of Occupation.' Harashima spat the last word as if it stung his mouth. 'This was a time of terrible suffering in Japan and many people were forced to sell family treasures to survive. Some of these treasures were more . . . significant than they seemed.'

'Uh, I really don't know why you're –'

'Kuromori-*san*, your grandfather rescued some of

these treasures and hid them away. He sent you here to help find one of them.'

'No, he sent me here to spend time with my dad, that's all.'

Harashima arched an eyebrow. 'Really? Then why did he ask us to keep an eye on you after you arrived?'

Kenny opened his mouth to protest, but then forced it closed. 'Er, I can see . . . *things*. Is that a part of this?'

'What sort of things?' Harashima's eyes shone with interest.

'Well, there was this raccoon thing on the plane, who seems to live here – he's in the next room – and this huge *oni* thing at the airport.' Kenny's cheeks burned. 'I know it sounds stupid.'

The man smiled and his body relaxed slightly. 'Yes,' he said, 'that is, as you say, a part of this.'

A huge wave of relief flooded through Kenny, pushing out more words. It was all still weird, but at least this man was taking him seriously.

'Really? This guy, Sato, at the airport, he turned my voice off. And, after, when this ninja biker dude was chasing us, he made fire. And this police guy turned into a badger. What's that all about?'

Harashima looked away and pursed his lips. 'The word you would use in English isn't one I would choose, but I cannot think of a suitable alternative, so "magic" will have to suffice.'

Kenny's eyebrows shot upwards. 'Magic?'

'Please think of a better word to explain what you saw.'

Kenny ignored him, his face reddening again. 'Where is that biker guy, anyway? You can ask him. The one who brought me here.'

'After rescuing you and saving your life, yes?'

'I wouldn't have been in any danger if he hadn't come along in the first place.'

Harashima smiled again. 'Kuromori-*san*, you would be dead by now if my . . . associate had not helped you. But yes, I should introduce you.' He clapped his hands once and the biker came in, still wearing the helmet with the mirrored visor. Without his boots, the rider was five centimetres shorter than Kenny.

'Kenny Blackwood,' Harashima said, 'please say hello to my daughter, Kiyomi.'

Kenny stood weakly as the biker removed the helmet and shook out her long black hair.

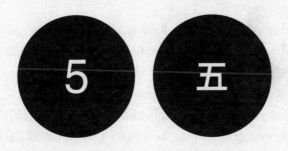

'You're a girl?' Kenny hadn't meant it to sound like an accusation, but that was how it came out.

'Last time I checked, yes,' Kiyomi said, smiling at his awkwardness. Her almond eyes looked directly into his and he blushed, turning away.

Harashima cleared his throat and addressed Kenny. 'Your grandfather gave you a message, did he not?'

'How could you possibly know about that?'

'Poyo told me,' Kiyomi said, setting her motorcycle helmet on the table. The visor faced Kenny and he saw his own distorted reflection looking in bewilderment back at him.

'Who's Poyo?' Kenny was floundering; too many new things were happening to him at once and he felt the urge to scream, just to drown it all out.

'This is Poyo,' Kiyomi said and the furry animal squeezed through the doorway and scampered up to her. She knelt and gathered it up in her arms. 'Ooh, you're getting fat,' she cooed. 'Is Poyo missing Mama?'

'That thing told you?' Kenny said, struggling to keep up.

'Mm-hm,' Kiyomi nodded, tickling Poyo under his chin.

'The message, if you please,' her father insisted.

'I don't have it,' Kenny shot back. 'That Sato bloke took it from me. He's still got it.'

'Did you make a copy?' Harashima said quietly. 'If I know your grandfather, he would have allowed for this.'

'A copy? No, with wha–?' Kenny's voice trailed away. 'Wait. Yes. I do have a copy. It's on here.' He held out his phone. 'I took a picture.'

'Kiyomi-*chan*,' Harashima said.

Kiyomi nodded and took the phone from Kenny, her fingertips brushing his. She clicked open a panel on the wall, pulled out a USB lead and plugged in the phone.

'Poyo,' she said. The animal waddled over to a shelf, picked up a remote control and tapped the buttons. This may have been the freakiest thing yet, but Kenny said nothing as the wall panel slid aside again and the enlarged snapshot of his grandfather's letter appeared, spread out over numerous TV screens. Both Kiyomi and her father scanned it quickly.

'Hm,' Harashima said. 'Hardly worth the effort of writing, do you not think, Kuromori-*san*?'

Kenny hesitated. 'I did think it was a bit strange . . .'

'Didn't you see the hidden message?' Kiyomi said.

Kenny blushed again. Not only was the girl very beautiful, but she was also making him feel very stupid.

'What hidden message?' he asked.

'Take another look,' she said. Her spoken English was

flawless, with a slight American accent. 'Your grandfather typed this up in a cute font and it's all nicely done, right?'

Kenny stared at the letter, grateful for something else to focus on. He nodded. 'Yeah . . .'

'*Bzzt*! Sorry, wrong answer. Thank you for playing.'

'Huh?'

'Look, Ken-*chan*. Look harder.'

Kenny looked again, as carefully as he could, searching for hidden shapes and patterns. 'I don't see anything.'

Kiyomi walked up to the screens and pointed. 'Didn't you notice the wonky letters? Some of them are in italic. Look. Here, the "p" in "place" leans to the right. Two lines down, the "h" in "that" and then the "l" in "feelings" are irregular. Do you see it now?'

Kenny stared again. 'Oh, wow,' he said, as the pattern became clear, like a 3D Magic Eye picture coming into focus. 'You're right. I never saw any of that before.'

'That's because your brain irons out the wrinkles,' Kiyomi said. 'Here, let me underline the italics.'

'It's an old trick from World War Two,' Harashima said. 'Prisoners would send hidden messages this way in their letters home.'

'So,' Kiyomi said, arms folded in a teacher-like pose, 'what does it say?'

To my dearest grandson, Kenneth,

Yes, I know you hate being called 'Kenneth'

but it could have been worse – your
grandmother wanted to name you 'Aloysius'.

If all is well, you will be reading this upon
an aero plane high above the Pacific Ocean,
making your final approach to Japan,
where I have arranged for you to spend the
summer with your father.

I remember what it was like for me,
travelling alone to a strange and unfamiliar
place, but, once I adjusted to the local
customs, I found it a place of magical
wonder. I suspect that you too may be
embarking on a similar journey of self-
discovery.

If I have any advice for you, it is this:
believe in yourself; trust your feelings;
do what is right, especially when it is most
difficult; and always carry a cucumber near
fresh water.

With all my love,

Your grandfather, Lawrence

Kenny read down quickly. 'It says . . . open . . . the

'. . . enve . . . lope. Open the envelope. Open the – Hey, I already opened it, otherwise how would I have got the letter out? This is stupid. It makes no sense.'

'Do you have the envelope?' Harashima asked.

Kenny patted down his pockets, heard the paper rustle and took it out. 'Yes, here it is. They took the letter, but left this.'

'May I?' Harashima drew closer and held out his hand to take the paper. It was then that Kenny noticed that the last joint was missing from the man's little finger. He stared for a moment, trying to remember what that signified. Harashima gave no indication that he had noticed.

'Kuromori-*san*, your grandfather went to a lot of trouble to tell you to do something you have already done. Is that not so?'

Kenny nodded. He was feeling stupider and stupider, and getting weary of everything being phrased as a question.

'Except you have not done as he instructed.' Harashima carefully ran his fingertip under the sealed edges of the envelope, gently lifting as he went, and flattened it into one large sheet of paper. 'Now it is opened,' he said, sniffing at the paper and holding it up to the light.

He took a silver cigarette lighter from his jacket and struck the flint. He ran the flame beneath the envelope, scorching it in spots, trying to avoid burning his fingers. 'Lemon juice makes a good invisible ink,' he said. 'So do onion and vinegar, but the smell gives them away.'

When he had finished, he snapped the lighter shut and handed the paper to Kenny. There, clearly written in brown lines, were the symbols:

N/Ca Al:Fm

Harashima smiled. 'Your grandfather has done well to narrow it down. It is as we thought.'

Kenny stood up again. 'OK, obviously, whatever's going on here, you don't need me. I'm way too dumb for any of this fun and games, so I'm just going to get my backpack and go, all right? I need to find my dad.'

Harashima adjusted a cufflink. 'Kuromori-*san*, you are wanted by certain authorities who, no doubt, have you listed on their records as a threat to national security. You have no money, no friends, no contacts; you cannot speak, read or write Japanese. As of now, the only people who have helped you are us.'

'I can call my dad, just as soon as I get a signal.'

'Your father was arrested this afternoon, just before your plane landed. If you call him, it will lead Sato straight to you.'

Kenny's hands closed into fists and he felt a scream starting low down in his stomach.

'I know how difficult this is for you,' Kiyomi said, 'and believe me, I'd love to tell you more, but you're going to have to trust us. You're safe here. I saved your life once already. Why would I do that if I meant you harm?'

'Look, I get it, OK? Something crazy is going on. I can see . . . weird creatures. My stupid grandad is somehow mixed up in this. You think I can help you, but you're wrong. That's not me. I don't belong here and I don't want to be involved in any of this, whatever it is.'

'Kenny, you're already involved,' Kiyomi said. 'As am I. We were involved in this before we were even born. Choices were made for us years ago, and now we have to decide whether to accept those choices or not.'

'You're kidding me, right?' Kenny took a deep breath, placed his fists on the table and rested his weight on the knuckles. 'OK, one question before I go: what does it mean? N, Ca, Al, Fm?'

'Chemical names,' Harashima said. 'Nitrogen, Calcium, Aluminium and Fermium. They're not important. What is important is their position in the periodic table. Nitrogen is 7, calcium is 20, aluminium is 13 and fermium is 100.'

Kiyomi looked expectantly at Kenny.

'What? I don't get it,' he said. 'I'm stupid, remember?'

'Seven, twenty, thirteen, one hundred,' she said. 'It's a date and time: July the twentieth, thirteen hundred hours.'

'What's the big deal about that?'

'Ken-*chan*, that's nine days from now. Unless you help us to stop it, that's when fifty million people on the West Coast of America are going to die.'

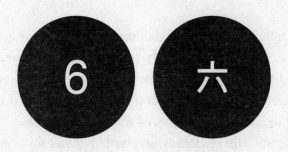

Kenny's legs buckled and he sat down hard.

'Say that again,' he said. 'I don't think I – I couldn't have heard that right.'

Kiyomi sat down across from him and leaned closer. 'Kenny, there is a plan to kill millions of people in America in nine days' time to avenge something that happened many years ago.'

'In nine days?'

Kiyomi nodded and leaned back.

'How?'

'We are not exactly sure, although I have a good idea,' Harashima said.

'And are you going to tell me?'

'Not yet, Kuromori-*san*. You have not yet chosen sides, therefore it would be dangerous to tell you more.'

'Sides?'

'Ken-*chan*, there is a war still being fought,' Kiyomi added. 'There are some who would gladly turn back the clock and return Japan to its pre-industrial state.'

Her father turned off the television screens. 'You are tired. Sleep will help.'

Kenny's stomach growled and he put a hand over his middle to muffle it.

'You're still hungry?' Kiyomi said. 'Oyama said you ate everything. And I mean everything.'

Kenny cast a wry look in the direction of the furry animal. 'Not me,' he said. 'It was him.'

'Poyo!' Kiyomi said. 'But you had dinner already. No wonder you're so fat. That was naughty.' The creature lowered its head in shame.

'Um, what is that thing anyway?' Kenny asked.

'Poyo? He's *tanuki*. Japanese raccoon dog.'

'Do you know why he was on my plane?'

Kiyomi paused. 'I sent him. He's been watching over you.'

Poyo nodded vigorously.

'What do you mean, "watching over me"?' A gnawing suspicion was growing in Kenny's mind.

'We sent him to America a few months ago, when we . . . We thought you might be in danger.'

Kenny rounded on the *tanuki*. 'So you're the one who's been raiding my fridge at school? I thought I was going mad and kept blaming my room-mate. I got into a huge fight over that.'

Poyo's ears drooped and he slunk away to hide under the table.

Kiyomi nodded. 'I know. Poyo told me.'

'What else did he tell you?' Kenny's ears were heating up.

Kiyomi exchanged a glance with her father. 'Oh, nothing much. Just that you're, er, very independent. He likes you, by the way. Says you're much cleverer than you look.'

Kenny's stomach rumbled again and he stood up, eyeing the door.

'So why did I need this?' he asked, holding up the bamboo whistle. 'If Fatso's been spying on me the whole time?'

'Because here you're going to need all the help you can get. In America, you were pretty safe,' Kiyomi explained.

'You just said I was in danger.'

'It was your grandfather's idea,' Harashima said. 'And it worked. We protected you and brought you here.'

'And that makes it all right, does it? You know what? I've had enough of being here, wherever here is. I'm off. See ya.'

Kenny went to the door, slid it open and stopped. His path was blocked by the huge servant he had encountered earlier. The man was holding Kenny's backpack.

'No one is going to prevent you leaving,' Harashima said, 'but know that you do not choose your path; the path chooses you.'

Kenny rolled his eyes. 'Isn't that what Yoda said to Luke?'

Kiyomi took the backpack and held it out to Kenny.

'Tell you what,' she said, 'let's go get some air. I'll buy you a burger, so at least you're fed, and then I'll drop you off wherever you want to go.'

Kenny's eyes darted between the people in the room. 'No strings?' he asked.

'No strings.' Kiyomi held up three fingers, palm outwards with thumb and little finger touching. 'Scout's honour,' she said.

Kenny allowed himself a smile. 'I'll bet you were never a Scout, or even a Girl Guide.'

Kiyomi handed Kenny his backpack. 'See? Poyo was right: you are smarter than you look.' She returned the smile.

'Kiyomi-*chan*,' her father said in a low voice, 'be careful. They know he's here.'

'So,' Kiyomi said, leading the way past the huge servant, 'do they have McDonald's where you're from?'

The cool night air ruffled Kenny's hair as he clung to the motorcycle. They rode down a long thoroughfare which seemed like a canyon made of light. Glass-fronted buildings towered on either side, brightly lit from within. On the outside they were decked with huge illuminated signs advertising cosmetics, electronic goods, soft drinks, cars and countless other products.

Pedestrians milled around everywhere, patiently waiting for the traffic lights to change; when they did, the crowds

45

would break and spill across the roads in great waves.

Kiyomi passed a small temple, the reflected lights of skyscrapers glinting in the *koi* pond in front. She pulled into the car park of a McDonald's restaurant and glided to a stop. Kenny dismounted and crouched to take a closer look at the motorcycle.

'This bike,' he said, 'has no exhaust pipes.'

Kiyomi stood with her arms folded and watched, a smile playing on her lips. Poyo plopped to the ground and sprawled beside Kenny.

'It's also completely silent,' Kenny said, finally working out what it was that had been bugging him ever since he had first set eyes on the bike and its mysterious rider. 'What? How –?'

'Ken-*chan*, I'd love to tell you, but I can't since you'll be leaving soon. Poyo, you stay here. And no going through the trash cans.'

Kiyomi pushed open the glass doors and went to the counter to order. Kenny caught up with her in the queue. 'You know, you're not fooling me with this whole I-don't-need-anyone lone-wolf routine,' she said. 'You should trust us to help you.'

'I can handle myself,' Kenny said.

'Really? So, Mr Independent, why don't you order for us?'

'*Irrashaimase!*' said the girl behind the counter, looking expectantly at Kenny.

He stared at the illuminated photos of hamburgers

above the counter with Japanese writing underneath, before flashing Kiyomi an embarrassed grin. 'Um . . . could you do it, please?'

Kenny found a table by the window and watched his fellow diners. There were office workers on the way home, school pupils still in uniform, a couple of punk rockers, an old lady wrapped in a long raincoat. The place was much brighter and cleaner than fast-food restaurants at home.

'Did you want a shake?' Kiyomi asked, placing a tray on the table.

'Sounds good,' Kenny said, reaching for a fry. 'Chocolate for me.'

'Well, now it's summer, so you can have melon, peach, banana or green tea.'

'Oh . . . maybe later then.'

Kenny bit into his burger, savouring the taste. 'I haven't had one of these in years,' he said, wiping a dribble of ketchup from his chin.

'How come?' Kiyomi dipped a fry into her peach shake.

'It's something . . . My mum would treat me, but . . . I stopped.' Kenny put the burger down, blinking several times.

Kiyomi put her hand on Kenny's. 'It's OK. I know about your mother.'

Kenny pulled his hand back and wiped a knuckle over his blurring eyes. 'I don't think about her much any more.' He sniffed.

'I lost my mother too,' Kiyomi said, gazing into space. 'But I was too little to remember her.'

'I was six,' Kenny said. 'You?'

'I was two.'

They ate the next few bites in silence.

'Thank you,' Kenny said.

'Huh? For what?'

'For not giving me the usual "I'm sorry" routine.'

Kiyomi laughed. 'Oh God, I hate that. Everyone says it and I just want to say, "Don't be sorry, it's not like you're responsible."'

'Exactly. I was so sick of all the pats on the head, people telling me how brave I was, saying she's in a better place – like they know anything.'

Kiyomi shrugged. 'They mean well. They just don't know what else to say.' She took a slurp of peach shake. 'They can't imagine what it's like to grow up without a mum.'

'You know what the worst thing was for me?' Kenny looked away, his cheeks pink. 'It's kind of silly . . .'

'Come on,' Kiyomi said. 'Who am I going to tell?'

Kenny stared down at his meal. 'I miss the cuddles and the hugs. You know, with my mum, it didn't really matter what I did. If I was upset, she would just give me a hug and it was all better. With my dad . . . let's just say it's different.' He popped the last of his burger into his mouth and licked his fingers. 'How about you? What was the hardest thing . . . growing up?'

Kiyomi's smile vanished. 'It would have been nice to get tips on what to wear and make-up. Stuff like that. My dad isn't –'

'Hey, at least your dad is there for you, every day. He didn't dump you like a bag of dog poo first chance he got.'

Kiyomi reached for Kenny's hand again. 'Your father fell apart afterwards. Papa told me. He couldn't cope. You know that. I think seeing you was too painful for him, reminded him too much of your mum.'

'And that's an excuse to shut me out, is it?' Kenny drew his hand back. 'Anyway, you seem to know a lot about me. How come?'

Kiyomi dunked her last chicken nugget into a small pot of sour-plum sauce. 'Our families go way back,' she said. 'You didn't know that, did you? My grandfather and yours were friends. They worked together after the war.'

'They did? Doing what?'

'Sorry, can't tell you that. You're leaving, remember?' Kiyomi wiped her fingers on a paper napkin. 'We should go.'

'Allow me,' Kenny said, gathering the empty containers. He wrestled the rubbish into an overflowing bin and stowed the tray. He wasn't ready to leave just yet. For one thing, he had nowhere to go; Kiyomi's father was right about that. And he had so many questions. How could his grandfather have kept all this from him? He straightened up, as if adjusting the weight of a burden, and caught Kiyomi staring at him.

'Neodymium alloy magnets,' Kiyomi said, when he returned to the table.

'Huh?'

'My bike. It's a prototype. Lithium-ion batteries and super-magnets drive the motor. That's why it makes no sound. It's electric. My father borrowed it.'

'Stole it you mean?' Kenny regretted the words as soon as they left his lips.

'No. Borrowed it. From a business associate.' Kiyomi stressed each word. 'Do you really think I'd be riding around on a stolen bike?'

'Well, your dad is, um, a gangster . . .' The accusation was out of Kenny's mouth before he could stop himself.

'What?'

'He's a *yakuza*, right? Japanese mafia. I saw his missing little finger.' Inside Kenny's head, a small voice was screaming at him for messing up what was almost a pleasant meal.

Kiyomi grabbed her handbag and stood up. 'Maybe it's better you're leaving us, Kuromori. I mean, you obviously know everything already. You don't need us and we certainly don't need you.' She strode towards the door, watched by the old woman in the raincoat.

Kenny stood up. 'No. I'm sorry. Look, that's not what I meant. I, er . . .'

'Get lost!'

Kenny watched numbly through the window as Kiyomi

marched to her bike and swung a leather-clad leg over the seat. As she leaned forward to pull on her helmet, four dark shadows emerged from the gloom of the car park and swarmed at her. One of them swung something at Kiyomi, catching her around the head, and she fell from the bike, her helmet bouncing away over the tarmac.

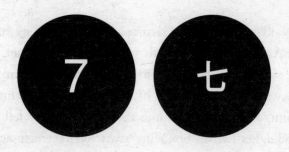

Kenny was on his feet before he realised what he was doing.

By the time he was out of the glass doors, his mind had finished arguing with itself. One side was saying to keep out of it, that this was nothing to do with him, that it was dangerous and that he was leaving anyway; the other side said simply that someone was in trouble and he had to do something.

'Hey! What are you doing?' Kenny shouted. 'Leave her alone!' He made his voice as loud and as deep as he could while he fumbled for the whistle.

'Hnh? *Nandayo?*' The four shapes moved back from the fallen girl and Kenny saw a jumble of black jumpsuits and leather jackets with Chinese writing on them, biker boots, long red sashes tied in an X-shape across the chest, headbands – and a baseball bat, a wooden sword, a metal pipe and a length of chain.

'Oh, crap,' Kenny muttered, looking around for anything he could use in defence. Suddenly, this wasn't such a great idea.

Two of the bikers moved behind him, cutting off his escape. He glanced into the restaurant, but the diners were oblivious. The lead biker slapped the metal pipe against his open palm and sized up the teenage boy standing before him.

'*Ki demo kurutta ka?*' he said, dragging the last word out into a sneer.

Kenny fought the urge to run. Instead, he pointed at the pipe and broke into maniacal laughter, quick and high-pitched, like a hyena. The biker blinked and took a step back from this foreign lunatic. In that moment, Kenny moved. He threw the whistle hard, aiming at the man's face, and closed in, grabbing for the pipe before he could swing it.

'*Aiee!*' the man shrieked as the whistle hit his eye. His grip loosened and Kenny wrenched the pipe free.

'Duck!' Kiyomi screamed and Kenny dropped, feeling the rush of air as the baseball bat swept over his head. It smacked into the man who was clutching at his eye and knocked him to the ground. Still crouched, Kenny swung the pipe hard to his left. There was a sharp crack as it connected with a kneecap, another scream, and the biker holding the bat crumpled to the floor. Kenny sprang up and saw the remaining two, one with the chain and the other with the *kendo* sword, rushing him. Kiyomi dragged herself across the ground towards her bike.

Kenny twirled the pipe – like a baton – and edged away from the biker with the chain. Thinking quickly, he lowered the weapon, offering his opponent an opening. The man took it and swung the chain. Kenny brought the steel tube up to meet the flail. With a rattling clang, the chain wrapped itself round the pipe and Kenny pulled back sharply with all his strength. Caught off balance, the man stumbled and fell, releasing his grip on the metal links.

Three down, one to go, Kenny thought, but he was too late. The man with the sword bore down on him, raising both arms high above his head and then bringing them down. Kenny raised an arm to protect himself. There was a snarl, a flash of fur and then more shrieking. The man fell backwards, his hands clawing to fend off Poyo whose sharp little teeth were clamped to his crotch.

The last biker standing, the one who had been wielding the chain, looked at his companions – one on the ground with cracked ribs, one writhing with a broken kneecap and one with an angry *tanuki* attached to his privates – and decided it was time to go. He turned on his heel. And stopped.

The old lady in the raincoat had emerged from McDonald's and was directly in front of him. She swayed gently and stared at him hungrily. Her eyes were small and beady, glinting red in the street lights, and her long grey hair was waving even though there was little breeze.

The biker looked from Kenny to the old woman and back. He shrugged and continued marching towards her, an arm raised to shove her aside.

That was when Kenny's stomach lurched as he caught sight of a forked tongue flickering over the old lady's lips. Something was horribly wrong here. 'Wait!' he shouted at the biker, raising a hand in warning. 'Stop!'

The biker hesitated and the thing in the raincoat pounced. He was flung to the ground, spread-eagled, with the creature on top of him, its mouth clamped to his.

'Ew, gross!' Kenny said, backing away.

Kiyomi shook her pounding head to clear it and hauled her bike into an upright position. She heard Kenny's warning shout, looked up, and her blood chilled. 'Kenny . . . ' Kiyomi said, her voice low but in a tone not to be argued with. 'Get back here, now . . . We can still get away. Poyo, *jubun da*.'

Poyo unclamped his jaws from the biker and sniffed the air. His eyes grew wide and he bounded over to Kiyomi, whimpering. She picked bloodied, matted hair out of her eyes and pulled herself up on to the bike.

The creature released its lips from the now-still biker and leered up at Kenny, who was rooted to the spot. Blood dribbled down its chin and it began slithering towards him.

'Run!' Kiyomi yelled.

Kenny sprinted to her, hurdling the fallen bikers who lay groaning on the ground.

The creature reared up again. Its coat flapped open and Kenny glimpsed rippling coils covered with tiny scales.

'What is that thing?' he said, scrambling up beside Kiyomi.

'*Nure-onna*,' she said, wobbling on to the bike. 'Bad news. Let's go.'

'What, and just leave those guys here for its dessert? We can't do that.'

'OK, it was just an idea.' Kiyomi groaned and reached down into a side panel. 'Here,' she said, withdrawing a can of Pringles.

'You're going to eat crisps *now*?' Kenny said.

Kiyomi pressed her thumb against the end of the can; the fingerprint reader bleeped and it popped open.

'Whatever you're doing, can you hurry it up?' Kenny said. 'That thing's getting closer.'

The *nure-onna* slithered over the three bikers and advanced towards Kiyomi and Kenny. The scritching sound of its scales on the asphalt set Kenny's teeth on edge.

'Aim for the head,' Kiyomi said, handing Kenny the contents of the Pringles can: a short sword in a scabbard as long as his forearm.

'This? You want me to fight that thing with this – this pocketknife?' Kenny said, pulling out the blade halfway. It was exquisite, brightly polished, with Japanese lettering engraved on it.

'Well, duh,' Kiyomi said, putting her hand to her head and pulling it away, sticky and red. 'Look, it's your idea to stay and fight. I've got blood in my eyes and I'm seeing two of everything, otherwise . . .'

'All right, all right,' Kenny said, moving away from the bike. 'But I'll take any help you can give.'

The forked tongue licked at the air. Kenny backed away and the *nure-onna* closed in. He clutched the wooden scabbard tightly in one hand and gripped the short sword in the other.

'Uh, you,' he said. 'Freaky snake-woman thing. You probably can't underst–'

'*I know who you are, Kuromori-child*,' it hissed.

Kenny froze. The awful serpentine voice had sounded *inside* his head; its lips hadn't moved.

'*And I know why you are here . . . but you will not succeed. A thousand starving* yurei *cry out for vengeance. You will not stand in their way.*'

The *nure-onna* slithered closer, swaying as the snake body undulated beneath the raincoat. Kenny held his ground, trying not to look at the beady eyes, the long wicked fangs or the flickering tongue. He glanced into McDonald's, through the windows behind the creature, but no one seemed to have noticed anything unusual happening in the car park. He was on his own.

Turning and running seemed a good idea, but the *nure-onna* was almost upon him. 'Kiyomi . . . now would be a good time to do something . . .' he muttered.

'Poyo! *Kame!*' Kiyomi said.

The *tanuki* shot across the car park like a guided missile and sank his sharp little teeth into the creature's tail. It shrieked and in that instant Kenny rammed the

57

scabbard into its open mouth, forcing the wooden case down the open gullet. The *nure-onna* gagged and Kenny whipped the blade across its neck, slicing through flesh. A startled expression stayed on the *nure-onna*'s face as its head bounced across the ground and the body flopped at Kenny's feet, writhing and churning.

Poyo spat out a chunk of tail and retched in disgust, trying to dislodge the taste. He leapt back, startled, as the body crumbled to a fine dust.

Kenny lifted the raincoat with the point of the sword, but it was empty. He wiped the blade on the coat, picked up the scabbard, slotted the sword home and handed it back to Kiyomi. She started up the motorcycle and the engine hummed softly.

'Come on, we should go,' she said, scooping up Poyo. 'One dead biker is going to attract attention. Or are you still going it alone?'

Kenny took in the scene around him: three wounded bikers lay moaning on the ground; one was still; the empty raincoat flapped; and the fine dust eddied away. 'That thing, it was after *me*, wasn't it? These guys just got in the way.'

'Something like that, yes.'

'And there are more . . . things out there too? More of them after me?'

Kiyomi nodded, her lips pressed tightly together.

'OK, I'll come back with you. You're very persuasive,' Kenny said and he climbed on to the motorcycle behind her. 'Besides,' he said, 'look at the trouble you get into when I'm not around.'

Kiyomi elbowed him, hard, and then opened the throttle, pulling out of the car park so fast that Kenny had to fling his arms round her waist to keep from falling off.

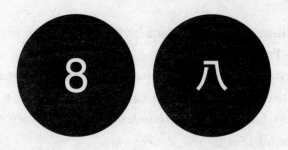

'**O**ww!' Kiyomi said, squirming away from the huge servant's grip as he applied antiseptic to the cut on her head.

'Oyama used to do *sumo*,' Harashima said, as if this explained everything. He was pacing the floor in front of the screen covering the TV monitors.

'So who were those guys, the ones who jumped you in the car park?' Kenny said, putting down his hot chocolate and pinching his nose to stifle a yawn.

Kiyomi's face twisted in disgust. '*Bosozoku*,' she said. 'A biker gang.' She glanced up at her father, whose face remained impassive. 'I got into a race with one of them a while back, beat him easily. He said I'd cheated and wanted my bike as payment. Fat chance.'

Kenny nodded. 'So they were waiting for you?'

'Yeah, bunch of cowards. I could have handled them if they hadn't snuck up on me.' Kiyomi touched her scalp, felt the broken skin and pulled her hair back down to cover it. 'Feels like a *taiko* drummer inside my head, but I'll live,' she said. 'You did pretty well, though. Where'd you learn to fight like that?'

Kenny turned away. 'You don't spend seven years getting shunted from one boarding school to another without learning how to defend yourself.' He was unable to keep the bitterness out of his voice. 'Plus, my grandad taught me a few moves last summer.'

Kiyomi tilted her head to appraise him. 'You were lucky. You have poor technique, no balance. If those guys could fight properly, you'd be mincemeat.'

Oyama cleared the medical kit from the table, bowed and left.

Kenny waited for someone to say something, but both Kiyomi and her father seemed comfortable with the silence.

'Sir?' Kenny said, when he could stand it no more.

Harashima inclined his head to acknowledge him.

'I came back, like you wanted, right? So, what happens now? I mean, you must have a plan, to stop this thing. How's it going to happen? How are all those people going to die?'

After a long pause, Harashima replied, 'I don't know . . . exactly.'

'Then what *do* you know? If I'm supposed to help you, I need to know what I'm being asked to do.'

Harashima nodded. 'You are right, Kuromori-*san*. You deserve answers and you will have them, only not now. You are exhausted. You have had a long and . . . eventful day, with much to take in. You will rest now and in the morning you shall have answers. Is that acceptable?'

Kenny yawned a huge jaw-splitting yawn that made his face hurt. 'OK. I'm too knackered to argue.'

'Oyama will show you to your room.'

The huge servant returned and motioned for Kenny to follow him.

'As for you, my child, remain where you are,' Harashima said to Kiyomi, who had been sneaking towards the door. 'You have some explaining to do.'

Kenny awoke. Light was bleeding into the room through small square windows and he knew he was dreaming. He had always been able to tell when a dream was a dream. 'Lucid dreaming' was what scientists called it. Sometimes Kenny was able to influence the outcome of a dream, but not tonight.

He was lying on a camp bed in a metal hut with corrugated-steel walls that curved overhead. The tinny sound of Frank Sinatra crooned from a radio outside. Kenny rolled off the cot, yawned and stretched. He was wearing an olive-drab service uniform with brass buttons.

Outside, under a forbidding grey sky, he saw that he was in an army compound with chain-link fences, barbed wire, jeeps and off-duty soldiers heading out in small groups. The American flag drooped from a pole.

Kenny strolled out through the gate and the contrast couldn't have been greater. He had crossed into a devastated wasteland where once a city had stood.

Rubble from burnt-out homes and shattered roof tiles covered the ground to such an extent that Kenny could not tell where the road was supposed to be. He wandered past hundreds of silent, hollow-eyed Japanese people, huddled in groups, dressed in little more than rags. The luckier ones had fashioned huts from cardboard, rocks and chicken wire. An old man bathed in rainwater collected in an oil drum. A young girl accepted a kiss from a teenage American soldier in return for a Hershey chocolate bar. An elderly man traded a priceless Japanese sword for a bag of flour.

Quiet sobbing carried across the gloom. Kenny listened and followed the sound to the nearby ruins of a house, picking his way through the wreckage. He pulled open the broken door and saw a girl crying inside. She knelt with her back to him, but he could see that her hair was long and black and she was wearing a plain, white kimono.

'Kiyomi?' he croaked, his throat dry. 'Is that you?'

The girl slowly turned towards him and Kenny cried out. She had no face; only a blank, featureless mask, as smooth as eggshell. He backed away, but the ground crumbled beneath him and he felt himself falling, dropping into an endless black void, tumbling over and over.

After what felt like an eternity, he landed with a crash at the bottom of a huge chasm. Kenny gingerly picked himself up, dusted down his fatigues and peered into the gloom. That was when he realised he wasn't alone. There was something down there with him in the dark. Something huge. Something ancient. Something evil.

Kenny woke with a start. His heart was pounding and his clothes were heavy with sweat. He was lying on a *futon* but the house was dark and still. He checked his watch, which was still set to Pacific time. 12:23. That meant it was almost four thirty in the morning, local time. The night sky was a pale indigo, heralding the approach of dawn. Kenny sat up and rubbed his face, afraid to go back to sleep. He had never experienced a dream as vivid as this before. It was unnerving, as if his subconscious mind was trying to tell him something – but what?

Six kilometres to the east, in Shinjuku's skyscraper district, lights burned in the corporate headquarters despite the earliness of the hour. The visitor exited the lift on the sixtieth floor and knocked once on the heavy walnut door.

'Enter,' came a voice from within and the visitor hurried inside.

Seated behind a mahogany desk and dressed in a black pinstripe suit was a stocky Japanese man. His thinning hair and sagging jowls placed him near retirement age. He set down the dossier he was reading. 'Miyamoto-*san*, it is good of you to come at short notice. What news?' the older man said.

Miyamoto bowed deeply. '*Shacho* . . .' he began, then hesitated. 'The boy, sir, he got away.'

The older man cocked his head. 'He . . . escaped? From Sato? How? He must have had help.'

'He did, sir. Details are as yet unclear, but it would appear that Harashima-*san* may have been involved.'

'How can you be sure?'

'Two police cars, one truck and two motorcycles were destroyed. We had a road closure for three hours.'

The senior man nodded. 'Yes, that sounds like Harashima all right.' He sighed and stood stiffly. 'Do we know where the boy is now?'

'He is hidden from us. His being *gaijin* makes him harder to track.'

The older man dabbed his forehead with a silk handkerchief. 'What of the boy? Is it true?'

Miyamoto nodded. 'Sato tested him. He has the Gift of Sight.'

'And to think we had him in our hands.'

The man shuffled round to a small cage perched on a filing cabinet. Inside, a fluffy, toffee-coloured ball lay curled on the sawdust. 'The father?'

'Arrested yesterday afternoon. He doesn't know anything. He was simply there to meet the boy at the airport.'

The older man reached into the cage and gently lifted out the hamster. It sat up sleepily in his palm. He tickled it beneath the chin and fed it a pumpkin seed. 'What charges are you holding the father with?'

Miyamoto shrugged. 'We'll probably go with possession of drugs. No one ever questions that when it comes to *gaijin*. We can make it stick.'

The man carried the hamster to a sideboard opposite. A fish tank sat on top, but no water was inside.

'So, here we are – a few days away and now this boy arrives . . . this boy who can *see*,' the older man said.

'It doesn't mean anything,' Miyamoto ventured. 'It doesn't mean he is the one, does it, sir?'

The man lifted the lid from the fish tank and set it aside. 'I don't believe in prophecies,' he said. 'You've read *Macbeth*. Prophecies only come true when men act on them. Do nothing and who can say if anything will happen?'

'But, sir, if there is any chance . . .?'

Something unfurled itself from within the tank, light reflecting from its tiny scales. The man dangled the hamster by one leg.

'We have the boy's father,' he said. 'Even if, by some miracle, the child is able to retrieve the sword, he will never be allowed to use it.'

There was a flash of movement, a piteous, muffled squeak and the hamster was gone, held in the jaws of the snake, which settled down to digest its meal.

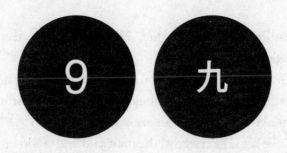

Kenny pushed the plate away and wiped his mouth on a napkin. Breakfast had been bacon and eggs with a stack of pancakes on the side, doused in maple syrup. With a night's rest and a hearty breakfast, he was feeling much better.

Oyama came into the room and cleared away the small table. Kenny knew the route well enough by now to make his own way to the main business room. Kiyomi and her father were talking in Japanese, but fell silent when Kenny came in.

'Kuromori-*san*, I trust you slept well,' Harashima said. He was wearing an open-necked black shirt and white linen trousers.

'Yeah, apart from a really weird dream.'

A glance flashed between father and daughter.

'What sort of dream?' Kiyomi asked. 'Do you remember anything?'

'My dreams can wait. You promised me some answers.' Kenny pulled out a chair and sat facing his hosts.

'Just like your grandfather,' Harashima said, steepling his fingers. 'Let us begin.'

'OK, first off, who are you?' Kenny said, trying not to stare at the man's missing finger joint. 'I don't just mean who are you, but also who are *you*? Does that . . .?'

'Make sense? Perfectly,' the man said and stood up. 'As you know, my name is Harashima. I am an independent businessman.' He nodded towards Kiyomi. 'And this, as you also know, is my daughter, Kiyomi.'

Kenny hesitated, not sure if he wanted to know the answer, but the question was bothering him and he had to ask. He held up his little finger. 'Um, I know this might seem rude, Mr Harashima, but what's with your finger? I mean, are you . . .?'

'*Yakuza*? A Japanese gangster, like in the movies? Yes, sort of. Let us say that I do not always work within the strict confines of the law.'

'But you're helping me – and trying to save lives?' Kenny said, his eyebrows raised.

Harashima spread his hands. 'Mine is an honourable organisation. Sometimes, however, one has to work outside of society in order to protect it.'

Kenny let this sink in. 'So what's with this Curry-Murray thing you keep calling me?'

Kiyomi laughed. 'You say it "Koo-roh-mor-ee". It's your family name, Ken-*chan*, in Japanese.'

He looked at her blankly.

'*Kuro* means black and *mori* means wood,' she said,

'so Kenny Blackwood becomes Ken Kuromori. You have a Japanese name.'

'I do? Oh. Uh, that's cool.' Kenny paused, trying to order the multitude of questions stampeding through his mind. 'So, what's happening in nine, uh, eight days' time that's so major? How are all those people going to die?'

Harashima pressed a button on the remote. The wall slid aside and the TV monitors blinked to life. This time, they were all tuned to news channels and covering the same event.

'An earthquake?' Kenny said, his eyes skipping over the screens. 'But how is this related?'

The pictures changed to form one large shot of an orbiting satellite.

'There is a weapon in space at this very moment,' Harashima said. 'It is experimental, but it works, as you can see from the news.'

'And it does what? You're telling me it caused that earthquake?' Kenny tried not to laugh. 'No way! I'm sorry, but that's bull.'

'It fires a low-frequency ultrasonic pulse which is calibrated to resonate within certain rock strata. The result is an earthquake.'

Kenny remained incredulous. 'You're telling me that someone snuck that thing up there and is now test-firing their weapon ahead of a biggie?'

'Yes. In eight days' time, the weapon will be used to trigger a massive earthquake on the West Coast of the

United States. It will destroy Los Angeles, San Francisco, Seattle, Portland and much of the Pacific North-west. The attack will be revenge for something that happened in 1946, after the war.'

'You're serious about this?'

'Deadly serious.'

'But this is . . . nuts! It sounds like a plot from a James Bond movie.'

Harashima glanced at Kiyomi. 'Yes, I agree, it does. But is that any harder for you to believe than a human snake, or the *oni* you saw at the airport?'

'Or Sato switching off your voice and making a wall of fire,' Kiyomi added. 'Surely an orbiting satellite is easier to believe than magical creatures?'

Kenny's mouth twisted in doubt. 'I . . . suppose,' he said. 'But what does any of that have to do with me?'

'As Papa said, there is a resonant frequency carried within the pulse,' Kiyomi said. 'Well, there's a rare type of crystal which can disrupt that frequency. We need you to help us find that crystal.'

'Uh-huh. Rare crystal. Disrupts frequency. *Riiight*. Do you realise how crazy this all sounds?' Kenny protested.

'Your grandfather once had that crystal,' Harashima said, 'and he hid it here, in Japan. That's why he sent you – to help us find it and to prevent this massacre.'

'But how am I supposed to . . . Oh, wait a minute! Does this have anything to do with me being able to see those things?'

Harashima clapped his hands. 'Brilliant! Yes, that's exactly it. Courtesy of your grandfather, you have a rare Gift, and that is what is needed to help us find the swo—'

'Crystal!' Kiyomi interjected.

Kenny's mind was racing. 'Last night,' he said, 'nobody in McDonald's noticed the *nure-onna*. The only ones who saw it were us and the biker it killed.'

'Ken-*chan*, the mystical creatures from these islands are hidden from most people. They can show themselves if they choose to, but otherwise they are invisible,' Kiyomi said. 'Only a few people with the special Gift of Sight can see them when they wish to remain hidden.'

'And you have this Gift?'

She nodded.

'And I know I do. What about Sato?'

'No, but he has other Gifts.'

'What about you? Can you see them?' Kenny asked Harashima.

'No, I cannot, but my father could. The Gift, you see, skips a generation each time. Otherwise, there would be none left to pass it on – the burden is great.'

Kenny examined the picture of the satellite once more. 'So, who are these people we're up against and how do you know so much about them?'

'You will recall what I said last night about choosing sides,' Harashima said. 'Well, there are some who have never accepted Japan's opening up to the west and subsequent modernisation. They feel it has made us weak.

71

There are not many, but they are powerful. They have chosen to fight progress. That is who we are up against. As for how I know, I make it my business to know. I have eyes and ears everywhere.'

'You have spies in their camp?' Kenny said. 'Cool.'

'Are we done with the questions now?' Kiyomi asked. 'There's still a lot to do.'

'All right, one more thing,' Kenny said. 'Who's this Sato dude?'

'Sato is a loyal public servant who believes he is doing what is right,' Harashima replied, his voice tinged with sadness. 'I doubt he fully understands who he is working for.'

'OK. One more thing: what's a *yurei*?'

Harashima abruptly turned off the monitors. 'Where did you hear that word?' he said, looking around.

'From the *nure-onna*, when she spoke inside my head. She said that a thousand starving *yurei* were crying out for revenge and that I wouldn't be allowed to stop them.'

'So they also know you are here,' Harashima said. 'This is much more serious than I thought. Maybe your grandfather should have kept you away from all this.'

'You still haven't told me what a *yur–*'

'It's a ghost, a spirit of the dead,' Kiyomi said quickly. 'If someone dies horribly, unjustly, and their body isn't laid to rest properly, or with the right prayers said, then they might return to seek revenge on the living.'

'But what's that got to do with– ?'

72

'Ken-*chan*, don't you see? Thousands of people died in the aftermath of the war. There was no time or money for proper funerals.'

'And that means you have a lot of unhappy spirits out there?'

'Exactly. And some of them want nothing more than revenge.'

'So, this crystal thing you want me to find,' Kenny said. 'Where is it?'

He was hurrying to keep up with Kiyomi as she strode along a path through the gardens surrounding the house. The air was thick and humid; sweat prickled his scalp.

'We don't know. No one knows. The only person who might know is your grandfather, but he isn't here.'

'Couldn't you just call him and ask?'

Kiyomi stopped. 'It's not as simple as that.'

'Why not?'

'Sato is Japanese Secret Service, Paranormal Investigation Division. That means the government can monitor or intercept every communication we send; that's why your grandfather used you as a messenger. The only reason any of us is still here is that we've managed to keep what we know a secret.'

She resumed walking.

'Where was this crystal last seen?' Kenny tried again.

'Just after the war. Your grandfather went on a mission to retrieve it before it could fall into the wrong hands.'

'Why? What else can it do?'

Kiyomi hesitated, tightening her brow as if deciding how much to say. 'I don't know. But the *yokai* are scared of it.'

'*Yokai*?'

'The creatures you've been seeing, like the *oni* and the *nure-onna*.'

'And the other one, the *yurei*, they are . . .?'

'Ghosts, pretty much. But still dangerous.' She stopped abruptly. 'Here we are.'

Kiyomi stepped out of her Hello Kitty sandals and padded up the stairs of a large open-sided summer house. It was a low, wooden octagonal building, with a packed earth floor. Four of the walls had paper screens in them; the other four were completely open. Timber poles supported the roof and it made Kenny think of a wooden tent.

'And this is . . .?'

'A *dojo*. A training area. Take your sneakers off before you come in.'

Kenny kicked off his footwear and stepped into the *dojo*.

'Training area? For what?' he asked.

'Last night, against the *nure-onna*, you got lucky. Very lucky. You're brave, I'll give you that, but stupid. Now the *yokai* and the *yurei* know you're here, they'll try again to kill you, so I need to teach you how to take care of yourself.'

'You crack me up, you know that?' Kenny said with a smirk.

'You think this is funny? Laugh at this.' Kiyomi dropped and punched him, just above the navel.

Kenny fell to his knees and doubled up, his hands clutching his middle.

'Not so funny now, is it?' Kiyomi said, standing over him. 'Listen, Ken-*chan*, my job is to teach you how to take care of yourself and stop you getting us all killed. It's not my idea of fun, but Papa figures that because we're the same age, I can communicate better with you. How am I doing so far?'

Still on the ground and groaning, Kenny managed a thumbs-up sign.

'Good. You need to learn how to fight, properly, and how to act while you're here. Otherwise, we're all screwed. Got me?'

Kenny nodded and Kiyomi helped him up. 'Feeling better? Ready for more?'

Kenny nodded weakly.

'Good. You think what you did last night wasn't luck? Then hit me. You know you want to.'

'I . . . don't . . . hit . . . girls . . . ' Kenny said.

'Wrong answer.'

Kiyomi smashed the heel of her palm into Kenny's jaw and, once more, he sprawled on to the dirt. The ground was cool and comfortable beneath his cheek. This time he decided to stay where he was until he stopped hurting.

Back at the house, Oyama was preparing lunch. He looked up from grating a *daikon* radish and raised an eyebrow at Kiyomi who was storming past.

'He's useless,' she muttered. 'Teaching him to fight is like putting Poyo on a diet. Twenty minutes and he hasn't learned a thing.'

Oyama listened to her rummage around and held out an apple. Kiyomi grabbed it as she stomped past carrying an assortment of swords and other weapons.

When she arrived back at the *dojo*, Kenny was lying half-comatose on the dirt floor. He jumped when Kiyomi dropped a wooden sword next to his head.

'Is it break time yet?' he groaned into the floor.

'You remember that *oni*? What would you do if he decided to tear your head off and keep it as a souvenir?'

'Uh, not a lot. You?'

'I'd rip his guts out, tie them round his neck and strangle him.'

'*Niiice*. Remind me never to ask you out on a date.'

'OK, playtime's over. Get up, pick a weapon and let's see if you can hold the right end.'

Kenny inched himself up like a caterpillar and rose painfully to his feet. Kiyomi was standing with her arms folded. At her feet was a stack of daggers, knives, sticks, swords, axes, poles, clubs, chains and more exotic items that Kenny had never seen before.

'Whoa! Are you nuts?' he said.

'We haven't got all day.'

'Um, aren't I going to hurt you?' Kenny asked, picking up a short, heavy length of wood.

'You wish. You'd have to hit me first, if you even can. Now hurry it up. Or are you still too scared to fight girls?'

'For you, I'll make an exception.'

Annoyed, Kenny stepped forward with the *jo* staff. He swung it low, aiming for the girl's hip. Kiyomi leapt into the air, easily vaulting the blow, and lashed out with her right foot. She caught Kenny on the side of the head and sent him flying.

Three hours later, a battered, bruised and bloodied Kenny limped back to his room to clean up.

'This is so not worth it,' he said, fishing the last clean T-shirt from his backpack.

'You need to learn some Japanese,' Kiyomi said, after Oyama had cleared the empty *bento* lunch boxes from the table in the main room.

'Why?' Kenny asked, pressing an ice pack to his chin.

'Because not all *yokai* can speak inside your head, and I won't always be there to translate for you.'

'You won't? How do you –?'

'There are some things you'll have to do on your own, Ken-*chan*. Some things no one can help you with.'

Anger overcame exhaustion. 'What sort of things? Is this more stuff you can't tell me? I'm not stupid, you know.' He caught the look on her face. 'Well, not completely stupid.'

Kiyomi softened, almost appearing sorry for him. 'Ken-*chan*, when the time is right, you will know everything. To tell you too much now would only place you in more danger.'

Kenny took a sip of green tea and laughed to himself. 'More danger? I've got a thousand ghosts plus all their monster friends wanting me dead, you kicking my ass and I should worry about more danger?'

Kiyomi laid a large sketch pad on the table. 'Let's start with simple things.'

'I have a question,' Kenny said.

Kiyomi sighed.

'How come your English is so good? Who taught –?'

'I had an English nanny when I was little. Later, Papa sent me abroad to study. I've spent time in the States, Australia, Canada, Singapore, loads of places. Plus, I've had lessons here.'

'Oh. That sucks.' Now it was Kenny's turn to feel sorry. 'Getting bounced from one place to the next, like nobody wants you, huh?'

Kiyomi shrugged. '*Shoganai*.'

'What does that mean?'

'It is what it is. Can't be helped.' She looked away, her eyes moist, then took a deep breath. 'So, Japanese then. You know Roman numerals, right? Do one, two and three here on the paper, going down in a line.'

Kenny scowled and drew the figures:

I

II

III

'OK, look at this.' Kiyomi rotated the page a quarter turn to the left so that the figures were lying on their side: 一 二 三 . 'Now you've just written one to three in Chinese characters.'

Kenny blinked. 'Wow. That's . . . impressive.'

'You know the number ten as a Roman numeral? Turn that forty-five degrees and what do you get?'

Kenny squinted to visualise the number. 'A cross.'

'And that's ten in Chinese too. Here, what number is this?'

Kiyomi drew: 三十

'That's three and ten. Thirty?' Kenny said.

Kiyomi smiled. 'And this is: 十一?'

'Ten, one. Eleven.'

Kiyomi grinned. 'Ken-*chan*, we've finally found something you're good at!'

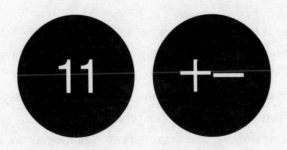

Sato entered the police interview room and motioned for the officer standing guard to leave.

The man sitting at the spartan table watched Sato closely. When the door clicked shut, Sato placed two items on the table: a business card and a thick dossier.

The seated man, a westerner, pulled a pair of rimless glasses from his pocket and slipped them on. He reached for the card and held it in both hands, examining the Japanese writing on it.

Sato sat, taking in the other man's appearance: in his mid-fifties but younger-looking; highlighted shoulder-length hair fell against his suit; a trimmed beard edged his tanned face. He was visibly agitated.

'You're from the *koanchosa-cho*?' the man said. 'I don't – Why . . .? What would the Japanese Secret Service want with me?'

'Professor Charles Blackwood . . .' Sato began.

'No. Listen, I don't care who you are, you can't just arrest me without saying why. And where's my son? I was supposed to meet Kenny at the airport yesterday.

Where is he? Is he safe? Is he with you?'

'Professor, it would help us both if you remained calm,' Sato said. 'I am here to help –'

'I want my lawyer, or someone from the embassy. You can't just lock me up without due process.'

'Professor, we can detain you for as long as we wish. Suspected terrorists have no rights. You can be held for as long we want, without any evidence. Isn't that how it works these days?'

Charles opened his mouth to protest, but thought better of it.

'You are being held for your own safety. There are forces at work that may wish to harm you and your son.'

'This is absurd. You know I've done nothing wrong. Do you know who I am?'

Sato patted the dossier. 'I know very well who you are, Professor Blackwood. You teach history and comparative anthropology at Tokyo University. Well respected by both students and faculty. You have a flat in Shibuya. You have lived in Japan for the last three years. Need I go on?'

Charles narrowed his eyes. 'Who are you? What do you want from me?'

'My name is Sato, as per my card. What I want is information.'

'About what?'

'Let us start with the Occupation of Japan.'

'The Occupation? What's –? Ah, I see.' Charles smiled in resignation. 'What's my father's done this time?'

Sato interlaced his fingers. 'Why don't you tell me what you think you know about your father?'

'I want to talk to my son.'

'First, you help me. Now, about your father . . .'

Charles shrugged. 'What's to say? It's all in the public domain. He majored in oriental studies, as they called it back then, at Oxford. Got the tap on the shoulder to go to Japan with MacArthur's mob, helped advise the Americans while he was here.'

'And?'

'And what? He got drawn into collecting and preserving Japanese artifacts. Without him, many ancient treasures would have gone abroad as souvenirs.'

'Did he tell you about any of these treasures?'

'No, not really. Enough to make me interested in the subject, I suppose, but he held a lot back. A man of many secrets, my father.'

'And you, Professor Blackwood, what secrets do you keep?'

'Look, I don't like the direction this conversation is taking,' Charles said, rising to his feet. 'I demand to see a lawyer. I have work to get back to. And I want to see my son. He's –'

'Gone missing.'

Charles sat down, eyes darting in bewilderment. 'What do you mean, "missing"?'

'He . . . ran away from my protection. I have every reason to believe that Kenny's life is in great danger. Do you know anywhere he would go? To find help?'

Charles shook his head slowly. 'No, he's never been to Japan before. He doesn't know anyone.'

'Hm. Let me tell you what I think is happening. Then you will see why I am talking to you. Your son is, I believe, trying to carry out some work on behalf of your father.'

Charles laughed. 'That's ridiculous. How? My father's in England, in a retirement home six thousand miles away. He's ninety-five years old, for heaven's sake. How can he possibly –?'

'So you have no knowledge of your son's whereabouts?'

'I've already told you, no. Why would –?'

Sato traced a shape in the air and Charles stopped speaking.

'You will now tell me the truth,' Sato said. 'Everything you know about your father, his work, his contacts here and your son Kenny.'

Charles felt his head drop, rise, drop, rise: he was nodding. Gritting his teeth, he formed the word 'no' but when he spoke it came out as 'yes'.

'Good,' Sato said. 'Let us begin.'

A soft tap sounded on the *shoji* screen door.

'Come in,' Kenny said. He was lying on his *futon* mattress, hands behind his head, staring at the ceiling.

Harashima slid the door open and peered in. 'Kuromori-*san*, I would like you to join us for dinner in the main room.'

84

'Uh, OK.' Kenny tried to sit up, winced and pressed a hand against his ribs.

'How are you feeling?' Harashima asked, his eyes tinged with concern.

'Everything hurts. But no worse than after a game of football.' The boy sat up. 'I've had worse beatings than that. She hits like a girl.'

Harashima smiled. 'I won't tell her you said that. I think you have had enough punishment for one day.'

They walked together to the main room and Kenny took his seat next to Kiyomi, while her father sat opposite them.

Oyama came round with a tray of hot, tightly-rolled hand towels. Kenny watched Kiyomi unfurl one and use it to wipe her hands. He followed suit and then mopped his face. He was considering cleaning his ears too, when Kiyomi snatched the cloth from him.

'Just your hands,' she hissed, rolling her eyes.

'Sorry,' he whispered.

Oyama set a large shallow serving dish in the middle of the table. Upon it lay a colourful assortment of neatly-cut rectangular shapes, each the size and width of a matchbox. These were artistically arranged on a nest of grated white strips, interspersed with green leaves and lemon slices. There were hues of deep red, light pink, a delicate orange, smooth white, silver-edged, rose purple and a pumpkin-coloured blob.

Kiyomi picked up her chopsticks. 'Shall I serve you,

Ken-*chan*, or are you going to take your own?'

'Erm, what is all this stuff?' Kenny ventured.

'*Sashimi*,' Harashima said, rubbing his hands. 'A traditional Japanese delicacy. Very good for you.'

'Isn't that, like, uh, raw fish?' Kenny was dreading the answer.

'Oh, yes.' Harashima took up his chopsticks and indicated as he spoke. 'This here is tuna, this is salmon, over there is octopus, this is squid, that is mackerel, this is . . .' He looked to Kiyomi. '*Uni*.'

'Sea urchin,' Kiyomi said.

'You're going to eat *raw* octopus and squid and sea urchin?' Kenny said, deciding he was no longer hungry.

'No, Kuromori-*san*, *we* are going to eat. Here, try this.'

Before Kenny could stop him, Harashima had deftly loaded his plate with one sample of each fish and set it before him. He poured soy sauce into a tiny side dish. 'You dip your fish in the sauce before eating it,' Harashima said and began to serve himself.

Kenny sat back, staring at the plate. He imagined the fish glaring back at him reproachfully.

Kiyomi eyed him with amusement. 'Do you need me to feed you?' she asked.

'No.' Kenny picked up his chopsticks. 'Um, what do I do with these?'

'Here. Hold one like this, between your thumb and the webbed part where your thumb meets your hand.' She showed him. 'Hold the other with your first two fingers,

86

the way you hold a pencil. Now, if you move your fingers, you'll open and close the two ends of the chopsticks and you can pick things up. Watch me.'

Kenny studied Kiyomi's technique and tried to copy it. 'Hey, wow. I can do it,' he said, surprising himself.

'Good. Give it a few days and you'll be picking up individual grains of rice.' Kiyomi placed some *sashimi* on her plate, lowered her chopsticks and said, '*Itadakimasu*.' It sounded to Kenny like 'eat-a-dakky-mass'.

'*Itadakimasu*,' her father repeated and looked expectantly towards Kenny.

'You say it too,' Kiyomi prompted. 'It's good manners, like saying *bon appétit* or grace before a meal.'

'Oh, OK. Eat a messy duck or whatever it was.'

'Close enough,' Harashima said and dipped a piece of fish into soy sauce before slipping it into his mouth.

'Here goes,' Kenny said, taking a deep breath. He was famished after the day's training, even though he had serious reservations about the food in front of him. He managed to get both chopsticks round a slender piece of pink flesh and lifted it, wobbling, towards his mouth.

It fell and plopped into the soy sauce, spattering his T-shirt. Annoyed, Kenny speared the fish with one end of a chopstick and jammed it into his mouth. It was cool, soft but firm, almost creamy in the way it melted when chewed. There was nothing slimy or fishy about it, just a subtle meatiness that reminded Kenny of a very rare steak he had eaten once.

'Wow,' he said. 'That is delicious. Can I have some more?'

Oyama served green tea, rice and *miso* soup while Kenny tried each type of seafood on offer. The squid, he decided, was crisp and rubbery, as was the octopus, but Kenny forced it down. Finally, he was faced with the sea urchin, which looked to him like cat poop.

'You don't have to eat it,' Kiyomi said. 'Most *gaijin* can't eat *uni*.'

'Really? Well, I'm not most *gaijin*.' Kenny scooped up the blob and dropped it into his mouth. It was slightly sweet, which he did not expect, but it also had a soapy, salty bitterness. He gave a tentative chew and almost gagged on the texture which was like grainy custard. Kenny decided it was quite simply the most disgusting thing he'd ever eaten, but he wasn't going to admit defeat. Holding his breath, he swallowed it and glugged some green tea to wash away the taste.

'Bravo, Kuromori-*san*, bravo,' Harashima said.

Kenny wiped his mouth on a cloth napkin and set down his chopsticks. Time to get back to business. 'Sir,' he began, 'this crystal I'm supposed to find . . .?'

Harashima lowered his cup. 'Yes?'

'Where do I start? I mean you're saying Grandad hid it somewhere safe after the war and told no one about it. How am I supposed to know where to look?'

'Ken-*san*. Do you know why I insist on calling you Kuromori?'

'Uh, no, not really.'

'Because your grandfather's blood flows within you. You think of yourself as a unique individual, and yes, that is what you are, but you also have roots which go deep into your family. You are no more separate from your grandfather than a tree which shares a common root system with others.'

'I don't get it,' Kenny admitted.

'What Papa is trying to say is that there are some creatures out there who will look at you and see your grandfather,' Kiyomi said. 'Any enemies he might have made are now your enemies.'

'Oh, great. That explains a lot.'

'It explains why you mustn't leave this compound without a bodyguard,' Kiyomi said.

'But, on the other hand, your grandfather's allies are now also your allies,' Harashima said. 'Like us. You have other friends here, as well. I fully expect that one or two of them will be contacting you soon to help you.'

'And all we have to do is keep you alive long enough for that to happen,' Kiyomi said and touched her cup against Kenny's. 'Cheers.'

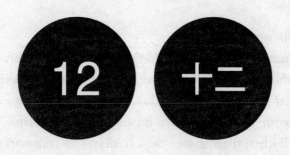

That night, Kenny had the dream again, only this time there was more.

He was in the Quonset hut, in his military uniform. Wandering off base, he passed hundreds of starving, destitute Japanese people living amid the ruins of their city. A diesel engine rumbled from behind and a cheery voice shouted, 'Hey, buddy! Hop in!'

A US army jeep stopped and one of the three teenage servicemen inside offered Kenny a hand. He climbed into the back beside his new friend and the car bounced along the rubble-strewn road.

'I'm Floyd,' the soldier said, with a wide grin. 'This here's Elmer, and Dale's driving. You are?'

'Kenny. I'm kind of new here.'

'Smoke?' Floyd said, offering Kenny a cigarette from a packet marked Chesterfield.

'No thanks,' Kenny said. He watched two small children clearing a square of dirt to use as a vegetable patch. 'So, where are you guys going?'

'Shinjuku black market. We've had a report of trouble.

Rival gangs are muscling in from out of town.'

'Is that a problem?' Kenny asked.

'You bet it is. We've already agreed rates with the Ozu Gumi. We don't need to go through all that again.'

'Agreed rates?' Kenny repeated.

'Man, you're greener than a cornfield in May. Here, take this. It'll help you get acquainted with a nice girl.' Floyd held out two Hershey bars.

After twenty bone-jarring minutes, Kenny saw a small crowd ahead, queuing near a cleared space.

'Here we go, rookie. Just follow my lead,' Floyd said, jumping out and pushing his way through the waiting Japanese.

Kenny followed him to where a number of wooden crates and mats were set out, displaying foodstuffs, sandals, clothing, cooking utensils and other goods, many of them marked with a *US Army* stamp. Impoverished Japanese men clustered round the makeshift stalls, haggling and bartering for wares.

Floyd, Elmer and Dale went from stand to stand, collecting cash from the vendors. One of them, a balding older man who held his head high, refused to part with his money. Dale slapped him round the face, but the man glared in stubborn silence.

'Come on, you stupid Jap,' Dale said. 'Just pay up like everyone else and nobody has to get hurt.'

The crowd was silent, waiting to see what the soldiers would do.

'He isn't going to play ball,' Elmer said. 'We're going to have to make an example of him.'

'Man, I hate that,' Floyd said. 'You always get one, don't you? Come with us, boy. Time to teach you a real good lesson.' He patted his service pistol, slung in a holster.

'Wait,' Kenny said, stepping in between the servicemen and the trader. 'What are you going to do?'

'It's just business, buddy, nothing personal,' Floyd said, as if this explained everything.

'Out of the way, you.' Dale barged Kenny aside.

He sprawled on the ground and felt cracks open beneath his palms. 'No!' Kenny yelled. The earth crumbled away from under him and he fell once more, deep into the bowels of the earth.

Back in the familiar part of the dream, Kenny rose to his feet, straining to see and hear in the dark. Water dripped all around him and the dank chill of the air permeated his bones. A warm breeze ruffled his uniform, then died away, before returning at intervals. *A way out?* Kenny thought, moving towards the wind. He pulled out his phone and switched it on, sweeping it around to cast some light.

An odd rock formation lay ahead and Kenny moved closer. It was smooth, shiny and its surface was etched with thousands of curves. It moved. Kenny stared as the rock seemed to swell and subside, in time with the breeze. His mind reeled in shock as the pieces fell into place: the etchings on the rock were overlapping scales and the wind was the breathing of some immense creature trapped in the darkness with him.

Kenny wanted to scream and run, but where could he go? He took one horrified step backwards, then another. He backed away until he reached the rock wall of the chasm and felt something poke into his hip. Reaching down, Kenny felt the smooth edge of a door handle. He turned it and a portal opened in the rock.

He stepped through into a blinding radiance and held a hand over his eyes until they adjusted from the gloom. He was standing on a narrow bamboo bridge which stretched over what seemed to be a lake of grey gravel. The tiny stones had been shaped into gently lapping waves and small grass islands supported large rocks. Dwarf trees and sculpted bushes lay beyond the lake and wind chimes tinkled in the fragrant air.

Kenny followed the bridge. It curved upwards and then down on to a wide circular clearing. In the centre was an animal that Kenny recognised as a fox, but it was the strangest one he had ever seen. Its fur was pure white and it sat on its haunches, licking a paw, its tails fanned out behind on the close-cropped grass. *Tails?* Kenny counted twice to be sure; the fox had nine tails, all bushy and white.

Fascinated by the exotic creature, Kenny stepped off the bridge and slowly approached the fox, moving carefully so as not to startle it. If the fox was concerned, it made no sign, and Kenny drew close enough to be able to touch the silvery fur. He reached out to stroke it, but the fox faded away like a wisp of smoke. Kenny blinked and looked at his hand.

Without knowing why, he felt deeply saddened by the fox's absence and gazed around. To his left was a small stand of six pine trees. On his right was an earthenware jar of spring water beside a cast-iron tea kettle. Behind him was the bridge. The fox had been sitting centrally to the three sets of objects, but now it was gone and Kenny was alone.

Kenny woke up and checked his watch: 06:21 Tokyo time. Too early to get up, but too late to settle back to sleep.

'Bloody typical,' he muttered to himself.

Two hours later and Kenny's day was steadily getting worse.

'You've got to be kidding me,' he said, eyeing the breakfast that Oyama had set before him. 'Can't I just have cornflakes?'

'Stop being such a baby,' Kiyomi said, looking up from a thick *manga* comic book she was reading. 'That's a traditional Japanese breakfast. It's a lot better for you than a full English fry-up.'

Kenny sighed and picked up his chopsticks. On the lacquered tray was a bowl of *miso* soup, steamed rice, a slice of grilled salmon, assorted pickles, a raw egg and some slimy, sticky beans which smelled like cheesy toes.

'I can't eat this. It's gone off.' He prodded the beans, lifting strings of white mucus from their surface.

Kiyomi rolled her eyes. 'In the same way that yogurt and cheese are rotten milk and wine is rancid grape juice. Try it, you might like it.'

Kenny grimaced as the beans slipped off his chopsticks.

'But don't worry if you can't,' Kiyomi added. 'Most *gaijin* can't eat *natto*.'

At that, Kenny dug his chopsticks into the slimy mess, held his breath and scooped in a mouthful. He chewed tentatively and was relieved to find that the taste was savoury, slightly nutty, with a hint of yeastiness.

'Hmm, not bad,' he declared. 'I've eaten worse.'

Kiyomi set down her *manga* and watched Kenny eat the rest of the *natto*. A blob splotted on to the front of his T-shirt as he finished.

'Wow. You did really well,' Kiyomi said. 'I hate the stuff and many Japanese can't eat it either. I'm impressed.'

Kenny wiped his mouth on a napkin. 'You tricked me?'

Kiyomi shrugged. 'Maybe a little.'

'I liked it. Shame about the mess, though. This is my last clean shirt.'

Harashima looked into the room. 'Kuromori-*san*, I wanted to ask you if – *Uwa!* You ate the *natto*? When Oyama said he was serving it, I thought he was joking.'

'He liked it, too, Papa,' Kiyomi said, looking disappointed.

Harashima smiled. 'You are becoming what we call

henna gaijin. It means "strange foreigner".'

Kenny frowned. 'Why strange?'

'Japanese culture can be difficult for visitors to understand, so it is unusual for a guest to adopt our ways so quickly.'

'When in Rome . . . ' Kenny turned to Kiyomi. 'So, what are we doing today? More Japanese lessons, or are you going to smack me around again?'

Kiyomi glanced up at her father. '*Otosan*, I was thinking I could take Ken-*chan* into the city today.'

Harashima shook his head. 'No, it is too dangerous. He is a target.'

'He's a target with nothing to wear. Look at the state of him.'

Kenny smiled weakly and tried to wipe the blob of slime from his T-shirt. 'It's OK, I can wash my clothes in the sink. I'm used to living out of a bag.'

'No way,' Kiyomi said. 'You might like looking like a dork, but I'm the one stuck with babysitting you.'

'Oyama can go for him,' Harashima said.

'What, and have him wear a kimono all day long?'

'All right,' Harashima said after a long pause. 'He does need more clothes than those he brought with him. But be careful.'

Kiyomi clapped her hands in delight. '*Yatta*! Sure thing, Pops. You know me.'

'Which is precisely why I said to be careful.'

*

After a short walk to Nezu Station, Kenny and Kiyomi took the Tokyo Metro for eleven stops on the Chiyoda Line to Meiji-Jingumae Station.

'Ta-daa!' Kiyomi said, as they emerged on to a busy intersection. 'Welcome to the world famous Harajuku, fashion centre of Japan. Forget New York, Paris, London or Milan; if it isn't happening here, it isn't happening anywhere.'

As if to illustrate the point, a teenage girl wobbled past on dangerously high platform boots with a shredded leather ensemble topped by a shock of rainbow hair.

'I have a bad feeling about this,' Kenny said, as Kiyomi grabbed his arm and steered him down the pedestrian-only Takeshita Street, swarming with people and lined with colourful boutiques and pancake cafes.

After spending a day cooped up in the Harashima compound, Kenny was glad to be out in the city, with all its vibrant sights and sounds. He tried not to stare but the unique fashion statements all around him – everything from neon pink furry leg warmers with ski goggles, to a zebra-striped onesie with a spiked dog collar - made him wonder if he hadn't stepped on to a science-fiction movie set.

At the end of the lane, they turned right on to the more sedate Meiji Dori with its international designer label stores, and then left on to the upscale Omotesando which was lined with leafy zelkova trees. Lastly, they went right on to Aoyama Dori, past the five-storey indoor play centre, and they walked down to Shibuya, with its famous pedestrian crossing.

'How about this?' Kiyomi said.

Kenny took one look at the lime-green hooded cagoule and mimed gagging.

'You need some kind of top in case it rains,' Kiyomi persisted.

Kenny was dazed from the retail assault. He had lost count of the number of boutiques Kiyomi had steered him into, the racks of clothes, the fitting rooms, the pairs of jeans, the jackets. Judging from the many overflowing carrier bags nestling around Kiyomi's feet, Kenny suspected that he had been used as an excuse for her own shopping spree, and he wasn't pleased.

'Why can't I just get myself some trainers, a pair of jeans, a few more T-shirts and a jacket?' he pleaded. 'It's a universal style, fits in anywhere in the world.'

'No. I don't want to be seen with you looking like some *otaku* dweeb.'

'*Otaku*? Is that like a geek?'

'Worse. Look, we can dress you better than that.'

'What's this "we" business? You're shopping and I'm just following you around and carrying the bags. I've had enough! If I see one more Hello Kitty top, I'm going to puke *natto* on it.' Kenny stormed out of the boutique and on to the hot pavement.

Crowds swept past in orderly lines. Across the road, Kenny caught sight of a large wedge-shaped building with two huge pillars in front and the words *Tokyu Hands* going vertically up the outside, like the spine of a book. Kenny made straight for the store, using the wide zebra crossings, and merged with the crowds.

'Kenny! Wait up. Where are you–? That's a hobby shop.' Kiyomi's voice faded as Kenny jogged away.

Once inside the air-conditioned coolness of the store, Kenny lost himself gazing at the displays. There were bicycles hanging on the wall, a rainbow of wellington boots, enamelled tea kettles, waxed paper umbrellas, sewing kits, candles, hair-care products, pet food, power tools, stationery, curtains, fancy-dress costumes, wedding supplies, briefcases, stepladders and thousands of other practical items, spread over eight floors.

The shop wasn't crowded and, without thinking about where he was going, Kenny ended up in the sports section. He picked up a football and bounced it on the floor to see how firm it was. Satisfied, he dropped it on to his instep, flicked it up, bounced it on his thigh and headed it into his hands. This was more like it. He'd finally found something familiar, something he was good at. He could easily mark out a pitch back at the Harashima house and it would be his turn to show Kiyomi a trick or two.

Kenny tucked the ball under his arm and went to the nearest cash register. No one was there. He looked around and was surprised to see that the floor was deserted.

'Was it something I said?' he joked to himself, craning his neck for signs of life.

The air temperature seemed to drop by ten degrees, making him shudder. Overhead, the fluorescent lights went out, followed by other lights flicking off, one by one, leaving Kenny alone in the dark.

'Hello?' he called. 'Anyone there? Don't tell me you're closed alread–?' His voice died as footsteps came from behind. He spun round to see – not a member of staff, but the figure of a young woman striding towards him, her form silhouetted in the dim light. Something was odd about the way she moved. She was followed by another girl, then another.

Kenny took a step back. More noises from behind. He turned and saw two more young women. He was surrounded.

All five were in their late teens and dressed in a bewildering assortment of eccentric clothing. One was wearing a frilly black dress with lace trim, a pillbox hat, white stockings and platform boots. Beside her was a punk, with a shock of scarlet hair, a sleeveless blouse, tartan miniskirt, stripy tights and red Dr Marten boots. The third was dressed as a pink bunny rabbit, complete with stick-on whiskers and fake ears. The last two were a caped *anime* superhero in a minidress and a walking accessory stand, plastered with brightly coloured necklaces, hair clips, bangles and badges.

Kenny was too startled to speak.

The pink bunny smiled at him, revealing wicked rows of sharp, pointed teeth.

'*Ken*-chan,' she said, in a sing-song voice, '*You've led us quite a chase, all the way from Harajuku to Shibuya.*'

'*Yeah*,' chimed in the Goth. '*We had to wait ages for you to ditch your girlfriend, but now we've made sure you're all alone. That's too bad.*' Her claw-like hands reached out for Kenny who was rooted to the spot, frozen in horror.

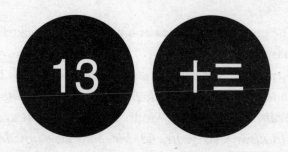

Instinct took over. Kenny dropped the football and volleyed it, smashing it at full power into the Goth's midriff. She screeched and crumpled to the floor, winded.

Kenny dived for a neatly stacked pyramid display of golf balls and upended the lot, sending a cascade of balls clattering across the floor. He ran, his eyes searching for the nearest exit.

The other four Harajuku girls scrambled after him but they hadn't counted on the golf balls. Like Bambi on ice, their legs shot out in all directions and they crashed to the ground.

Kenny reached a fire door leading to the stairs. He wrenched at the handle, but it wouldn't budge.

'*There's no escape for you*,' said the punk. She had regained her footing and was fast approaching, Doc Martens squeaking on the vinyl.

Fumbling in his pocket for the *tanuki* whistle, Kenny positioned himself next to another display, eyes darting to keep track of the monsters pursuing him. Seeing him raise the whistle to his lips, the creature rushed at him.

Kenny dropped the whistle, thrust a hand out behind him, felt it close on a narrow cylinder, and then swung it with all his strength.

There was a dull thud and a slight metallic ping as the baseball bat connected solidly with the punk girl's head and, to Kenny's shock, the head tore off, ripping free, and sailed through the air to smash into a glass display case. The body tumbled to the floor.

'Oh my God! I didn't mean to –' Kenny started to babble. He froze at the sound of a horrible sucking, squelching noise. As he stared in mute horror, the heads of the other four creatures detached from their bodies and gathered as they rose into the air, trailing squirting, sloppy blood vessels and floppy ligaments. The bodies slumped.

'*You can't stop all of us,*' hissed the floating head of the superhero. '*And one bite is all it takes for you to join us.*'

Kenny recoiled and fought the urge to be sick. With blood dripping on to the vinyl flooring, the four heads converged on him.

They were quick, much faster without their bodies to hinder them. Kenny swung the bat, time and again, but it was like swatting at houseflies; the creatures zoomed away each time, out of reach, hovering and looking for an opening.

'*You're slowing down, Ken-*chan,' the bunny said, her lilting voice setting Kenny's teeth on edge. '*Your arms are getting tired.*'

Kenny swung again, missed, and the Goth head rushed at him on his exposed side, fangs bared. He slid his hands down the barrel of the bat and jabbed backwards with the handle. There was a crack and a screech as the knob connected with the thing's nose, crushing it.

Kenny was now at the edge of the sports department and approaching the camping goods section. Several ideas flashed through his mind at once. The first was to duck behind a life-sized cut-out of the tennis player Andy Murray, and Kenny held the bat out in his left hand and fished around with his right.

The floating heads approached cautiously. The spangly one saw the baseball bat sticking out from Murray's waist and surmised the boy was crouching, waiting to swing. It changed direction and swooped in from the other side, just as Kenny had hoped. The tennis racquet slammed into the creature's face; there was a twang of elastic tension and then – *whoosh* – it rebounded, flew across the room, bounced off the wall in a hail of barrettes and dropped through a basketball hoop into a bin.

'Three to go,' Kenny muttered under his breath and burst from cover. He pumped his legs as fast as he could.

'*There he is! Kill him!*' the bunny screeched and the three heads soared after him, flying swiftly over display tables stacked with merchandise.

Kenny dived over a camping table, sending the tableware and cooking equipment crashing to the floor. He pulled the table on to its side and ducked down behind the makeshift shield, grabbing at the items rolling on the floor around him.

'*Come out, come out, wherever you are,*' gurgled the Goth head, blood oozing from its nose.

'*We do so love foreign food,*' added the superhero, its eyes sweeping from side to side.

Kenny picked up a metal plate, weighed it in his hand and flipped it upside down. He held his breath, listening to the *drip-drip-spatter-spatter* of the creatures as they floated towards him. His heart hammered against his ribs and his stomach was doing somersaults.

'*He is close,*' the bunny head growled. '*I can smell his fear.*'

'*I see him!*' the Goth head shrieked and it soared towards Kenny's hiding place.

Kenny sprang to his feet and hurled the plate like a frisbee. It smashed into the flying head's mouth, sending fragments of teeth down through the hole where its neck would have been.

'*Aaahcch!*' it howled, but Kenny wasn't finished. He whipped out a can of insect repellent and sprayed it, catching its eyes and nose. '*Mmmbbphlgh!*' it gurgled, unable to remove the plate.

'*You'll pay for that!*' screeched the bunny head and it flung itself towards the boy.

'Send me the bill!' Kenny retorted and, keeping his finger firmly pressed on the aerosol nozzle, he clicked the safety gas lighter in his other hand. *WHOOMPH!* The fine spray ignited and Kenny thrust the jet of flame into the monster's face.

It shrieked and spun away, its whiskers and hair ablaze.

The last one hovered, just out of reach, the sputtering flame reflecting in its dead, black, shark-like eyes.

'*You are running out of tricks, boy,*' she spat. '*I will enjoy feasting on your marrow.*'

Kenny backed away, edging towards a small canvas tent which stood beside a plastic tree.

The can felt lighter by the second and he knew it was almost empty. Abruptly, the gas died and the fire went out. Eyes glinting in triumph, the superhero's head rushed towards him. Kenny flung himself backwards and into the tent. He had only seconds. His hands scrabbled at the rear flap as the head poked inside.

'*There's nowhere left to run,*' it said.

Kenny waited until it entered the tent. He then dived through the flap at the back, jumped to his feet and stamped on the plastic support struts, snapping them all. The tent collapsed, trapping the screeching head under the canvas. Kenny watched it flail around inside, like a bouncing lottery ball.

He grabbed the loose ends of the tent, held them closed and dragged them over to a display of angling equipment. Ignoring the hissing and cursing from within the canvas, Kenny looped a length of fishing line round the top and tied it securely. He then deposited the package in a freezer box and locked the lid.

Satisfied, he retrieved his football, scooped up the wooden whistle and started towards the emergency exit. He froze at the sound of something approaching from behind the door. An intense light blazed around the frame and the door exploded into matchstick-sized fragments.

'Kenny!' Kiyomi screamed, charging in with her short sword in her hand. 'What are you –? I was so worried! Papa would kill me if anything happened to . . .' She trailed off, taking in the wreckage lying around: broken glass, golf balls, overturned tables, torn canvas.

She glared at him. 'Have you been trashing the place? Is this you having a stupid tantrum or – *mmmph*!' Kenny grabbed her and kissed her, squishing his mouth against hers. He hadn't planned it – high on adrenalin, he felt reckless and exhilarated; at that moment, it just felt right, and it was the quickest way to end the tirade.

Kiyomi slapped him, hard. 'What was that for?' she demanded, wiping her mouth on her sleeve.

Kenny blushed a shade of beetroot. 'Erm, it seemed like a good idea at the time?' He shrugged. 'Sorry.'

Kiyomi raised her hand to slap him again, but this time Kenny caught her wrist. 'Enough, OK?' he said. 'I've had my daily kicking already.' He headed for the stairs.

'Now what're you talking abou–?' Kiyomi's eyes went wide as she saw a stripy pair of legs sticking out from behind a counter.

'And you know what else?' Kenny's voice echoed from the stairwell. 'You have some bloody weird monsters in this place.'

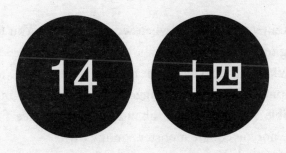

14 十四

'Five? Five *nukekubi*? On your own?'

Kenny shrugged. 'Yeah, I suppose. Why? Are they dangerous?'

Kiyomi rolled her eyes and mimicked him. '"Are they dangerous?" Hell, yes. Think vampires that hunt in packs.'

'That bad?'

Kiyomi shook her head. 'I can't work out if you're still alive because you're incredibly stupid, incredibly lucky or –'

'Let's stick with incredibly stupid,' Kenny said. 'I had no idea they were that bad.'

They were seated in the middle carriage of a green-liveried Chiyoda Line subway train, heading north, deep below the frenzied streets of Tokyo. With it being between lunch break and rush hour, they had the carriage to themselves.

Kiyomi sat opposite Kenny, her shopping bags jostling around her feet like lapdogs. Colourful banner advertisements ran above her head and from poles across the carriage.

'Kenny,' she began, 'when we get back . . . You're not going to tell my father –'

'What? That you used me as your excuse to go shopping? That you dragged me around a million horrible shops and then abandoned me to face five of those nookie-cookie monsters on my own?'

'*Nukekubi*.'

'Yeah, them, whatever.' Kenny leaned back and smiled. 'No. No, I'm not going to tell. I owed you one, remember? Now we're quits.'

His eyes lit on a poster above Kiyomi's head. It was a cartoon picture of a brown fox licking its lips and holding out a cup of noodles.

'What's that ad about?' Kenny asked, indicating the poster.

Kiyomi looked up and wrinkled her nose. 'That? Instant noodles. Why, do you want some?'

'No. It's just the fox . . . Do you have foxes here?'

'Like, duh. Of course we have foxes.'

'How many tails do they have?'

Kiyomi was across the carriage, with her knee in Kenny's stomach and her arm across his throat, in the time it took him to blink.

'You've seen a fox with more than one tail?' she whispered.

Kenny managed to nod.

'This fox, what colour was it?'

'White,' Kenny gurgled.

'How many tails did it have?'

'Nine.'

Kiyomi released her chokehold and rolled on to the seat beside Kenny.

'You've seen Genkuro-*sensei*,' she said, eyes shining with excitement. 'When? Where? Tell me.'

'Get lost! You just tried to strangle me.' Kenny rubbed his throat.

'I had to be sure you weren't messing around. This is very, very important.'

'So important you couldn't ask me nicely? Man, I thought I had anger-management issues. Has it ever occurred to you that you might get better results if you tried being nicer to people instead of always attacking them?'

Kiyomi opened her mouth to deliver a stinging retort. Unable to think of one, she closed it again. Arms folded, she slumped in the seat, lips pressed tightly together. They rode on in silence. The train pulled in to Nijubashimae Station; they had four more stops to go.

'This fox,' Kenny said, in a conciliatory tone, 'you gave it a name, said it's important.'

Kiyomi nodded. 'Genkuro-*sensei*. Yes.' Her gaze turned downwards. 'Kenny, look, I'm sorry, OK? You're right. Sometimes I act before I think. I would never really hurt you.'

Kenny's cheeks were uncomfortably hot. 'All right, all right,' he said. 'Apology accepted. Don't go all mushy on me, OK?' He loosened a button on the neck of his new polo shirt and told her about the last part of his dream; he decided not to mention the black market or the creature in the dark.

'You idiot! Why didn't you tell us this before?' Kiyomi said, when he had finished.

'Why? It's just a stupid dream.'

Kiyomi's hands closed into fists. She took a deep breath and opened them again. 'Ken-*chan*, you remember when my father said that friends would try to contact you?'

'Yes.'

'Well, they're not going to send you a text message. This is how it happens. Genkuro-*sensei* is telling you something.'

'Are you serious? This . . . fox thing has hacked into my head, while I'm asleep, and left me a message in a dream?'

'Something like that, yes.'

'Do you know how crazy that sounds? OK, assuming that's true, you still haven't told me who or what this Genkuro dude is. Or what he wants with me.'

'Genkuro-*sensei* was your grandfather's teacher here in Japan. He taught me some of my skills and, if we can find him, he will teach you.'

Kenny let out a low whistle. 'Wait, a *fox* taught my grandfather? To do what? Raid a henhouse? How old is this guy?'

Kiyomi jumped up and began pacing. 'We have to take

you to him, as soon as we can. Time is running out.'

Kenny shrugged. 'OK, let's go then.'

Kiyomi stopped. 'No one knows where he is. He keeps moving, always changing location. That's why he comes to us, not the other way round.'

'Then how do we find him?'

'I don't know. It has to be something in your dream.'

Kenny stood up and looked round the carriage, as if expecting to see the answer written somewhere.

'We're looking for a specific place,' he said. 'The fox was sitting in the middle of a circle and there were three things around him: a kettle with a jar of water, the trees and the bridge. Does that mean anything to you?'

Kiyomi shook her head. 'If you're asking me if there's a park with a giant kettle inside, then I'd say no. A whale, yes, but a kettle, no.'

'So it has to be something about the trees and the bridge and the kettle. All made of wood? No. All to do with water? No, the lake was gravel. Numbers? Wait – that station we passed. The one which began with two . . .'

Kiyomi looked blankly at him. 'What station with two?'

Kenny went to a subway map on the wall, counted back and jabbed a finger at Nijubashimae. 'Here, we did this yesterday. The first part of this name is the number two. Two horizontal lines.'

'It's just a place name.'

'Yes, but it must mean something. Nothing gets named by accident.'

Kiyomi looked closely at the four Chinese characters. 'Ni. Ju. Bashi. Mae.'

'Those are the names, right? What are the meanings?'

'Two. Solid. Bridge. Before. I don't get it.'

Kenny's hands were on his head now. He was so close, he could feel it. 'Different angle: what's actually there? At Knee-jerk-bash-my-eye? You said a bridge. Is there a bridge?'

Kiyomi's eyes widened as understanding dawned. 'Yes, it's a double-arched bridge made of stone. I never thought about it before.'

'So are there any other places with numbers or bridges in the name? What does the number six look like?'

Kiyomi took out a lipstick and wrote on the window:

Kenny looked doubtful. 'A hat with legs?'

Kiyomi glared at him.

'OK, looking at this map, do you see anywhere named after six bridges, six kettles, six trees?'

'Oh my God.' Kiyomi clapped a hand over her mouth. 'Roppongi. It means six trees.' She clapped her hands in delight, then stuffed them under her armpits. Her feet started jumping instead. 'I never thought about what it meant; we've always just called it that.'

Kenny nodded, his mind working furiously. 'That's

OK. I always wondered why there were no clowns at Piccadilly Circus.'

'That's easy. Circus as in circle. It's named after the round bit where the statue is.'

They looked at each other for a second, held their gaze and started laughing.

'Where's Roppongi?' Kenny asked, once the giggles had stopped.

'Down here.' Kiyomi pointed to the bottom of the map. 'It's nightclub central, really cool. It'll blow your mind. One day, I'll take you there.'

The train pulled in to Nezu Station.

'This is us, isn't it?' Kenny asked, looking out of the window at the signs in Japanese and English.

'Stuff it,' Kiyomi said. 'Let's figure this out first. It's far more important.'

A grumpy-looking schoolboy in a navy-blue uniform stomped into the carriage. He pulled his cap further down over his ears and slumped, turning the volume up on his music player.

Kenny returned to the subway map. 'We know the things in my dream represent places, so we should be able to find the other two.'

'Got it!' Kiyomi said.

'That was fast.'

'The bridge, you said, was bamboo?'

Kenny nodded.

'It's here. Takebashi.' She pointed to a spot on a sky-blue line near the centre of the map. '*Take* means bamboo and *bashi* is bridge.'

'Brilliant. So that just leaves the kettle and the water jug. They have to be here somewhere.'

They huddled over the map, fingers tracing lines. They were so absorbed in their task that neither noticed the schoolboy remove his cap and stroke his horns.

Kenny jumped when a guttural voice thundered through the carriage.

'Fo-fee-fi-fum!' it roared.

The schoolboy was gone. Standing in his place, wearing tattered shreds of uniform, with his head squished against the ceiling and outstretched arms touching either side of the carriage, was a huge blue *oni*. His muscles rippled and ugly veins squirmed over his arms like electric cables.

'I smell blood of Englishman!' The *oni* grinned, displaying great yellow teeth with chunks of rotting meat stuck in between. 'My English is good, *ne*? I study! My name is Kenichi. Pleased to eat you.'

And with that, the *oni* charged.

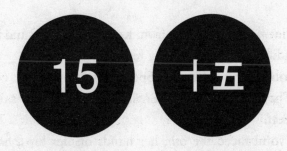

15 十五

The *oni* slammed into the seats, only to find itself wedged under the armpit by the vertical hand rail. Kenny had leapt aside at the last moment, whereas Kiyomi had dived straight between the creature's legs, rolled and sprang to her feet behind it.

The *oni* trampled the shopping bags as it tried to regain its footing. The Pringles can rolled loose from a squashed bag and trundled towards Kenny's feet.

The *oni* wrenched itself free and twisted round.

'Kenny! The *tanto*! Throw it,' Kiyomi said, taking two steps back from the *oni*.

'The what?' Kenny said, grabbing the canister.

'The sword, in the –'

Kenny flung the Pringles can. The *oni* stuck out a huge, three-fingered hand, caught the can and tossed it into its mouth, swallowing it whole.

'Urgh! You idiot!' Kiyomi screamed. 'What kind of crap throw was that?'

'How was I supposed to know it was going to catch it?' Kenny said.

The *oni*'s head swung from Kenny to Kiyomi and back again like it was watching a tennis match.

'Too fast!' it bellowed. 'Speak slow.'

'It wants to practise English *now*?' Kenny said in disbelief.

Kiyomi faced the *oni*, her hands on her hips, hatred twisting her face. 'Give me my sword back, puke-face, before I kick your ass out through the top of your head.'

The *oni* cocked its head to one side and its lips moved as it worked on translating.

'I don't think it underst–' Kenny began.

'That. Not. Nice,' the *oni* roared.

'Then again.' Kenny shrugged.

The huge creature snapped the handrail from its fixings and held it in both hands like a club. It glared at Kiyomi. 'You bad girl. Kenichi teach manners.'

'Yeah, yeah, whatever.' Kiyomi traced a shape in the air, which Kenny realised for the first time was a Chinese character. '*Chikara*!' she shouted and, stepping forward to close the gap, she landed a piledriver fist into the *oni*'s midriff.

The blow lifted the monster off its feet and sent it flying down the central aisle of the carriage. It would have continued down the length of the train, had it not stuck out both hands and grabbed on to the carriage wall.

'Not nice!' it roared again and struggled to its feet.

'I asked you nicely: give me back my sword,' Kiyomi repeated.

'*RRRAARRGGHHH!*' was the *oni*'s answer and it charged towards her again, with the force of a locomotive.

Kiyomi ran to meet its charge, leapt high into the air and landed a flurry of blows to a host of nerve centres, working her way up with a kick to its knee, another to its crotch, a punch to the solar plexus, elbow to the sternum and a heel of the palm below the jaw. To Kenny, she almost seemed to clamber up the creature's body.

The *oni*'s head snapped back and it crashed to the floor, eyes rolling back and tongue lolling. Kiyomi landed with her knee in its stomach. It gagged and spat out the Pringles tube.

'Ugh,' Kiyomi said in disgust, picking up the can. She opened it, removed the sword and bent over the twitching monster. 'This is for my mother,' she said and brought the sword down. The *oni* crumbled to dust.

Sato knelt by the mound of ash under the counter in the *Tokyu Hands* sports department. He touched it lightly, rubbed a little dust from his fingertips, watching how it fell, and then smelled his fingers.

The floor manager wrung his hands and hopped from foot to foot as he watched.

Sato put a small sample of ash in a ziplock bag and slipped it into his jacket pocket. 'Thank you,' he said to the manager. 'I have finished here. You may reopen the floor.'

'After we clean up, of course,' the manager said, pulling out a handkerchief and mopping his face.

'One last thing,' Sato said. 'You have security cameras, yes?'

'Please, come with me.' The manager led Sato away, allowing the clean-up crew to take over.

Once in the security office, Sato leaned closer to the television monitor. On screen was monochrome footage of Kenny swinging the baseball bat around in the sports section as if chasing flies. There was no sign of anything untoward, like flying heads, just a teenage boy smashing up the place.

'This is vandalism,' the floor manager said. 'These *gaijin* have no respect.'

'Thank you,' Sato said. 'That will be all.'

The manager bowed and left. Sato waited for the door to close before putting on his sunglasses and viewing the disc again.

'*Nukekubi*,' he said. 'Taro?'

'I see them,' the red *oni* said, peering over Sato's shoulder. 'Five of them.'

'Yes. The boy is clever . . . resourceful. He learns fast.' Sato watched the film again.

'But he doesn't kill them,' Taro noted.

'No, that would be this one.' Sato froze the picture on Kiyomi plunging her sword into one of the headless bodies.

Taro blinked. 'Isn't that . . .?'

Sato sighed, with deep resignation. 'Yes, it is. I always knew it would come to this one day.'

'What are you going to do about it?' the *oni* rumbled.

'Find the boy. Nothing has changed. He is the key to it all. Find him, find the sword.'

Kiyomi swayed and her legs started to buckle. Kenny caught her before she fell and lowered her on to a seat.

'Kiyomi, are you –?'

'I'm OK, just a little woozy. That one really takes it out of you.'

'What does? That . . . thing you did?'

'Yeah. It's kind of like borrowing energy in advance. But then you've got to pay it back.'

Kenny sat down beside her. 'You know, you were pretty awesome back there.'

Kiyomi shrugged. 'It was him or us.'

'I heard what you said. Before . . .'

Kiyomi looked up at him, a steely edge to her eyes. 'I don't want to talk about it.'

'Your mother –'

'I said I'm not going to talk about it. Let's go home. I've had enough for one day.'

'This is worse than I thought,' Harashima said. '*Nukekubi* almost never attack in daylight, and then for an *oni*.' He glanced at Kiyomi but she looked away. 'They are getting desperate and that means it is too dangerous for you to go out again.'

It was late afternoon and the three of them were sitting

121

on wicker chairs in the garden. The trees, high above, vibrated with the songs of cicadas. The air was hot and sticky, and the shade from the parasol was of little help.

'But sir, aren't I supposed to find this fox-person?' Kenny asked. 'How can I do that if I'm stuck here?'

'Kuromori-*san*, the only reason you have not been captured yet is because the wards placed on this land keep you hidden. And you being a foreigner makes it much more difficult for them to trace you . . . by other means.'

'Father means *yurei*,' Kiyomi said, still gazing distractedly into space. 'Spirits are excellent trackers because they can go almost anywhere, but they can't read your *ki*.'

'My key?'

'*Ki*,' Harashima said. 'Energy, spirit, life force. The thing that powers your body.'

'Being alive, you leave traces of energy wherever you go,' Kiyomi said, 'like a scent. Certain beings can follow that scent.'

'But you being an outsider makes it difficult,' Harashima continued. 'The wavelength of your energy is beyond their range.'

Oyama came out of the house with a tray, balancing a jug of iced tea and three glasses, which he set down on the table.

Kenny scratched his head. 'You mean, it's a bit like the dog whistle in reverse? You can see me, but they can't?'

122

Harashima smiled and handed Kenny a glass. 'Yes, something like that.'

Kenny pondered this for a few seconds. 'So how come these things are always popping up and trying to eat me?'

'They're flooding the ground,' Harashima said. 'It spreads them thin, and it's a big risk, but that shows how important you are to them.'

'I still don't see why everyone thinks I'm any use,' Kenny said, half to himself, and took a gulp of tea. He frowned at it and held it up to the sun.

'Is something wrong?' Harashima asked.

'No, not really,' Kenny said. 'It's just my tea. It tastes a bit . . . soapy, that's all.'

Oyama scowled in Kenny's direction.

'That would be the soft water we have here,' Harashima said. 'London tap water is much harder and it makes tea taste —'

'Oh my God. Papa, you're a genius!' Kiyomi shrieked, leaping up and bounding into the house.

Kenny and Harashima exchanged puzzled glances and shrugged, before following Kiyomi indoors. They found her in the main room, furiously tapping the keys on a laptop plugged into the bank of monitors.

An aerial map of Tokyo flashed up on the wall, showing vast grey areas of conurbation with a blue river snaking through to the sea.

Kiyomi continued to type as she spoke. 'There I was thinking how important it is that we find Genkuro-*sensei*, while all you men can do is discuss whether hard or soft water makes better tea, and then it hit me: water for tea.'

Kenny waited for it.

'Duh! Ochanomizu. Kenny, your dream. It wasn't the kettle or the water jug that was important, it was what the water was *for*.'

Kenny looked to Harashima for help.

'Ochanomizu is a place in Tokyo,' he said. 'Literally, it means "water for tea".'

Kenny's eyebrows shot upwards. 'You have a place called "tea water"?'

'Don't you start,' Kiyomi said. 'There's a place called Catbrain in England and a Monkey's Eyebrow in the States.'

Harashima stroked his chin. 'There was a spring once, very pure, which was used to make the tea for Toku–'

'Papa, not now!' Kiyomi said. 'Look.'

The map zoomed in and blobs of green appeared amid the grey. Kiyomi adjusted the picture again and Kenny could make out roads, city blocks and parks.

'If I key in Takebashi, Roppongi and Ochanomizu, we get a very thin triangle, running north-east to south-west,' Kiyomi said, drawing the vectors between the three places. 'And if I calculate the centre of that triangle . . .we get – Oh, no! You've got to be kidding me.'

Kenny looked and saw a small island on a lake set inside a lush expanse of green.

Harashima smiled. 'Genkuro-*sensei* still likes his

tricks. Where better? It's green, it's safe. Perfect.'

Kenny looked over Kiyomi's shoulder at the laptop screen. 'This Genkuro bloke is on the island?' he said. 'That's great, then. Let's go see him.'

Kiyomi groaned. 'Kenny, a patch of green in the centre of Tokyo? Do you have any idea where this is?'

Kenny shook his head.

'It's the gardens of the Imperial Palace – where the Emperor lives. Talk about mission impossible. It's got armed guards, motion sensors, watchtowers, you name it. And all we have to do is break in.'

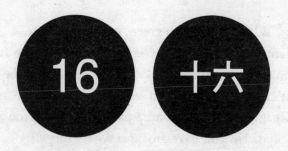

'I'm sorry,' Kenny said, 'I must have misheard you.'

'Which part?' Kiyomi asked.

'Try all of it. Did you say the Emperor's Palace? Motion sensors? Guards with guns?'

'Yeah, like I said, impossible.'

'Difficult, yes. Impossible, no,' Harashima said, tracing his index finger over the map and examining it closely. 'I have an idea.' He checked his watch. 'There is still time. Go, please. I must make some telephone calls.'

Kiyomi knew better than to argue with her father. Instead, she went to her room to fetch a flat wooden box, which she tucked under her arm, and started out to the *dojo* in the garden. Kenny trotted after her, a question nagging at his mind.

'Kiyomi, wait up,' he called, jogging to catch up. 'On the train, with the *oni*, how did you do that . . . thing?'

'What thing?' She didn't slow her pace for him.

'When you drew in the air, it was a Chinese character, wasn't it? You drew it and then . . . ' He twiddled his hands. 'You know.'

'Oh, that. I don't know if I can explain it properly. Perhaps Genkuro-*sensei* will be able to. Anyway, you won't be able to do it. Even if you could, it'd be very dangerous. Until then, let's stick to what I *can* teach you.'

She kicked her slippers off and stepped on to the cool, dirt floor. Setting the wooden box down, she opened it and removed a number of flat metal discs, their ends cut into starlike points with sharp, bevelled edges.

'Whoa,' Kenny said, stepping into the *dojo*. 'Don't you ever play with Barbies or make-up, like normal gir–' He stopped as a metal star swooshed past his ear and thudded into the wooden post beside his head.

'These are *hira-shuriken*,' Kiyomi said. 'Very useful against *nukekubi*. I'll show you how to throw one properly.'

Kenny stared at the razor-sharp throwing star which had shaved his ear, while Kiyomi went out back and returned with a straw dummy. She slammed it down into position against the far wall. It was clear that her mood had taken a sharp turn for the worse.

Before Kenny could wonder why, she stomped over to stand beside him. 'Are you saying I'm abnormal?' she asked.

'No, no. Just that you're . . . different from other girls.' Kenny wished his mouth had waited for his brain; he'd obviously hit a nerve.

'Different? Thanks. Another way of saying abnormal.' She launched a *shuriken* across the space, landing it in the dummy's head. 'Here, see what you can do.' She handed him a throwing star.

'Oh, man. Must you twist everything? I just meant that most girls –'

'Throw it.'

Kenny held the *shuriken* and then swore as it sliced his finger.

'Hold one of the points flat between your thumb and first finger. Like this. You pinch it.' Kiyomi demonstrated the grip.

'You see? This is what I mean,' Kenny said. He threw the star and it slammed straight into the floor. 'Most girls I know don't play with these kinds of things.'

'Play? You think this is a toy? Try again. Since you're a beginner, I'll show you an easy throw.' She handed Kenny another *shuriken*. 'Hold it up, beside your ear. Lift your elbow and point it at the dummy.'

Kiyomi stood so close to Kenny that her scent gave him goosebumps. She positioned his arm and stepped back.

'I suppose most girls you know spend their time worrying about their friends, their clothes, their hair,' she said. 'I'll bet none of them know the first thing about the real nature of the world.'

Kenny snapped his arm down, releasing the star as his arm extended out straight and pointed at the target. The *shuriken* whistled past the dummy's shoulder.

'Better,' Kiyomi said. 'Try shifting your weight from back foot to front while you throw and flick your wrist at the end. Go for accuracy, not power. *Shuriken* are meant to distract, not kill.'

Kenny took another star from the box. 'Kiyomi, listen. You and I both have this ability to see these *yokai* things. It sets us apart, right?'

'You mean it makes us into freaks, isn't that what you're saying?'

'No, no, not at all. It's good that we can see these things, isn't it? It means we can help people.'

'But Kenny . . . ' Kiyomi's eyes were welling up, her voice breaking. 'Who helps us?'

'Wh – What do you mean?' Kenny was caught off guard by the show of emotion.

'You think I wouldn't love to be able to forget about all this, to live my life like a normal person, thinking monsters are just in fairy tales? Why do I always have to be the strong one?'

She bowed her head and her hair fell forward as she covered her face. Kenny wasn't sure what to do. Run away? Wait for her to cry it out? Hide? He made himself inch closer and reached a tentative hand towards her. Kiyomi moved a step nearer, and Kenny's hand rested on her shoulder. He felt silly, standing like that, so he placed his other arm round her and gently drew her close. He felt her tears dampen his shoulder but he didn't mind.

'Because it's either you or Poyo, and he isn't much use in a fight,' he whispered.

'*Ahurm.*' Kenny looked up to see Oyama blocking the

doorway. The servant beckoned for Kenny to follow and turned away, his face as impassive as a stone Buddha's.

Back in the house, Harashima was sitting at the table. He gestured for Kenny and Kiyomi to join him.

'I think I have found our way in. On most days, there is a guided tour of the Imperial Palace,' he said. 'It is very popular and you have to book weeks ahead. Fortunately, I have been able to call in some favours and so you two will be joining the group tomorrow. Here, you will need these.'

He handed Kenny a thin dark blue booklet and gave Kiyomi a black one. Kenny looked at the gold lettering on the front. It said PASSPORT and, below the image of an eagle clutching arrows in one claw and an olive branch in the other, was the lettering: *United States of America*. Kenny thumbed it open and looked in the back to see his picture.

'You need identification to get in,' Harashima said, 'and Sato has your real passport.'

'But sir,' Kenny said. 'How did you –? You didn't have enough time . . .'

Harashima smiled. 'I had this passport made three years ago. That is why you look so young in the photo.'

'Who gave you the picture?' Kenny suspected he knew the answer.

'Your grandfather. He said it would come in useful one day.'

Kiyomi smiled. 'So, Richard, what do you think?'

'Richard?' Kenny read the name in the back. 'Oh, no.'

'Yep. Your name is Richard Head, but I'll call you Dick.' Kiyomi beamed, waiting for the penny to drop.

'Thanks. Let me guess, that was your idea. And who are you supposed to be?'

Kiyomi showed him her passport. 'I'm Candice Wong, from Kowloon, Hong Kong. My friends call me Candy, because I'm so sweet.' She smiled winningly and fluttered her eyelashes. 'Am I right?'

'No, you're Wong.'

'I've got it all worked out. We met on the plane coming over. You're here visiting family on the naval base at Yokosuka. I was in the next seat and we got talking. I didn't like you at first, because you're such a dweeb, but then you offered to carry my bags and you –'

Harashima held up a hand for silence. 'Why don't you two go and practise your lines somewhere else? I need to discuss some things with Oyama.'

Kiyomi's ears pricked up. 'Why Oyama?'

'Because he is going with you. Children have to be accompanied by an adult. Poyo will go too.'

'Sir, you said you have a plan to get us into the palace grounds,' Kenny said. 'When are you going to tell us about it?'

'Soon enough,' Harashima said. 'Soon enough.'

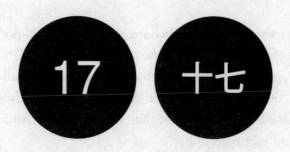

The taxi pulled up on Uchibori Dori at 09:30 the following morning. Oyama eased himself out of the passenger seat and thrust a handful of crisp brown notes at the white-gloved driver.

Kiyomi opened the rear door and Poyo bounded out. He lounged on the pavement while she knelt to ruffle his ears and give him a small tube of toothpaste, which he took in his paws.

'You know what to do, right?' she said. Poyo nodded and raised a paw in salute. 'Go, then. And be careful.'

'What's that for?' Kenny joined her and watched the fat, furry animal scurry away, weaving between the legs of unsuspecting pedestrians, with the skyscrapers of downtown Tokyo punctuating the horizon.

'You'll find out.'

Oyama led the way, past squat concrete bollards and up to a checkpoint on the right. He handed the visitor passes and fake passports to a white-gloved official who checked the names against a list and waved them through. The path led over a tree-lined stone bridge which crossed the moat.

'This is the Kikyo-mon, the Bellflower Gate,' Kiyomi said, pointing in front.

Two massive stone walls rose up on either side of the bridge with a dark-tiled, gable roof crossing the open space between. A white-walled watchtower with a curving roof stood to the right.

Kenny grinned. 'Finally, I get to see some of the real Japan, not just burger bars and shops.'

Over the bridge was another checkpoint where their bags were examined and paperwork scrutinised again. The path curved under the watchtower and led to a squat single-storey visitors' centre. Tables and benches stood in neat lines opposite a large flat screen.

Kenny groaned to himself. 'Here's where we get the video, right? Telling us everything we're about to see?'

Kiyomi smiled. 'You've been here before?'

While they waited, the room filled up and Kenny estimated there were over a hundred visitors taking the tour, most of them Japanese by the look of it.

As he had feared, the video was in Japanese, without subtitles, but Kenny did his best to follow the pictures.

The film over, uniformed tour guides herded the visitors out and back into the courtyard. The route led past an old government building, a white-walled three-storey keep towering above a stone embankment, across another bridge overlooking a moat choked with a carpet of lotus leaves, and on to a long, narrow, paved courtyard which lay in front of the Imperial Palace. The guides spoke in Japanese but Kiyomi translated for Kenny's benefit.

'Japanese people gather here at New Year and on the Emperor's birthday,' she said. 'Like you guys do on The Mall in London. Over there is the palace and the royal family appear on that balcony.'

The tour group marched past another white-walled keep, down to the Nijubashi bridge and then doubled back on itself, passing the palace again, this time on the left.

'We're almost where we need to be,' Kiyomi said. 'Get the whistle ready.'

The guides directed the crowd to make a sharp turn down the side of the palace and under an interconnecting passage linking the residence with an administration building. The path merged on to a long tree-lined road, bordered on both sides by earth embankments with sculpted bushes.

'Blow the whistle now,' Kiyomi said.

Kenny slipped the *tanuki* whistle from his pocket and blew hard on it. A crashing came from the undergrowth and Poyo burst out of the bushes in an explosion of twigs and leaves.

Screams of terror tore through the air and a ripple of panic surged through the crowd as someone yelled, '*Kyokenbyo!*' The tourists, who had been moving in orderly lines up till now, broke ranks and stampeded in all directions, leaving bags, umbrellas, lunch boxes, guidebooks and other items behind in the rush.

Kenny grinned to himself. Poyo was leaping around,

snapping and growling at the nearest visitors, minty-white froth foaming from his jaws. He looked exactly like a rabid animal on the rampage.

A tour guide hung back and gestured frantically for Kenny to follow him. Kenny hesitated, knowing he was being watched. Oyama suddenly threw his hands in the air like a damsel in distress and ran smack into the guide, sending him flying into the bushes.

'Now!' Kiyomi said and she bolted off the path, up the embankment and into the thick trees beyond.

Kenny looked back long enough to see Oyama lift the stunned guide on to his shoulders and begin carrying him back to the gate before he charged after Kiyomi into the trees.

A hand grabbed his trouser leg. 'Shh! Down here.' Kiyomi pulled Kenny into a hollow at the base of a tree where they crouched low.

'We wait for the fuss to die down and then we move,' she whispered. 'The island's about three hundred metres due west, but we'll need to go round the moat pond first. If we keep to the trees, no one will see us.'

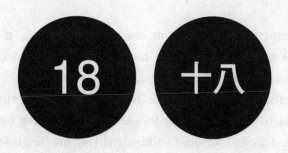

Sato placed the mobile phone on the table in the police interview room. 'Remember, Professor, Kenny's life is in great danger.'

Charles Blackwood nodded and picked up the phone. After spending three days in police custody, the strain was beginning to show. Sato sat opposite and observed him the way a cat watches a mouse.

Kenny's father scratched his stubbled chin and punched in a string of numbers, then waited for the international connection to go through.

The receiver picked up after one ring. 'Hello?' An old man's voice, but strong and authoritative.

'Dad? It's Charles.'

'Charles! How the devil are you? Long time no hear. And how's my precious grandson? Is he settling in well?'

'Yeah, he's doing fine, just fine. Uh, Dad . . . is there something you haven't been telling me? About this trip?'

'No, not at all. Why do you ask?'

'Oh, just something Kenny said about running an errand for you.'

'He said that? Really?'

'I know, it's absurd, isn't it. To think you'd send a teenage boy all this way just to complete your unfinished business. Ridiculous idea, isn't it, Dad?'

Sato counted the pause that followed: seven seconds.

'May I speak to Kenny?' said the voice on the line.

'You could if he were here.'

'Charles, I'm sorry. You have no idea how sorry I am. If there was any other way.'

'Dad, are you out of your mind? He's a child! He's –'

'A lot more talented and resourceful than you give him credit for.'

Charles was on his feet by now. 'Listen, Dad, they've arrested me and there's a manhunt under way. The Secret Service are involved, for God's sake. What the hell have you got him doing?'

'Charles, believe me, the less you know about this the better for everyone.'

'Is he stealing some treasure for you? That's what they think is happening, you know.'

Charles's father sighed. 'Put Sato on the phone.'

Sato raised both eyebrows quizzically as Charles thrust the phone at him.

'Yes?' he ventured.

'You and I both know that my son has nothing to do with any of this,' Lawrence said, his voice low. 'Kenny is the one you want. Let Charles go. Put him on the next plane back to England, if you must.'

'Kuromori-*sama*, it is an honour to speak to you at last,' Sato said, bowing. 'However, you are in no position to make demands. Professor Blackwood will remain as my guest unless you return the stolen treasure or Kenny gives himself up.'

'You know I can't do that. There are millions of lives at stake.'

'Then you have made your choice and I have made mine.' Sato ended the call.

Kiyomi moved through the thick undergrowth. Stretching out a slender leg, she tested the earth beneath her foot and, only when satisfied that there were no twigs to snap or dry leaves to scrunch, she transferred her weight forward. It made for slow going but it was nearly silent. The only sounds were birds singing overhead, the wind rustling through the trees and Tokyo traffic in the distance.

Kenny tried to work out far how they had come. He stopped by the trunk of a Japanese maple to view his surroundings: all around was thick growth at each level – grasses, shrubs, bushes, trees. Something sparkled ahead, through the leaves.

'Psst! Kiyomi,' he whispered.

'What is it?' she hissed, balancing in mid-step.

'What's that shiny thing in front?'

'That's the old moat pond. We need to stay well away from it. Come on.'

Kenny took a last look at the murky brown pool,

overgrown with water lilies. For a moment, he could have sworn he saw something looking back at him. There was a splash and a plop as a frog returned to the water.

They continued circling clockwise round the pond, keeping as far from the water as they could. Kiyomi raised a hand to signal a stop.

'Problem,' she whispered.

Kenny looked. They had come to the edge of the treeline. To the left was an open road leading to a cluster of traditional Japanese buildings. Ahead, on the right, was the moat pond. A narrow bank ran between the two.

'That's the Kyuchusanden, the Three Palace Sanctuaries,' Kiyomi whispered, indicating the buildings. 'Very special, very holy places. They'll be crawling with security.'

'Which means what?'

'It means we'll have to risk the pond. Do exactly what I do and, whatever happens, make sure you get to Genkuro-*sensei* on the island. Nothing else matters, you understand?'

'It's only a pond.' Kenny had never heard Kiyomi sound so uneasy before.

'It's not the pond I'm worried about. Now come on.' She led the way along the narrow strip of bank, keeping a watchful eye on the water, which was smooth and placid. Marshmallow clouds shimmered in reflection.

They were halfway across when Kiyomi stopped. 'Kenny, don't move,' she said, looking down. A tiny indentation appeared in the fine soil beside her feet. She watched in growing horror as the dimple rapidly deepened and dilated, becoming a crater in seconds. Her arms shot out to grab at nearby branches and tree roots as the bank collapsed, dropping her waist-deep into the murky water. 'Kenny, run!' she said. 'It's a trap.'

Kenny caught a glimpse of something gliding beneath the surface, heading straight for Kiyomi.

'I said, go!' she repeated.

'No way! I'm not leaving you,' Kenny said.

'You must. You're too import– *bleurghh*!' Kiyomi disappeared beneath the water, leaving only bubbles and a hand desperately reaching upwards, clawing the air.

Kenny flung himself forward, grabbed her hand and wrapped his other arm around a slim tree trunk. Kiyomi's hand pulled away from his. Kenny dug his fingers into her wrist and hung on. His left arm was wrenched at the socket and he felt the young tree start to move in the loosened earth. Whatever it was that had grabbed Kiyomi was strong and a powerful swimmer.

Kenny's face twisted in pain and he felt like both of his arms would be torn out. He heard his shoulder ligaments creak and his arms burned, but he refused to let go. Just when he thought he couldn't hold on any longer, the thing released its grip and Kiyomi's head burst through the lilies as she drew in a huge lungful of fresh air. Kenny dragged her towards the bank.

'*Nandaro?*' said a high, whiny voice.

A head was sticking up out of the pond, its two bulbous eyes glaring at Kenny. The face was green, with features like those of a wizened monkey; small nostrils sat atop a protruding, beak-like mouth and a ring of black hair fringed a sunken bald pate.

Kiyomi splashed her way to the bank and tried to clamber up, but the creature disappeared again beneath the water, resurfacing to wrap its scaly webbed fingers round her trailing ankle.

'Let her go!' Kenny shouted.

'Will not!' the thing said. 'Me catch dinner. Me hungry. Me eat now.' It tugged the ankle. Kiyomi was dragged back, grass tearing loose in her hands.

'No, wait!' Kenny said. 'No, you don't want to eat that.'

The thing stopped and its eyes swivelled from Kenny to Kiyomi and back. 'Yes, me do,' it said. 'Girl pretty.' It squeezed Kiyomi's hip. 'Nice and soft. Yummy.' She twisted away, trying to kick out with her other foot, while still clinging to the grassy bank.

'No way, man, uh, thing,' Kenny tried again. 'Not that one. She's tough and mean, all stringy and gristly.'

'Hey!' Kiyomi said. '*She* can hear you.'

'I'm trying to help you here,' Kenny muttered.

'Oh, yeah, sorry.' She kicked out at the creature, splashing it with water. 'He's right,' she said. 'I'm yucky. You don't want to eat me. I'd make you –'

'Quiet!' the thing said. 'Not talking to you.' It hawked and spat a swampy green glob of phlegm into Kiyomi's face. The blob splattered over her mouth and instantly hardened, sealing her lips shut.

'*Mmmfff mff mffffm ffffffffffmmmm!*'

'See? Told you,' Kenny said. 'Not nice at all. I'm sure we can find you something much tastier to eat.'

'Like you?' The thing cocked its head and appraised Kenny's worth as a meal.

'Me? No, no, I taste worse. Besides, who likes foreign food anyway? I'd probably give you bad gas and then how would you swim?'

'Me hungry!' the thing shouted. It looked from Kenny to Kiyomi and its eyes lit up. 'Me eat you both.'

'How about I get you something else – like a sampler plate?' Kenny said. 'You know, a tasting menu. That way, if you find something you like, you can have more of it, instead of us.'

The creature looked doubtful.

'Have you ever had a Big Mac? No one's ever hungry after one of those.'

The monster slithered out of the water and parked its rear on Kiyomi's chest. '*Gnnff!*' she protested. Kenny shuddered. The thing was the size of a large child, with a domed shell on its back, like a turtle's, and a necklace of monkey skulls rattling against its chest.

'No tricks,' it said. A strong smell of fish emanated from the creature.

Kenny reached for the whistle, blew hard and stepped back, positioning himself beside a thick fallen branch. A rustling came from the bushes and Poyo sprang forward. He took one look at the pond creature and recoiled, whimpering.

'Poyo,' Kenny said. 'Go find some food as quickly as you can. Only good stuff, OK?'

Poyo turned tail and bolted back the way he had come.

The creature leaned over Kiyomi, keeping its head level, and brought its beak closer to her face to sniff at her. It repositioned itself and placed a clawed hand on her middle. Kenny watched in fascinated horror. Its movements were very odd, as if balancing a book on its head.

'Mmm, lots of yummy sausages in there,' it said, patting Kiyomi's belly. 'Me cannot wait.'

Kenny decided to try and keep it talking. 'So, uh, what do you normally eat around here?' he asked.

'Frogs . . . lotus roots . . . fish . . . worms . . . sometimes squirrel, or duck.' It laughed: a series of short barks. 'Duck funny. Head goes down, chomp, head goes down.' It shook with laughter and sunlight sparkled off its bald head. Kenny looked closer: on the top of its head was a bowl-like depression, and in the hollow was a shallow pool of pond water.

'Not monkeys?' Kenny offered, pointing at the skulls around the thing's neck.

The creature scowled. 'No. No monkey near pond.'

'Then what're those . . .?' Even before it answered, Kenny felt his stomach churn.

'Yes! Baby! Yummy. Soft and juicy. Babies best.'

Kenny eyed the heavy branch by his foot. But the creature was close to the water and Kiyomi wouldn't have a chance. He would have to wait.

There was a crashing through the bushes and Poyo tumbled head over heels, skidding to a stop by Kenny. He was holding a fast-food takeaway bag in his mouth, and in his paws was a *bento* box. He lay on his back, panting from his efforts.

'Thank you,' Kenny said, patting him. 'Good boy.'

The monster sat up, sniffing the air. 'Hungry!' it said again.

Kenny looked inside the bag. 'What have we here? Hot dog?' he said.

The thing pressed its claws against Kiyomi's throat. 'Me hate dog!' it shrieked. 'Smelly thing. Snappy, yappy, chasey.'

'OK, OK,' Kenny said, tossing the bag. He opened the lunch box. 'How about some *sushi* roll?'

'*Aaaagh*!' the pond creature howled, stamping its foot in fury. 'Me eat fish every day! You mock me. Promised me good food and – *aaaaahh*!' Its eyes grew wide and it jumped to its feet in excitement.

Kenny stared at the *sushi* he was holding. It was a thick slice of seaweed-wrapped rice with a glistening green middle. 'This? What's so . . .?' The answer came to him in a flash; after all, he was near fresh water. 'Grandad's letter!'

'Give it me,' the thing said, shuffling towards Kenny,

its eyes transfixed on the cucumber roll and its head held level.

Kenny took a step backwards. 'There's more in the box. You want it? Come on then.'

'Let me have it,' the creature said, sounding pained.

'That's the plan,' Kenny said, picking out three more chunks and holding them up. 'How many lumps do you want?'

The thing was now in front of him, its hands scrabbling at the air, reaching for the *futomaki*.

'Give it me!' it demanded.

'Catch.' Kenny dropped the *sushi* on the ground. The creature ducked to grab at it and the water spilled from the top of its head. It gave a loud croak of alarm and stiffened like a statue, still bent double.

'Hold that pose,' Kenny said, picking up the heavy branch. Fear filled the creature's eyes as Kenny drew back the club and took aim.

'*Ptoo*! Kenny, no!' As soon as the creature had moved away, Kiyomi had crawled up the bank and was scraping the goop from her face. 'No, don't kill it. It can't hurt us now.' She pulled herself up on to solid ground.

'This thing eats babies,' Kenny said. 'It deserves to die.' He readied the branch, lining it up with the creature's head.

'Kenny, no. It's a *kappa*. It does what it does. I'm not asking you to understand this right now, but it's not evil. It's just an animal.'

'It eats babies,' Kenny said again, hate twisting his face.

Kiyomi sighed. 'Babies who were drowned by their mothers a few hundred years ago because there wasn't enough food back then. Those skulls are ancient history. *Kappa* are clean-up crew, like vultures and things. Now they help keep the grounds clean.'

'Me . . . give . . . you . . . anything . . .' the *kappa* gurgled. 'Not . . . kill . . . me . . . ' Huge tears rolled down its cheeks and splashed on to the ground. 'Pleeaase.'

Kenny took a deep breath, his nostrils flared and teeth clenched. He closed his eyes and dropped the club.

Kiyomi crawled over to the stricken creature. 'Your life belongs to us now, you understand?'

'Yes . . . understand,' it said.

'Then go. Find another pond, far away. I never want to see you again.'

She gave the *kappa* a push and it plopped backwards into the water, disappearing from view.

Kenny helped Kiyomi to her feet. 'I've said it once and I'll say it again,' he said. 'You have some bloody weird monsters in this place.'

Relief flooded through Kiyomi and her knees buckled. Seeing her about to fall, Kenny caught her and she flung her arms round him for balance. He, in turn, held her tightly until she stopped shaking.

'You can let go of me now,' Kiyomi said. 'I know you were scared, but it's OK – the big, bad monster is gone.'

Kenny stepped back, the tips of his ears pink. 'What do you mean? I saved you there.'

146

'Nah, I just let you think that. We all know how fragile the male ego is.' She winked at him. 'Let's go find Genkuro-*sensei*.'

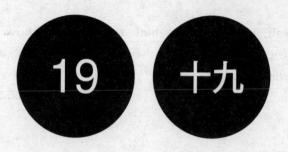

19 十九

The elevator stopped on the top floor of the Shinjuku headquarters and Miyamoto hurried to the Chief Executive's office. He knocked once and waited.

'Enter,' the older man said.

Miyamoto closed the door behind him and bowed low before the mahogany desk. '*Shacho*, you wished to see me,' he said.

'I want another test of the weapon,' the man in the pinstripe suit said.

'But sir, only last week –'

'Time is running out and we cannot afford any mistakes. I must be sure that we can control the weapon and that it can be properly targeted. The Americans must pay the price, not Mexico or Canada.'

'As you wish, sir. It will be done. Do you have a test subject in mind?'

The old man smiled: a cold, pitiless grimace. 'I feel that London would be . . . an educational target. What about the boy?'

'Still hidden from us, sir.'

'And Sato? Is he any closer to finding the sword?'

'No, sir. The path begins and ends with Kuromori. As prophesied.'

The older man leaned forward. 'I thought I had made myself clear: I will have no talk of prophecy.'

'But sir, if the boy is the one foretold, then all of this will –'

'If the prophecy comes true, then an enemy will die at the boy's hand. It will be a small price to pay. Now go and prepare the test.'

Miyamoto bowed deeply and left.

The old man waited for the door to click shut before he rose to stand in front of a portrait on the wall. It was an oil painting of a balding Japanese man, dressed in a traditional *kamishimo* ensemble. His head was held high and in his right hand was a closed paper fan.

The suited man bowed low before the picture. '*Otosan*,' he said, 'all is ready. Soon, your death will be avenged and your spirit will know peace. The Americans will learn for themselves what it is like to live among ruins.'

'There's the island.' Kiyomi crouched low, peering through the rushes at the edge of the small lake. A narrow footbridge led across to a small tree-covered hump of land.

'Let me go first this time,' Kenny said.

Kiyomi was about to argue, then changed her mind and nodded. Kenny checked that no one was around and stepped lightly on to the bridge. He quickly ran across and, once on the island, he was faced by a thick wall of vegetation.

'This is nuts,' he whispered to Kiyomi when she joined him. 'How can anyone live in this jungle? We must have got something wrong.'

'Shh,' she said and picked her way forward. 'There's something . . .' She reached out, brushing the air with her fingertips. The air shimmered and rippled like a curtain. Kiyomi smiled and pressed her hand against the invisible barrier.

Kenny gasped as Kiyomi's hand vanished. She pushed her arm through and then her head. It was the oddest thing Kenny had seen: half a body standing, the other half gone, as if slipping into a pool of watery light. Then Kiyomi disappeared completely and Kenny was wondering if he should follow when her head reappeared, floating in space like a *nukekubi*.

'What are you waiting for?' she said. 'Move your butt.'

Kenny pushed through the invisible barrier. He closed his eyes and it felt like being immersed in a thick gel. His body tingled with pins and needles all over and then he was through, standing at the entrance of a *Shinto* temple. Poyo squeezed his way next to Kenny.

In front of them stood a tall arched gate. A pair of stone columns rose to support two horizontal crossbeams, the uppermost of which curved gently upwards.

Kiyomi led the way, under the *torii* gate, up the stone steps beyond and on to a paved courtyard. Trees grew on three sides and in front was a magnificent, double-roofed, wooden building. Kenny could see balconies, pillars, intricate carvings inlaid with gold leaf, paper lanterns, *shoji* screen doors.

'Welcome, welcome,' said a strong, high voice. 'Please, won't you join me for some tea?'

Kenny looked for the speaker and saw a tall, thin Japanese man, wearing grey robes, standing at the entrance to the temple. His face was etched with wrinkles, but his eyes sparkled.

'Genkuro-*sensei*!' Kiyomi screamed in delight and ran to throw herself at him, almost knocking him over.

'Kiyomi-*chan*, you have grown,' Genkuro said, pinching her cheek and looking her up and down. 'You are almost a woman now.'

Kiyomi blushed.

Genkuro's kindly gaze fell on Kenny. 'And this is Kuromori-*san*. Welcome to my simple home.'

'You're human?' Kenny said, approaching the elderly man. 'I was expecting . . . something else.'

'Many things are not as they seem at first glance – like you, for example. I see your grandfather in you, young Kenneth. You have done very well to find me. Very well indeed. Your grandfather will be proud.'

'Thank you, sir,' Kenny said. 'You taught my grandfather?'

'Yes, I did. Lawrence was one of my most gifted students. You have much to live up to.'

'But that was over seventy years ago,' Kenny said, doing the maths in his head. 'If you don't mind my asking, sir . . . how old are you?'

Genkuro smiled and tucked his hands into the sleeves of his robe. 'Everything at its due time. Now, it is time for tea.'

Two hours later, Kenny finally sipped his tea. It was green, frothy and bitter, served in a bowl.

Genkuro had led his two visitors to a tea room inside the temple and meticulously performed *chanoyu*, the tea ceremony. Pouring freshly drawn spring water into a cast-iron kettle, he had set it on a charcoal fire to boil. When the water was hot, Genkuro took a bamboo ladle and transferred some of it into a tea bowl which held a measure of powdered green tea. Finally, using a bamboo whisk, he stirred the tea and presented it to his guests, each movement smooth and precisely executed.

'Mmm, delicious,' Kenny fibbed, passing the bowl to Kiyomi.

She bowed, took it in her right hand and placed it on her left palm. She then carefully rotated the bowl clockwise three times, before taking a sip. She wiped the rim with her thumb to remove the drip, turned the bowl three times anticlockwise and returned it to Genkuro.

'What do you think?' Kiyomi whispered to Kenny, while their host cleaned the utensils.

'That was pretty cool,' Kenny whispered back. 'Maybe one day I'll show you the English tea ceremony.'

Kiyomi shot him a puzzled look. 'Huh? I've never heard of that. How does it work?'

'First you warm the teapot. Then you chuck in a couple of tea bags – Hey!' He dodged the kick and grinned.

'Children,' Genkuro said, 'you will need to bathe and change clothes, you especially, Kiyomi-*chan*. Then we will have dinner and Kuromori-*san* will hear the truth about why he is here and what he must do.'

'Genkuro-*sensei*, forgive me for questioning you,' Kiyomi said, 'but is that wise? I mean, do you think Ken-*chan* is ready?'

Genkuro smiled his little smile. 'Kiyomi-*chan*, it matters not if Ken-*san* is ready or otherwise. He simply has to know.'

'Know what?' Kenny asked, uneasy at the direction in which the conversation was going.

'Know how to stop the weapon that will kill millions of innocent people,' Genkuro said. 'Only then can you choose to act or not.'

'I don't get it,' Kenny said. 'Why wouldn't I act if it would save lives?'

'Because there's a catch,' Kiyomi said. 'There's always a catch. Whatever you decide to do, people will die.'

Kenny flinched. 'Wait, are you saying that if I help you, people are going to die and if I don't help you, people are going to die anyway? What kind of choice is that?'

Genkuro pressed his palms together. 'Ken-*san*, it may not be a simple choice or a desirable one, but it is, nonetheless, a choice, and one you will have to make.'

After tea, Genkuro gave Kenny a tour of the building while Kiyomi went to clean up. All of the sliding doors opening on to room after room made Kenny think of a Chinese puzzle box he had seen once, with its many hidden panels. The strange thing was that even when he retraced his steps, the rooms seemed different, as if they had changed as soon as he had left them.

Kiyomi returned from her bath wearing a floral kimono that Genkuro had provided. Kenny tried not to stare, but this was a very different-looking Kiyomi to what he was used to seeing. Her spiky edge was gone, replaced by a softer, warmer glow.

'Your turn, stinky,' she said to Kenny, breaking the spell. 'Remember, it's a traditional Japanese bathtub, so make sure you soap yourself off *before* you get in for a soak.'

An hour later, Kenny pushed back his half-full bowl and dabbed his mouth on a napkin. Dinner was *chankonabe*, a hearty stew with chunks of chicken, fish, *tofu*, *enoki* and *shiitake* mushrooms, leafy greens, leeks, radish, carrots and noodles, all swimming in broth. It was delicious, but Kenny's appetite had diminished as his worries grew.

Genkuro put the lid back on the soup pot, rested the ladle beside it and settled back on his cushion.

'Thank you for the meal,' Kenny said. 'That's probably the most delicious thing I've tasted in my life.'

Genkuro bowed. 'And yet you ate so little. I thought you would be hungry, Ken-*san*.'

'Yeah, me too. Maybe if you'd saved the 'choice' thing until after I'd eaten . . .'

Poyo held his bowl up for a fourth helping and Kiyomi went to refill it.

'What have you been told about why you are here?' Genkuro asked, pouring Kenny a cup of oolong tea.

Kenny sighed. 'Something about a satellite weapon up in space that was going to fire an earthquake beam into the sea off the California coast,' he said.

Genkuro's eyebrows shot up and he smiled at Kiyomi, who blushed.

'That's . . . very creative,' Genkuro said.

'I had to tell him *something*,' Kiyomi said.

'Indeed. Ken-*san*, you do not sound convinced.' Genkuro handed him the cup.

'Well, it does sound ridiculous,' Kenny said. 'Like something out of Hollywood.'

'And how were you supposed to stop this satellite?' Genkuro asked. 'By hijacking a spaceship and flying up there to destroy it?'

Kiyomi collected the soup bowls and took them away, stamping as she went.

'There's supposed to be a crystal or something, that would absorb the rays,' Kenny said. He shrugged.

'Ken-*san*, Kiyomi-*chan* meant well, but you are not as foolish as she had hoped.' Genkuro swirled the tea in his cup, inhaling the steam. 'There is a weapon that will cause a terrible earthquake and there is a way of stopping the weapon, that much is true.'

'But it's not a crystal and there's no satellite?'

'No.'

Kenny relaxed. 'Thank God for that.' He took a sip of tea.

'It's a dragon and you need a sword to stop it.'

Kenny sprayed tea all over his lap. '*What?*'

Kiyomi looked into the room. 'You heard him right,' she said. 'Now you see why I made up the space story.'

'A *dragon*?' Kenny repeated. 'As in a real, live, giant, scaly, fire-breathing dragon thing?'

Genkuro nodded. 'Yes, although he doesn't breathe fire.'

Kenny's mind was racing. 'Wait a minute. My dream. *That's* the thing in my dream? The thing in the dark?'

'You know this to be true,' Genkuro said. 'After *oni*, *nukekubi*, *nure-onna*, *yurei* and *kappa*, why would a dragon be any less believable?'

Kenny was on his feet now, pacing. 'This dragon, it makes earthquakes?'

'Ancient legends tell of an enormous dragon

157

imprisoned beneath the earth. When it moves, it shakes the land above.'

'His name is Namazu,' Kiyomi said.

'How big is it?' Kenny asked.

'Pretty big,' Kiyomi said, glancing at Genkuro.

'How big?' Kenny glared at her.

'You've seen *Godzilla*?'

'Are you nuts? You want *me* to fight Godzilla?'

Kiyomi waved a hand in the air dismissively. 'No, don't be silly. Godzilla's not real.'

'And I have to do this, using just a *sword*? Are you out of your mind?' Kenny eyed the exit.

'Not just any sword,' Genkuro said, watching him. 'You must use Kusanagi, the Sword of Heaven. It was forged by the gods and given to mankind by the sun goddess Amaterasu. It alone can defeat Namazu.'

'I liked it better when we were talking about a satellite,' Kenny said.

Genkuro rose to his feet. 'Ken-*san*, it is good that you are fearful; it means you will walk with great care.'

Kenny scowled. 'So, where is this sword and why am I the one who has to do this?'

'The sword is lost. Hidden. The last man to possess it was Lawrence Blackwood, your grandfather. That is why it is you who must both find the sword and use it. Only a Kuromori can do this.'

Kenny pressed his palms against his temples as if trying to hold in his thoughts. 'My grandfather found this famous lost sword and then he hid it? And now I have to find it and use it, or millions will die?'

'That's about it,' Kiyomi said. 'Sucks to be you, eh?'

'You're not helping.' Kenny pursed his lips. 'Genkuro-*sensei*, do you know where the sword is?'

'No, but my mistress, the goddess Inari knows. When you leave here, you must travel to Kyoto, to the Fushimi Inari Taisha, her foremost shrine, and there you will ask her.'

'Sir . . .' Kenny struggled to choose the words. 'Do you think I can do this? I mean, I'm just a dumb *gaijin* kid who's way out of his depth here.'

Genkuro smiled and joined his hands. 'Ken-*chan*, I believe you can do this, because you must.'

That evening, Kenny sat next to Kiyomi, out in the courtyard, and they looked up at the stars twinkling high above.

'When are we going to Kyoto?' Kenny asked. 'We've got, what? Six days?'

'We go when Genkuro-*sensei* tells us. You can't go anywhere yet. You need some training first, things I can't teach you.'

Kenny nodded. 'Oh, you mean . . . that stuff. And then what? We talk to a goddess?'

Kiyomi shrugged. 'Ken-*chan*, I don't pretend to have all the answers. All I know is that I trust you to do what is right.' She reached over and brushed a few strands of

159

hair away from Kenny's eyes. Kenny squeezed her hand and they sat in silence for a few seconds.

'Kenny, I probably shouldn't be telling you this, but there's more . . . something that Genkuro-*sensei* didn't say to you.'

Kenny sighed. 'That would fit right in with the kind of day I've been having. You might as well go ahead and tell me.'

'There was a prophecy. Made by the goddess Inari, when she gave your grandfather the Gift of Sight.'

'She . . . ? Is that why I can see *yokai*?'

Kiyomi nodded. 'Yes, only one other *gaijin* was given this Gift before. The Americans had found the sword and were going to take it away. Your grandfather rescued it and she rewarded him.'

'Some reward,' Kenny said, shifting his weight. 'What's this prophecy, or do I even want to know?'

'I'll try and remember how it goes. It doesn't translate well from Japanese, but it's something like this:

When two suns dawn in the west
And spirits cannot find their rest,
The dead will rise to slake their thirst
For vengeance upon whom they cursed.'

'So, not too heavy,' Kenny said.

'There's more,' Kiyomi said. 'The next part goes:

From setting sun a child with Sight
Will come to claim his true birthright:
The Sword of Heaven, to subdue
The newly wakened Namazu.

In darkness deep, should he prevail,
In triumph he will also fail,
For victory carries a price so high:
One he loves must also die.'

'Are you kidding me?' Kenny said. 'Assuming that does mean me, I lose even if I win? What kind of deal is that?'

Kiyomi took his hand. 'Kenny, it does mean you. The sun sets in the west, which is where you're from, and you have the Gift of Sight. The sword is handed down to you from your grandfather. There is no one else it could mean.'

Kenny tried again. 'What's with the two suns in the west? That's never happened.'

'It's the two atomic bombs that ended World War Two. Survivors describe it like a sun being born. Nagasaki and Hiroshima are both in the west of Japan.' Kiyomi's voice was almost inaudible by now.

'Great. If I do nothing, bang goes half of America. If I do this, and somehow stop this freaking dragon, then what? Someone I care about is going to die? Like I haven't lost enough people already? Who's next? My dad? My grandfather?'

'Kenny, you don't have to shout. I'm right next –'

'Enough for one day,' Genkuro said softly. He had approached without making a sound. 'Ken-*san*, it is time to sleep. You will need to be rested for tomorrow.'

'Why, what's happening tomorrow?' Kenny asked, making no effort to hide his irritation.

'Tomorrow, you will learn to fight a dragon.'

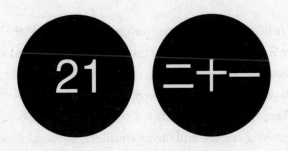

'Kiyomi-*chan* has taught you to throw *shuriken*, yes?' Genkuro asked, leaning on a *bo* staff.

'Uh, I wouldn't say that exactly,' Kenny said, absently touching the plaster on his finger.

'Just show him what you know,' Kiyomi said, handing Kenny four throwing stars.

They were in a makeshift *dojo* within the temple. Kenny could have sworn the large room had not been there the day before. He was barefoot and wearing a white *gi*, a martial arts training uniform, as was Kiyomi, although hers was tied with a black belt instead of a white one like his.

'I want you to throw and to aim for me,' Genkuro said. 'I will not come to any harm,' he added, seeing the look of concern on the boy's face.

'Are you sure about this?' Kenny said.

'I am sure,' Genkuro said. He smiled.

'OK then. Here goes.' Kenny held up a *shuriken*, took aim and flung it. It flashed through the air, towards his teacher's head.

THWUNK! Genkuro barely moved and the next thing Kenny knew, the metal star was embedded in the wooden staff.

'Wow. That was fast,' Kenny said.

'Again,' Genkuro said.

Kenny shrugged and threw another *shuriken*. Genkuro's fingers slashed the air as he drew something and the metal star vanished, leaving only an oily black wisp.

'Where'd it –?'

'Again.'

Kenny hurled the third *shuriken*. This time, after Genkuro wrote in the air, the star slowed as if the air had thickened to syrup around it and it bounced off the floor in front of the old man's feet.

'Again,' Genkuro said.

Kenny stole a glance at Kiyomi who was clearly enjoying his bewilderment. He threw the final *shuriken*, sending it spinning at Genkuro. The teacher traced a figure in the air and raised a hand, catching the star which was now a lotus flower.

'That's . . . that's . . . ' Kenny failed to find the words.

'In life, every moment presents a thousand choices. I showed you four,' Genkuro said. 'I could have caught the *shuriken*; I could have avoided it; I could have changed it into a butterfly. Our actions are only limited by our thoughts. Do you understand this?'

'Um, not really,' Kenny said, looking for pockets to put his hands in.

Genkuro leaned on his staff. 'Most of the time, people make the same choices, whether through habit or routine. This is good, otherwise they would be overwhelmed by all of the possibilities.'

'That happens to Ken-*chan* in McDonald's,' Kiyomi said, winking at him. 'He can't even choose a shake.'

'I could if they had normal flavours,' Kenny protested.

'Precisely,' Genkuro said. 'Comfortable choices are easy; it is the ones which stretch the mind that are hard. After all, how could you have chosen a green-tea flavoured milkshake if you did not know it existed?'

'See? That's what I said,' Kenny said to Kiyomi.

'In the same way, how could I change a *shuriken* into this flower?' Genkuro held out the pink lotus.

Kenny took it, turned it over, smelled it; it was real. 'Are you saying that it changed into a flower because you *decided* it would?'

Genkuro beamed. 'Precisely. It is good that you are able to make that connection so quickly. It took your grandfather a week.'

Kenny looked to Kiyomi. 'So, he's saying that you can make stuff happen by choosing it?'

'Not quite,' Kiyomi said. 'It starts with choice, then you focus spirit and will to enact that choice.'

'Kiyomi-*chan* taught you some Chinese characters, yes?' Genkuro asked.

Kenny nodded. 'Some basic ones. Some numbers.'

'Show me. Write the number one in the air.'

'That's easy.' Kenny swiped his hand horizontally.

'No. Too wide. Try again,' said Genkuro.

Kenny swiped again.

'No, you are sloping upwards. The line must be clean, neat, straight, level.'

Kenny moved his hand again.

'Japanese children learn to form their letters from an early age. It takes years to master the art and apply the correct precision and grace,' Genkuro said.

'I don't mean to sound rude,' Kenny said, 'but why should I care? I'm not planning to write in Japanese or Chinese or whatever.'

'Ken-*san*, some of these symbols are thousands of years old. As such, they have great power. The power to focus the mind is but one example.'

Kiyomi came closer. 'In your writing, letters represent sounds, right? Individually, they have no meaning. In Chinese writing, each character is also a little picture and it has a meaning as well as a sound. Let me show you.'

She knelt down and quickly drew three pictures on the dirt floor with her finger:

人 木 火

'The first one is a person,' Kiyomi said. 'Very simple, a body and two legs, like you make with your fingers walking.'

'OK, I can see that,' Kenny said.

'The second is a tree.'

Kenny smirked. 'Looks more like a cross with two ribbons hanging off.'

'Use your imagination,' Kiyomi snapped. 'The branches go across horizontally, the trunk goes straight down and its sides curve up. Can you see it now?'

Kenny squinted. 'Not really. What's the last one?'

'Fire.'

'It looks like your picture of a man with his arms floating.'

Kiyomi scowled. 'It's a bonfire, with two flames flickering up on each side.'

'If you say so. Now what?'

Genkuro raised a finger. 'Now you understand that when you write a character, you are also evoking a concept. Watch.' He drew the symbol for fire slowly in the air, exaggerating each movement so Kenny could follow. When he finished, he held out his open palm and a flickering flame appeared in his hand.

'No way,' Kenny said, coming closer and feeling the heat from it.

The old man closed his palm and the flame vanished.

Kenny looked from Genkuro to Kiyomi and back again. 'That's how you've been doing all that weird stuff,' he whispered.

'Now it is your turn,' Genkuro said.

'Do what I do,' Kiyomi said, raising her hand. She

made a short downward stroke, moved across and swept inwards, then down again for the central curve and finally a shorter move for the rightward curve.

Kenny tried to copy as best he could. 'That wasn't bad,' he said. 'How come there's no flame?'

'Were you thinking of fire?' Kiyomi asked.

He shook his head.

'Then how did you expect to create fire?'

'The last part is *ki*,' Genkuro said. 'Spirit. And will.'

'I thought that was just your life force,' Kenny said, trying to remember what Harashima had told him.

'*Ki*. Spirit. Energy. Life force. All around you, everything is spirit. The whole universe is made of energy. Some of it is locked up in atoms and these make the world you see and know,' Genkuro said.

'You know, like quantum physics?' Kiyomi said, trying to help.

'What sort of school do you go to?' Kenny said in horror. 'We don't study any of that.'

Genkuro ignored him. 'Everything is energy. If you use your own inner spirit, and will it strongly enough, you can direct the shape of that energy.'

Kenny stood, open-mouthed.

'But the most important thing is to believe that you can do it. Faith, you may know, makes all things possible,' Genkuro finished.

'This is nuts,' Kenny protested. 'I can't make fire with my mind.'

'Never heard of pyrokinesis?' Kiyomi said. She drew the symbol for fire in the air and a tongue of flame burst from the earth in front of Kenny, sending him sprawling backwards. 'I said you wouldn't be able to do it. You're too weak up here.' She tapped her forehead.

'Ken-*san*,' Genkuro said. 'If you do not believe you can succeed, then you never will.'

'And Mr Dragon will have you for a tasty supper,' Kiyomi added. 'If I were you, I'd start believing.'

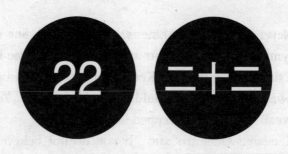

22 二十二

Several hours later, Kenny sat cross-legged in the courtyard, staring at the candle in his hands. He had spent most of the day practising the *kanji* characters, over and over, trying to form them correctly while picturing the associated meaning of each in his mind. Kiyomi, meanwhile, had been working on martial arts skills, combining these with her control of balance and aim.

'How did you learn to do this?' Kenny asked her, when she came out for a breather. 'I've been concentrating on this thing for hours and it still won't light.'

Kiyomi sat down beside him and dabbed a long white sleeve over her sweaty brow. 'It was easier for me. I was a very young child when Genkuro-*sensei* began to teach me. Children change reality all the time; their imaginations are so powerful.'

Kenny nodded. 'I remember. I built a rocketship in my room using an old cardboard box. It had a control deck, windows, everything.' He smiled. 'You try telling me I didn't go to Mars and fight off an alien invasion.'

'That's what I mean. You have to find that part of

yourself, the part that believes in those things. The problem is when you get older you start putting limits on yourself. Everyone tells you what you can and can't do. Stories, dreams, ideas – all these things – you start to shut them down. If you want to make fire, you have to *believe* you can make fire. You have to overrule your rational mind, which is telling you you can't do it.' She stopped and grinned. 'Oh, wow, listen to me. That sounds really heavy.'

Genkuro appeared on the front porch of the temple. 'Kiyomi-*chan*, rest time is over. We must continue.'

'Coming, *sensei*,' she called, rising to her knees. 'Kenny, you know when you take a shot in football and it goes wide, you tell yourself off?'

'Yeah.'

'Who's telling who off? Which part of your mind is angry at which? Think about that.'

She hurried back to her training session.

Poyo waddled up to Kenny and held out a paw. Kenny shrugged and gave him the candle. Poyo sniffed it, bit it in two and gave one half back to Kenny. He popped the other end into his mouth and chewed on it. When he was satisfied, he opened his mouth and stuck out his long pink tongue. On the end was the chewed stump of the candle, a small flame burning at the wick.

'No one likes a show-off,' Kenny said, scowling at him.

*

That evening, while they all sat round the dinner table, Kenny asked Genkuro, 'How long did it take for my grandfather to learn this stuff?'

Genkuro smiled, his face glowing in the candlelight. 'It took a long time. Once Lawrence mastered the idea, he learned quickly, but he began very slowly.'

'How long did it take him?' Kiyomi asked.

'Months.'

Kenny and Kiyomi exchanged looks. 'Months?' Kenny said. 'We've only got five days, max.'

'Your grandfather was very stubborn back then. It took him a long time to let go of his ideas of what the world is,' Genkuro said. 'You are not like him. You are angry, afraid to reach out, to free your heart.'

Kenny looked away, unable to meet his teacher's penetrating gaze.

Kiyomi decided to help him. 'Genkuro-*sensei*,' she said, 'how did Kenny's grandfather make the breakthrough? How did he come to believe?'

Genkuro chuckled. 'Finally, I grew tired of seeing him hold himself back, so I helped him to make his leap of faith: I pushed him off a cliff.'

'You did what?' Kenny's eyes were wide.

Genkuro nodded. 'He fell a long way. Once he understood that I was not going to save him, and that he was not ready to die, he believed.'

'What did he do?' Kenny was picturing the scene.

'He chose *numa*. Swamp. Changed the hard ground

below to soft mud. It was the first character he could think of. Very messy, but it worked.'

'Are you going to do that to me?' Kenny asked.

'No. There is no time for tricks like that.'

'But what if I can't do this?'

'You will.'

'Genkuro-*sensei*, it takes years to learn these skills,' Kiyomi said. 'How can Kenny do it in just a few days?'

'Kiyomi-*chan*,' Genkuro said, 'Ken-*san* will do this because I believe it to be so. You must believe it too. Then it will happen.'

'Great, so now it's my fault you're crap,' Kiyomi grumbled in Kenny's ear.

The night was warm and humid. After another long and tiring day, Kenny was grateful to return to his room. He lay back on his *futon* and tried to make sense of the jumbled thoughts colliding in his head. He was about to blow out the candle when there was a soft tap on the *shoji* screen door.

'Not now, Poyo,' he said. 'I haven't got any leftovers for you.'

The door slid open and Genkuro bowed. 'May I come in?' he asked.

'Uh, of course.' Kenny sat up. 'It's your house.'

'Thank you. I wish to share with you a story. Would you like that?'

'Sure. No one's read me a bedtime story since . . . it's been years.'

'This is a personal story. I tell it in the hope that it will help you to understand what belief can do.'

'OK,' Kenny said, chewing his lip.

'Many years ago, more than you would wish to count, these lands were empty of men,' Genkuro began, kneeling beside Kenny. 'When people arrived, they found the land hard and unforgiving. Many died. Some cried out to the gods for help. The goddess Inari took pity on them and came down to teach them many things. Under her guidance, men learned to grow rice for food, to shape metal for tools and to fight to defend these lands.'

Kenny leaned up on his elbow.

'Men in return built many shrines to Inari to thank her,' Genkuro continued. 'The first and the greatest of these was built on Inari Mountain.'

'Is that where we have to go, in Kyoto?' Kenny asked. 'To find her?'

Genkuro smiled. 'Yes. Men built the *torii* gate first, to mark the entrance to the shrine, and it was so beautiful, made of wood and painted red. One day, a *kitsune*, a small brown fox, came down from the woods to see what was making all the noise. When he saw the *torii* gate, he forgot his fear of men and sat beside it, like a guard, for many days. Inari saw this and spoke to the fox. "Would you like to serve me, little one?" she said. The fox answered, "With all my heart, but I am only a fox

174

and man is so strong. What can I do?" Inari smiled at the fox and said, "You can choose to be a fox and remain as a guard, or you can choose to be a man and serve me."'

'So, what did he do?' Kenny asked.

'As you can see, the fox believed and became a man.'

Genkuro wiped a tear from his eye.

'Was this a good bedtime story, Ken-*san*?' he asked, rising to his feet.

Kenny's throat felt constricted and he wasn't sure he could speak. He nodded instead.

'Goodnight, Ken-*san*,' Genkuro said and slid the door closed.

Kenny saw himself walking down a street. The sky was an unbroken slab of grey and the terraced houses on each side told him he was back in England. The street was familiar, like an old song.

He stopped outside a house with a short path and a privet hedge. The front door was slightly open and Kenny went up to it. He looked into the hallway. The beige carpet was as he remembered and the smell of cookies baking made his mouth water. His mother loved to bake and there were always cakes, muffins, scones and biscuits at the ready.

The living-room door opened and his mother peered out.

'Kenny! I thought I heard you come in,' she said.

She threw her arms round him and hugged him tightly.

Kenny held her for as long as he could, drinking in her fragrance and sinking into her embrace.

'Mum, I've missed you so much,' he said, blinking back tears.

'Oh, you silly thing,' she said. 'First day of school isn't that bad. Come, sit down and tell me all about it.'

Kenny went with her into the living room and sat on the floor beside her armchair. He told her all about the boarding schools he had endured, the teasing and the bullying, the long lonely holidays, the friends who he always had to leave and his trip to Japan. She listened as he unburdened his mind, stroking his hair and reassuring him.

'I'm so sorry that I haven't always been there for you,' she said. 'Can you forgive me?'

'Oh, Mum,' Kenny said. 'There's nothing to forgive. I've never been angry at you.'

'Not even a little?'

Kenny sighed. 'All right, a little.' He paused, hating himself for what he was about to say, but unable to stop it. 'Mum, aren't you supposed to be dead?'

A look of sad surprise crossed his mother's face. 'Oh, yes. So I am.' She faded like mist on a summer's day.

'Wait, don't go!' Kenny shouted, cursing himself for not keeping his big mouth shut. He had known all along that it was a dream, but he had been happy in it. Except now he had messed it up.

There was a bang and the house shook, as if a truck

had slammed into it. Pictures rattled on the wall and the television fell off its stand. A long crack opened in the ceiling and a plaster mist rained down. Kenny raced out of the house, into the street, dodging tiles that slid from the roof and exploded around him. An enormous crevasse opened in the road and a gigantic scaled claw reached out for him.

Kenny awoke, the sound of his heartbeat thumping in his ears, an icy sweat down his back and his breathing rapid and shallow.

Just a dream, he told himself. *Another stupid dream*.

He tried to settle down again, still wrapped in his shroud of longing.

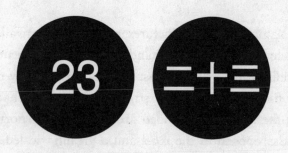

'I had a dream about you last night,' Kiyomi said to Kenny at breakfast. 'Not like that,' she quickly added, seeing the look on his face.

'So, what was it about? Were you beating me up again?' Kenny asked, stirring his *miso* soup.

'No, it was cool. You had mastered the five elements and were doing all this crazy stuff.'

Kenny took a sip of hot soup and held his chopsticks over a bowl of rice. 'Five? I thought there were only four elements: fire, water, air and earth.'

'We have five. The fifth is spirit, or aether. It covers all the weird stuff.'

Genkuro brought a tray of pickles and set it on the table. 'So, Kiyomi-*chan* now believes you will master your *ki*?' he asked.

'It was only a dream, *sensei*,' Kiyomi said before Kenny could reply.

'Dreams reveal our innermost feelings,' Genkuro said. 'They give voice to the heart, not the mind.'

Kiyomi blushed and concentrated on her omelette.

Poyo waddled in, a rolled-up newspaper in his mouth. He presented it to Kiyomi and then went in search of breakfast.

'I thought we should keep up with what's happening at home,' Kiyomi said, in response to Kenny's quizzical look. She opened the paper, which was the English-language *Japan News*, scanned the headlines and covered her mouth in surprise. 'Oh my God. Kenny, you should see this.' She thrust the newspaper at him.

Kenny took it and saw the headline: EARTHQUAKE HITS LONDON.

'Read it out,' Kiyomi said, pushing her plate away.

'The biggest earthquake to hit London for over four hundred years damaged famous historical landmarks and sent terrified office workers into the streets,' Kenny read. 'It was the largest quake in the south-east of England since 1580 and tremors were felt as far as Paris and Brussels.' He stopped. 'Is this related to what's happening here?'

'It is as I feared,' Genkuro said.

'Keep going. What else does it say?' Kiyomi asked.

'Uh, the British Geological Survey said the 5.3 magnitude quake struck just before 16:00 GMT and the epicentre was in the Straits of Dover. Extensive damage has been reported, particularly to many older buildings such as St Paul's Cathedral, Westminster Abbey and Hampton Court. No fatalities have been reported, with most injuries caused by falling chimney stacks.'

Genkuro's brow was knotted and his eyes swept the

floor. 'This is not good. Not good at all.'

'I dreamed this!' Kenny said, suddenly making sense of it and throwing down the newspaper. 'Last night. I dreamed about an earthquake hitting London.'

'This is a message,' Genkuro said. 'They are telling us that they control Namazu and that nowhere is safe.'

Kenny jumped to his feet. 'That's my home those scumbags are messing with!' he said, shaking with anger.

He unclenched his fist and drew the character for *fire* in the air, executing the strokes with precision. 'Now they've made this personal.' He focused his *ki*, concentrated his mind as hard as he could on the concept of fire and thrust out his hands.

Nothing happened.

'Come on!' he shouted at himself. He tried again, but still no flame appeared.

Staring at his empty hands, Kenny said, 'What *is* this? Even the dog can do it.'

Poyo looked hurt and slunk away.

'Ken-*san*. Anger is not the way to find your . . .' Genkuro pointed his fingers into his belly, pressing the tips above the navel and below the sternum. 'In here. Your core, your inner self, your *ki*.'

'I'm sick of this,' Kenny replied. 'The only "key" I want is the one that opens the door marked exit. I've had enough. I'm useless. You all know it. Go find someone else to fight your battles.' He stormed out.

'Kenny!' Kiyomi called after him.

'Let him go,' Genkuro said. 'Ken-*san* must find his own path.'

Kenny stomped down the stone steps, towards the *torii* gate marking the boundary of the shrine.

Poyo had slumped down in the middle of the path, but sat up in stages as Kenny approached. Kenny slowed to a stop, shuffled his feet and tried to avoid looking at the *tanuki*. 'I'm sorry I called you a dog,' he said. 'I was angry and took it out on you. I do that a lot and it's wrong.'

Poyo perked up, rested on his haunches and held out a paw. Kenny knelt and shook it. Poyo wagged his head and held out the paw again. Puzzled, Kenny shook it a second time. Poyo slapped a paw over his face in exasperation and put two fingers to his lips and mimed blowing.

'Oh, you want this?' Kenny said, taking out the whistle.

Poyo nodded.

Kenny looked at the object in his palm, with its Chinese character 狸 carved on the bottom. 'Is this you?' Kenny asked, showing Poyo the letter. 'This means *tanuki*?'

Poyo nodded, pointing a pudgy finger at himself.

Kenny sat down beside the furry creature. He was reluctant to part with the whistle. It had been the only thing he could depend on since he had arrived and, somehow, letting it go seemed too final. He sought to delay the moment.

'You were in Portland, watching over me, huh?' he asked.

Poyo nodded.

'Poor you. Getting sent all that way to watch a loser like me.'

Poyo shook his head emphatically.

'You don't think I'm a loser?' More head-shaking. 'Really? You want me to stay?'

Poyo nodded and scratched his rump.

'I want to stay too.' Kenny kicked at the dirt with his heel. 'It's just . . .'

The *tanuki* sniffed at the disturbed silt and poked a claw into it, sketching something.

Kenny leaned over. Poyo had drawn two stick figures: a boy and a girl, holding hands. The grinning creature puckered its lips and made kissing noises.

'Hah!' Kenny scoffed. 'You think –? What? Me and her?'

Poyo nodded, sending a string of drool in Kenny's direction.

'No way. She can't stand me. Thinks I'm a wimp.'

The *tanuki* shook his head.

'She likes me? Really? You know this?'

More nodding.

Kenny's cheeks flushed pink and his heart skipped. 'You think I can do this? Fight a dragon?'

Poyo nodded.

'How?'

The *tanuki* laboured to his feet, found an acorn and

picked up a stick. He threw the acorn into the air. It fell and landed as a *bonsai* tree twisted into the shape of a dragon.

'Cool. That's Namazu, right? Only a bit smaller?'

Poyo agreed. He pointed at Kenny then at his own furry body.

'And now you're me?'

Poyo nodded and began to mime a fight with the miniature tree. He showed more energy than ever before, growling, rolling, throwing himself around, parrying and feinting, using the stick as a sword. When he grew tired, which didn't take long, he walked up to the leafy dragon and poked the stick into its head.

Kenny laughed. 'As simple as that?'

Poyo panted, his pink tongue lolling.

'And that's his weak spot? Top of the head?'

More nodding, with drool for emphasis.

'And how do I learn to do all that, to get close enough?'

Poyo patted his hairy belly, lay down and pretended to fall asleep, complete with loud fake snores.

'That's your answer to everything!' Kenny said, suppressing a yawn.

Poyo sat up and pointed at Kenny, then pretended to sleep again.

'You think I'm tired and need a nap? And that'll help?' Kenny yawned again, and tried to shake off the drowsy feeling that was stealing over him.

Poyo nodded, took Kenny's hand and began tugging him back towards the temple.

'All right, all right, you win,' Kenny said. 'No rash decisions. I'll sleep on it, as Grandad would say.'

Genkuro, who was clearing away the breakfast dishes, pretended not to notice Kenny creeping past, back to his room. But he did allow himself a smile.

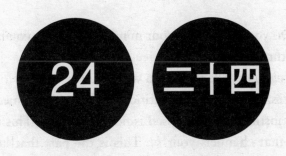

Even though it was mid-morning, Kenny fell asleep as soon as his head touched the pillow. Too many nights of broken sleep had finally caught up with him.

The sun was high when he awoke. He listened, straining for the sounds of Kiyomi practising her martial skills, or Genkuro's voice instructing her, but all was silent.

Puzzled, he rolled off the *futon* and went to the room used as a *dojo*. He looked in and jumped at the sight of a silvery fox with nine tails waiting for him.

'Genkuro?' Kenny asked.

'It is I,' said the fox. 'Do not be alarmed. Your mind will not harm you.'

'My mind?' Kenny relaxed. 'Oh, I see. Another dream.'

'Of course. That is why you see my true form, as you did before.'

Kenny looked around. 'Is my mum here?'

'Do you wish her to be?' asked the fox. 'It is your dream.'

Kenny was silent for a moment, then looked down, shaking his head slowly. 'No, it hurts too much at the end.'

'Do you know why your mind has brought you here?' Genkuro asked.

'I can guess. Is this to do with . . . ?'

'Yes. Your thinking, critical self is asleep, meaning your instinctive, feeling self is now in control. This is the part that channels your *ki*. This is the part that knows what you can do, if you allow yourself to do it.'

Kenny looked sceptical.

'Why do you doubt?' Genkuro said. 'This is a dream. You can do anything here. You can fly, you can score the winning goal at the World Cup, you can open a door to the Pyramids, anything you choose. Only your imagination sets the limits.'

Kenny grinned. 'I suppose so. Where to begin?'

Genkuro's tails swished behind him. 'Why not begin with fire?'

Kenny held out a hand and pictured a flame in his mind.

'Good,' Genkuro said. 'Now reach down deep inside; find your core; *feel* the fire. *Be* the fire.' His voice was calm, soothing, almost hypnotic.

Kenny's other hand traced the lines of the Chinese character:

火

He closed his eyes, concentrated on flame, imagined being fire, dancing and flickering, giving off heat and light. He pictured molecules moving faster and faster, energy being released, expanding into space. And then he felt it.

Deep inside something opened, like an eye or a window, and a rushing, rising feeling, of joy, of release surged through. Kenny felt like he was aglow from the inside and imagined light streaming from every pore.

He opened his eyes and felt perfectly calm, even though a flame flickered in his cupped palm.

'It tickles a bit,' he said.

The fox smiled.

'Oh my God! Kenny! *What are you doing?*' Kiyomi screamed from the doorway.

Kenny smiled at her. 'Just making fire. Now come over here and kiss me like I know you want to.'

'What is *wrong* with you?' Kiyomi demanded. Then her eyes widened. '*Sensei*? Is that you?'

The fox shimmered and the familiar form of the gentle old man returned.

'Relax,' Kenny said. 'This is a dream and I can do anything I want.'

'A dream?' Kiyomi repeated in disbelief. 'Kenny, trust me, you're wide awake.'

The fire in Kenny's hand died away. 'No, this is a dream. Look at Genkuro . . .'

The old man smiled and spread his hands in guilty surrender.

'No way. This is real?' Kenny's mouth hung open as

the implications sank in. 'This is *real*?'

'I am sorry, Kuromori-*san*,' Genkuro said. '*Kitsune* love playing tricks, however old we are.'

'This is real?' Kenny said again.

Genkuro nodded. 'It was necessary to trick you into channelling your *ki*,' he said. 'Now you know how to do it.'

Kiyomi approached cautiously. 'Kenny, you did it,' she said. 'If I hadn't seen it, I'd never have believed it. No one's ever made fire after, what, two days? It took me two years.'

'Kuromori-*san*, we should continue while the feeling is new,' Genkuro said. 'You have much to learn in a short time.'

'Yeah, this is great,' Kiyomi said. 'I want to see how –'

'Kiyomi-*chan*,' Genkuro said, 'you have *kata* to perform.'

Kiyomi's face fell. 'Oh. OK. Sure.' She bowed to Genkuro and hurried out.

'Kiyomi, wait –' Kenny started to say.

'No, Kuromori-*san*. You may talk later. Now you must learn,' Genkuro said.

For the rest of the day, Genkuro introduced Kenny to new Chinese characters, taught him to form the shapes, concentrate on the meanings and channel his *ki* to change matter. The work was exhausting and, by the end of it all, Kenny felt as limp and wrung out as a used dish rag.

Kiyomi was unusually quiet at the dinner table that evening and she avoided any eye contact with Kenny. As soon as she had finished picking at her meal, she got up and left.

Genkuro seemed not to notice and talked at length about the importance of inner calm, stillness, breathing, harmony, balance, *yin yang* and many other concepts that a drained Kenny struggled to keep up with. He found his eyes closing and his head nodding.

'Kuromori-*san*,' Genkuro said gently. 'You should go for a walk to clear your mind before sleep. You have had a long and tiring day.'

'OK.'

Kenny went out into the humid night air. Frogs were singing and bats wheeled overhead in the inky, star-speckled sky.

He found Kiyomi sitting on the stone steps near the entrance, her knees tucked up under her chin and her long hair falling over her face.

'What's up?' he asked. 'You're so quiet. Are you OK?'

No response.

'Hm. Mind if I join you here, then?'

Kiyomi remained motionless. Kenny shrugged and sat beside her.

'You're Kuromori now,' Kiyomi said into her knees.

'I'm sorry?'

'Genkuro-*sensei* calls you Kuromori. Haven't you noticed?'

'Yeah, I noticed, but everyone's always calling me something different. No one ever calls me Kenny.'

'I do.'

Kenny shrugged. 'When you're not calling me stupid, I guess. Or geek. Or dweeb.'

'You're not a geek any more,' Kiyomi mumbled. She still had not moved.

'No? What am I then?'

'You're Kuromori. The hero. Child of legend. Knight of Inari.'

'Oh. That.'

Kiyomi looked up at Kenny. He could see her eyes were red and her face wet, glistening in the soft light.

'I liked you as a geek. Now it's not the same. Now, it'll never be the same.'

'Why do you say that?'

'Because before, you needed me . . . to help you. Now you don't need anyone. Now, I'm the one who . . .'

'Shh.' Kenny put an arm round Kiyomi and pulled her closer. He thought she would resist but she was softer than he remembered. 'I promise you,' he said. 'I'll still be me, OK? I'll still dress badly and spill my food.' He reached out and drew her hair back from her face.

Kiyomi locked eyes with him. 'Were you serious when you asked me to kiss you?'

Kenny swallowed hard. 'I thought that was a dream.'

'I know, but did you mean it?'

'I meant it.'

Kiyomi raised her face to his and pressed her lips against his. Her touch made Kenny's skin tingle and he felt more alive than he ever had before. Their lips parted.

'What was that for?' Kenny whispered.

'For luck. You're going to need it. Now, if you die, I'll know what it's like to kiss you.'

'Oh. Me too. Kiss you, I mean, not me.'

Kiyomi smiled at him. 'Yeah, you're still you.'

She held out her hand and a firefly settled on her palm, its yellow luminescent tail lighting up her face.

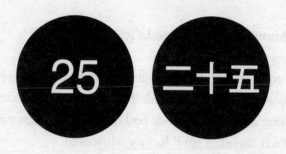

That night, Kenny had his best night's sleep in ages. All of his worries, his anxieties, his concerns had been swept away into a dreamless void. He awoke, feeling thoroughly refreshed and ready for the next challenge.

'Kuromori-*san*, you have taken your first steps, but you cannot walk yet,' Genkuro said, the following day.

They were back in the *dojo*, having spent the morning practising their skills.

'With regret, time has run out and I can teach you no more,' the aged *sensei* said.

'But I've only just started to get the hang of this,' Kenny said, his heart sinking.

'Only three days remain before Namazu will strike. If he does, there will be much suffering and death. Your new home, your friends, all will be gone. It is time for you to move on.'

'Genkuro-*sensei*, come with us,' Kiyomi pleaded. 'That way, you can still teach Kenny and help us do this.'

The old man shook his head. 'No, my child. I have my own path to walk. We will meet again, I promise you that, but now it is time for you to return to your world.'

Kiyomi ran up to the slender figure and hugged him. 'I'm going to miss you, *sensei*.'

'And I you, my child. Please give my regards to your father.'

Kenny smiled and held out his hand.

Genkuro looked at it. 'Show me fire,' he said.

Kenny traced in the air, closed his eyes and concentrated; a small flame danced in his hand.

'Metal,' Genkuro said.

Kenny signed again, focused and his hand changed to shiny chrome and back.

'Earth,' the teacher said.

Kenny held his palm out to the packed dirt floor, drew the character for earth, and a pillar of soil reached upwards to his hand, like a stalagmite of mud.

'Wind.'

Kenny made the sign for air, held out both hands and a gusty breeze rushed through the room.

'And water,' Genkuro said.

'Oh, I always struggle with this one,' Kenny muttered, whipping his fingers through the air to form the letter 水. He tried again.

'Remember, it's a river running between two rocks,' Kiyomi said.

'Why couldn't it be something simpler?' Kenny said, fighting his frustration. 'Like this?' He drew a drop ◗

without thinking about what he was doing.

The floor bulged, as if a mole was surfacing, and a small spring trickled upwards.

'Holy crap,' Kiyomi whispered.

Genkuro crossed the gap in an instant and knelt to touch the water. He looked up at Kenny, a startled expression on his face.

'Ken-*san*, this is something I have never seen before. You . . . changed matter in your own way.'

Kenny took a step back from the spring. 'Did I do something wrong?'

'No, not at all,' Genkuro said, trying to choose his next words carefully. 'But this is something only the gods are able to do.'

Nobody mentioned the incident again, which only made Kenny more intrigued. What did Genkuro mean? There was no way that Kenny could match a god, but he had summoned water without drawing any *kanji*. What did that mean?

'This way, please,' Genkuro said, escorting his guests to the *torii* gate marking the edge of the compound.

'*Sensei*,' Kenny said, 'how are we going to get out of the palace grounds? It was hard enough getting in the first time.'

Genkuro smiled. 'That will not be a problem, Kuromori-*san*. I wish you good fortune, and remember, you will succeed because you must.' He bowed deeply.

Kiyomi and Poyo both bowed; Kenny copied them as best he could.

They pushed their way through the invisible barrier and found themselves on a building site. Japanese construction workers hurried past, wearing hard hats, baggy canvas trousers with tool belts and split-toed boots. Bamboo scaffolding clung like a giant spiderweb to the front of a three-storey building that was being erected.

Kiyomi led the way along a worn dirt path and Kenny followed her out on to a busy Tokyo street. A sedate black limousine was parked there and Oyama sat in the front, reading the *sumo* section of a sports newspaper. On seeing the youngsters, he eased himself out, opened the passenger door and ushered them in.

'Genkuro-*sensei* sent Poyo with a message,' Harashima explained, once they were all back at the house in Nezu. 'That's how we knew where to meet you. Now tell me everything that has happened.'

When Kenny and Kiyomi had finished, Harashima looked at the boy as if seeing him for the first time. 'You are *madoshi* after only two days? *Subarashii.*'

Kenny looked to Kiyomi for a translation. 'Papa is calling you a sorcerer.' She rolled her eyes.

'It's really not like that,' Kenny said, trying to hide his embarrassment.

'If we had more time, I would ask you to show me

what you have learned. As it is, you must pack your bags and be ready to go in ten minutes,' Harashima said.

'Huh? We only just got back,' Kenny said.

'I have booked you tickets on the *Shinkansen* to Kyoto. You must hurry to the Fushimi Inari Taisha to speak with the goddess Inari and find the sword. Time is running out if we are to prevent the attack.'

'Papa, do we know where Namazu is yet, or how he is being controlled?' Kiyomi asked.

Harashima looked pensive. 'We have some idea. My spies have been able to find tiny pieces of the puzzle, but I am waiting for the senior Kuromori-*san* and Genkuro-*sensei* to unravel it. Then we can strike.'

'My grandfather's helping?' Kenny said.

'As best he can from so far away. I will do what I can here. You two must go, now.'

An hour later, Kiyomi and Kenny were pushing their way through the crowds at Tokyo Station, towards the Tokaido Shinkansen platforms. It was mid-afternoon, but the concourse was teeming with throngs of shoppers, businessmen, office workers, students and tourists.

'How far is Kyoto from here?' Kenny asked Kiyomi.

'I'm not sure. Around four hundred kilometres.'

'So, we'll be arriving at sunset?'

'Are you mad? We'll be there in two hours.'

A sleek, futuristic train, with an aerodynamically streamlined nose, glided silently past and slowed to a stop. The front reminded Kenny of a cross between Concorde and a fighter jet.

'That's our train?' he said, gawping at it.

'Duh. *Shinkansen* is the Japanese bullet train. Top speed's about three hundred kilometres an hour. Get in.'

They climbed aboard and found their reserved seats. The interior was like a passenger jet, with plush window and aisle seats.

Kenny sat next to a rounded window, across from an elderly Japanese woman wearing a kimono. He was amused to see earphone cords trailing from her tablet computer, on which she was watching a *samurai* soap opera.

The *Shinkansen* started to move, but were it not for the platform sliding past, Kenny would not have known it; the train was almost silent and the ride was so smooth that there was no sense of motion. He settled down to watch the city slide past the window as the train picked up speed.

Sitting at the far end of the carriage, Sato finished his call and put his phone away.

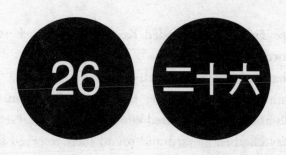

The bullet train sped through Tokyo and on to Yokohama, although Kenny was unable to tell where one city ended and the other began, such was the density of buildings. The urban sprawl finally gave way to countryside, farms, forests and hills.

Mount Fuji, the 3,776 metre tall volcano, with its elegant snow-capped cone, rushed by on the right hand side and the train followed the coastline, heading west.

After an hour of gazing out of the window, Kenny began tapping random beats with his fingers. Kiyomi noticed his fidgeting, unplugged her earphones and delved into her backpack.

'Here, I brought you something to read,' she said, handing him an American-import comic book.

'*Superman*?' Kenny said, glancing at the cover. 'Sorry. I can't stand that fat, hairy slob.'

Kiyomi wrinkled her nose at him. 'What are you talking about? Superman's ripped. Are you thinking of someone else?'

'No,' Kenny said. 'Think about it. He's always drawn

with huge, bulging muscles, right? How? He can lift an aeroplane, without any effort, so how does he build any muscle tone? You need to push against something for a workout, but nothing's heavy enough for him. He should have muscles like marshmallows.'

Kiyomi tried to hide her smile. 'OK, I'll give you that. Why's he so hairy, then?'

'Every part of him is invulnerable, right? So how does he get a haircut? How can he even shave? A blade would just break on him. Yet, he's always shown with a neat haircut and clean shaven. How?'

Kiyomi laughed. 'You think about this stuff way too much.'

'Here, I've got a better idea. Have you seen these before?' Kenny said, taking out his deck of trading cards.

'What're those?' Kiyomi said, taking the pack and riffling through it. 'Ooh, cool pictures. Is this some kind of giant robot fighting game?'

Kenny nodded. 'Yeah, it's called *MANDROID*. You build your robot, add armour and weapons and let them loose to fight each other.'

Kiyomi shrugged. 'Sounds geeky, but why not? How does it work?'

By the time the *Shinkansen* rocketed past Nagoya, Kenny was regretting his decision to teach Kiyomi the card game.

'OK, so if I hit you with a double *Napalm Blast* to melt ten points of armour and then launch all my *Hellfire*

Rockets, I blow up your fusion reactor, right?' Kiyomi said, placing three cards down in a row.

Kenny threw his hand down in disgust. 'Again? I thought you'd used all your rockets.'

'Must be beginner's luck,' Kiyomi said, gathering the cards to reshuffle. 'Want to play again or have you had enough?'

'I've had enough. Every time you deal, you get all the best cards and I'm left with crap.'

'I let you cut the deck,' Kiyomi protested.

'And a fat lot of good that did.' Kenny crossed his arms and slumped back, scowling.

'Ooh, is widdums upset that he can't win his widdle game?' Kiyomi looked up at Kenny from under her fringe. He tried to ignore her. She wiggled her eyebrows.

He smiled, in spite of himself. 'Grrr. You're so maddening. I can't even stay angry at you when I want to.'

Half an hour later, the *Shinkansen* pulled into the massive concrete, glass and steel behemoth of Kyoto Station.

Kenny gawped at the curved spine of ceiling which soared many levels overhead while Kiyomi led the way out, expertly navigating the arteries of walkways and escalators.

They transferred to the Nara Line and, after two stops, exited the local train at the tiny Inari Station.

Kiyomi dashed over the crossing and rounded a

corner. Kenny ran to keep up with her and stopped at the sight of a giant red *torii* gate straddling a paved path leading uphill. The setting sun pushed their long shadows towards the entrance. A second, equally massive gate stood further along the way, and beyond that were the shrine buildings.

They hurried under the *torii* and up a shallow flight of stone steps.

'Wow, this is definitely the place,' Kenny said, stopping at the top in front of the magnificent *romon* tower gate with its flared roof.

By the stairs, flanking either side, were two huge statues of foxes, each wearing a red bib. The one on the left held a stone key in its mouth, the other had a stone jewel.

'Too late,' Kiyomi said, looking back at the tangerine sky. 'We'll have to try again tomorrow.'

'It's shut?' Kenny asked.

'The *honden* is, yes.'

'What's the *honden*?' Kenny said.

'It's the main building, housing Inari's spirit. Well, that's not it exactly. It's more complicated.'

Kenny pursed his lips. 'So, what's the plan? We stop by tomorrow and she asks us in for a cup of tea and some biccies? Does she have a sofa and chairs in there?'

'How do I know? I've never met a goddess before. You're the one she wants to meet, not me. I'm just your dumb guide.' Kiyomi started down the steps.

201

'Whoa, wait a minute. Where'd *that* come from?' Kenny threw his hands out in exasperation. 'What's got into you?'

'Nothing's got into me. You're the special one, remember.' Kiyomi sped up.

Kenny hesitated, torn between chasing after her or turning his back and exploring the grounds of the shrine. He started running. 'Kiyomi! Wait up!'

She stopped and turned, her jaw set. 'What do you want from me?' she shouted. 'Haven't I done enough?'

The force of her anger took Kenny by surprise. 'Kiyomi, what I have done?' he said, drawing alongside. 'I'm sorry, OK? For whatever it is. I was just making a joke. Jeez, it's not like anyone's died. I didn't mean –'

'That's just it. I don't want to see you die,' she said, in a small voice.

'Oh. That.'

'For months now, all we've focused on at home is finding Namazu, getting you here, keeping you alive,' Kiyomi whispered. 'Only . . . now that we're finally about to meet her, it's all too real. Three days is all we have.'

Kenny spread his arms and shrugged. '*Shoganai*,' he sighed. 'Isn't that what you said before? Sucks to be me. It is what it is.'

Kiyomi wiped an imaginary smudge off his cheek. 'I'm sorry. You're knee-deep in this too, and you've had even less choice than me.' She raised her chin. 'Come on, let's go find our *ryokan*.'

'*Ryokan?*'

'Somewhere to sleep. Papa made us a reservation.'

The *ryokan*, it turned out, was a traditional Japanese inn. Brown clay roof tiles capped a wood-frame building. Inside were the familiar *tatami*-matted floors and *shoji* sliding doors.

'There's a *sento* down the block,' Kiyomi told Kenny after checking with the landlord. 'We can go clean up, grab some food and crash early, ready for tomorrow.'

'What's a *sento*?' Kenny asked.

'Public bathhouse. Come on, you could do with a scrub.'

Kenny followed Kiyomi, ducking under the blue curtain at the entrance of the *sento*.

Once inside, he was directed to the men's locker room. It reminded him of a changing facility at a sports centre, only with *tatami* mats on the floor. He stripped off, put his trainers and clothes into separate lockers and went through a sliding door to the tiled bathing area, a flannel in hand to preserve his modesty.

A row of taps was fixed to the walls on two sides with buckets and stools set out beside them.

Kenny took his place at one of these washing stations, soaped himself and rinsed off by filling the bucket from the taps and throwing it over himself. No one else was using the room and he began to relax, feeling less self-conscious.

In the centre of the room was a large square bathtub, sunk into the floor and full of clean hot water. It made Kenny think of football players sharing a bath after a match in the old days and he climbed in. He lay back, rested his head against the edge and relaxed into the soothing waters.

It was too good to last. While he soaked in the warmth, pondering what might lay in store the next day, he became aware of a quiet squelching sound: *sss-puck*, *sss-puck*. Kenny sat up and looked around. He was quite alone in the bathing area. The sound came again and this time Kenny looked up.

Something was crawling across the ceiling. The creature had long, spindly limbs, like a giant gecko, and it was the suction-cup fingers and toes that were making the strange sound. Its skin was a mottled green colour and, overall, it resembled a small child with an oversized head. The thing seemed not to notice Kenny and was working its way across the ceiling, its face pressed against the surface.

Kenny watched it scuttle down the wall and approach the far edge of the bath. Now he could see its large frog-like eyes and an enormous metre-long tongue which swept back and forth across the tiles, licking away any soap scum and dirt that had collected.

'So gross. Do you get paid for that or is it just a hobby?' Kenny couldn't help remarking.

The creature jumped back, startled, and its head

snapped round to see who was speaking.

'Oh, I get it.' Kenny laughed. 'I'm not supposed to be able to see you. Yeah, sorry about that.'

The filth-licker fixed its gaze on Kenny, inclining its head as if sizing up the boy in the tub. In a flash, the strange and repulsive creature transformed into something much deadlier. Rows of sharp, jagged teeth erupted along the length of the tongue and it advanced towards Kenny – *sss-puck*, *sss-puck* – lashing the tongue back and forth like a barbed whip.

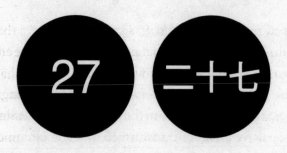

'Oh, crap,' Kenny said, sitting in the bath, naked and alone, while the monster closed in.

The spiked tongue whipping around was bad enough, but being stuck in a bathtub with nothing to use for defence was worse. He moved to the centre of the tub, trying to gain as much distance as he could from the filth-licker, but its tongue was easily long enough to reach him.

The tongue lashed down and Kenny flung himself aside. Hot water splashed upwards and the tongue retracted for another swipe. It whipped down again. Kenny caught a glimpse of jagged teeth and threw up an arm for cover. He had no escape. He screwed his eyes shut, grimacing in anticipation of the blow.

The tongue coiled round his arm and Kenny steeled himself for the stabbing pain from the rows of teeth, but felt nothing. He opened his eyes and was startled to see that his arm was shining metal. He'd somehow changed it, as Genkuro had taught him, only he'd done it without thinking. And if he could do that . . .

The filth-licker moved backwards, its suction toes

gripping the slippery tiles. It was much stronger than its skinny frame suggested and it dragged Kenny to the edge of the bathtub. The thing began to retract its tongue, hauling Kenny over the edge by his silvery arm and pulling him, slip-sliding on his front, towards its wide-open mouth.

Kenny focused, forcing down the urge to panic. He reached for the tongue with his free hand and grabbed the purple, fleshy mass. With an extra surge of concentration, his hand burst into flame.

The effect was instantaneous. With a hideous squeal, the filth-licker released Kenny's arm, whipped its scorched tongue back into its mouth and scurried backwards up the wall. It crawled across the ceiling and crouched in a corner, watching the boy with its unblinking gaze.

Without taking his eyes off the monstrous creature, Kenny backed up towards the door. His heel hit a bathing stool and he slipped. The filth-licker shot out its vicious, barbed tongue, aiming for Kenny's face.

'No!' Kenny cried, falling backwards, and a blast of raw energy crackled from his fingertips like a lightning bolt. It hit the creature, which shrieked and fell from the ceiling, its limbs flailing like a crazed disco dancer. It plummeted into the hot bathtub, sank for a moment and then exploded, throwing great green globs of stinking slime all over the bathing area – including Kenny.

He looked at himself in dismay. 'Oh, great,' he muttered. 'Now I need another bath and there's no way I'm going back in that tub.'

Half an hour later, Kiyomi walked Kenny back to the *ryokan* after he had cleaned up at another *sento*.

'Definitely an *akaname*,' she said, after he had recounted the whole episode once again. 'They don't usually attack people.'

'Lucky me,' Kenny said. 'Nice to know I get special treatment.'

'What I don't get is how you're able to do stuff without consciously focusing your will or tracing *kanji*. I've never heard of anyone doing that before. Not even your grandfather.'

'How come you didn't try and help me when you heard all the noise?'

Kiyomi screwed up her nose. 'Ew. What, and see you naked? No thanks. Besides, when I heard all that moaning and splashing and banging, I thought you were just, you know, doing . . . teenage boy stuff alone in the bathroom.'

Kenny was pretty certain he hadn't subconsciously set fire to his face, but it sure felt like it.

Early the next morning, Kenny and Kiyomi went back to the Fushimi Inari Taisha, which was already buzzing with visitors.

'Do what I do,' Kiyomi said. 'It's very important that you're respectful.' She went to what looked like a roof supported by four red pillars. Beneath was a large, curved, water-filled stone basin with a neat row of bamboo ladles resting on top. 'This is to purify yourself,' she explained, pouring water from a ladle over both hands and rinsing them. She then poured some water into her cupped hand, transferred it to her mouth, rinsed and spat into a gutter around the basin.

Kenny did his best to copy her exactly and was rewarded with an encouraging smile.

As they made their way further into the shrine, Kenny noticed that statues of foxes were everywhere, in all shapes and sizes.

'Come on, let's leave *ema*,' Kiyomi said. 'We're going to need all the luck we can get.'

She went over to a large wooden board which had hundreds of small wooden plaques hanging from it in tidy rows; long multicoloured streamers, made from thousands of tiny origami paper birds, were strung along the base.

'These must have taken ages to fold,' Kenny said, stooping to admire the handiwork.

'Those are *senbazaru*,' Kiyomi said. 'There's a thousand cranes on each string. They're a symbol of peace. Here.' She handed Kenny a small wooden tablet in the triangular shape of a fox's head. 'This is an *ema*. You write a prayer or wish on the back. Then we leave it here for Inari to read and answer if she chooses.'

'Well, my wish is an easy one,' Kenny said, taking a pen. 'Not to end up dead just yet. You?'

'I'm going to offer a prayer for my mother,' Kiyomi said, looking away.

Kenny watched her a moment before saying, 'You

don't talk about her much, do you? Whatever happened, it was bad, wasn't it?'

'Not as bad as what's going to happen to you if you don't stop asking me about it.'

They finished their messages, waited for their turn to hang up the wooden plaques and made their way uphill to the *gai-haiden*, an open-sided building with a gable roof curving inwards and a red picket fence around it.

'This is the outer hall of worship,' Kiyomi said. 'Follow me.' She went up to the fence, faced the middle of the building and bowed twice. She straightened up, clapped her hands loudly twice and bowed twice again, this time with her hands crossed over her chest.

'What's all that about?' Kenny asked, when Kiyomi had finished.

'You bow to show respect and clap to get Inari's attention. Got it?'

'Got it.' Kenny bowed, clapped and bowed again. 'Is that it?' he said. He waited for something to happen. Nothing did. 'So when does the goddess pop up?'

Kiyomi ignored him and walked to another smaller building, with an ornate carved roof, situated behind the *haiden*. She went up the steps to the front barrier, where short white curtains hung, and repeated the bowing and clapping. Lamps and candles burned in the dark interior of the *honden*.

'Is she in there?' Kenny whispered to Kiyomi, straining to see inside.

Kiyomi shrugged. 'I don't know. I've never visited a goddess before.'

'Greetings, most noble Kuromori-*sama* and Harashima-*sama*,' came a clear, high voice from behind them.

Kenny and Kiyomi turned round to see a Japanese man wearing the white robes, domed black hat, purple trousers and thick-soled black shoes of a *Shinto* priest.

'My mistress bids you welcome and awaits your presence,' the priest said, bowing towards them.

Kenny looked around and confirmed his suspicion that none of the other worshippers or tourists seemed to see the priest.

'Please, follow me,' the man said and clopped away on his platform sandals.

'Check out the shadow,' Kenny whispered to Kiyomi. In the bright morning sunlight, the priest's shadow cast the unmistakable shape of a fox, walking upright. 'Eight tails,' Kenny counted. 'What does that mean?'

'A fox who serves Inari grows a new tail every hundred years,' Kiyomi said, keeping her voice low.

'No way! You're saying Genkuro is nine hundred years old and this dude is eight hundred?'

'Ken-*chan*, didn't Genkuro-*sensei* tell you he was here when this shrine was first being built?'

'Yeah,' Kenny said, struggling to recall the details.

'Well, this shrine was founded in 711. Do the maths.'

'He's over *thirteen hundred years old*?' Kenny could hardly believe it.

'Yes. Nine tails are the limit.'

The priest stopped by a three-metre-high vermilion-hued *torii* gate, marking the entrance to a paved path leading up the wooded hillside, and motioned for his guests to enter. Kenny looked again and blinked. Behind the gate was another identical one, and then another and another, more than he could count, all standing close together to form a tunnel snaking gently upwards.

'Wow. There are millions of those things,' Kenny said.

'Closer to ten thousand,' Kiyomi said, 'if you count them all up. Each one marks a boundary to more sacred ground. This side is less pure; cross over and it becomes holier.'

Kenny let out a long whistle. 'So, if I go through a thousand gates I end up, like, in heaven?'

The fox-priest smiled. 'Sadly no, but you will arrive in a place sacred enough to meet my mistress. She is expecting you.'

Kenny swallowed hard. 'OK, then. I've come all this way. Might as well get on with it. Yep. Uh-huh.'

Kiyomi elbowed him. 'Quit stalling.'

Kenny led the way into the tunnel of *torii* with Kiyomi close behind. She drew level, put her hand in his and they walked together.

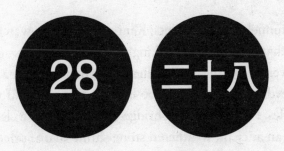

28 二十八

Kenny hiked up the path, his vision filled with the bright red of the *torii* gates, and he half-imagined he was travelling through an umbilical cord. He caught glimpses of the emerald forest on either side, but it felt like he was in another world, one untouched by time.

The path ended at a small shrine with stone lanterns and hundreds of small fox statues scattered around. Kenny and Kiyomi performed the ritual bowing and clapping and crossed to the next *torii* tunnel. Here the path forked and two tunnels led off in different directions, each looking like a mirror-image reflection of the other.

'Here's where you and I have to go our own way,' Kenny said, giving Kiyomi's hand a reassuring squeeze. 'Genkuro-*sensei* told me we'd have to see Inari separately.'

'OK.' Kiyomi took a deep breath. 'Good luck.' She gave him a quick kiss on the cheek. 'Let's go at the same time. Ready?' She counted to three and they headed into separate tunnels, holding hands for as long as they could before distance parted their outstretched fingers.

The tunnel seemed endless. Kenny checked his watch and saw that he had been walking for fifteen minutes.

Eventually the path ahead brightened and Kenny stepped out on to a bamboo bridge, over a lake of white pebbles. He followed the bridge which ended at a clearing with an ancient, weathered stone shrine to one side.

Sitting at the centre of the clearing, with her legs folded under her thighs and her hands resting, palm down, on her lap, was a Japanese woman wearing a pure white kimono. Her robes were so dazzlingly bright that they seemed to be made of light and Kenny immediately felt grubby in comparison.

As he drew closer, he saw that the woman was strikingly beautiful. Her eyes were closed, but her face was smooth and serene with strong, high cheekbones and full lips.

Kenny sat down opposite, unable to tear his eyes from her exquisite features. He felt as if he could spend the rest of his life there, gazing on this vision of perfection.

Inari opened her almond eyes. They were amber with vertical pupils, like those of a fox.

'Not long ago, another Kuromori answered my call,' she said. 'Now a new generation comes to take his place.'

'I, uh . . .'

Inari turned her vulpine gaze upon him and Kenny felt like she was looking through his physical self and into his soul.

'When I see you, child, I see the newest link in a chain

of life reaching back through time to the first stirrings of life on this world,' Inari said.

Kenny swallowed hard.

'Everything is spirit, or energy, if you prefer. All matter, all life. At the beginning, when the cosmos was born, there was spirit. Spirit took shape, became stars and planets, bound by laws. Do you understand this?'

Kenny nodded weakly. 'Just about,' he croaked.

'Spirit fashioned life and, from the first pairings of life's fragments, countless successful unions have led to you here today. I see you and I see an unbroken chain of life.'

'Oh,' was all Kenny could say.

'Two generations ago, a Kuromori championed my cause and served me well. Now he is passing that sacred duty to you, should you accept it.'

Kenny blinked, his mind snapping back into focus. 'You mean I have a choice?'

'Always,' Inari said. Her face showed no emotion, as if it was a mask she was concentrating upon to maintain.

'What if I say no?' Kenny asked. 'Millions of innocent people are going to die, right?'

Inari inclined her head a fraction. 'What is it to you, Kuromori? They are but strangers.'

'Yeah, but they're still people. I can't let them die for no reason.'

'Revenge is a reason.'

'No, it's not. It's an excuse.'

215

Inari's gaze swept over Kenny once more. 'I am calling you to put your life before the lives of strangers, even if it costs you dearly. Do you heed this call?'

'I know what it's like to lose those you love. Yes, I'll do it.'

Inari smiled. She reached out and touched her index finger to Kenny's forehead. He felt a surge of warmth wash through him from her fingertip and closed his eyes, swimming in the glow.

'It is done. Arise, Kuromori, servant of Inari.' She gestured for Kenny to stand and rose gracefully to her feet. 'In earlier days, the rulers of these lands appointed warriors to preserve order.'

'*Samurai.* I've read about them.'

Inari led the way towards the ancient shrine. 'The same happened in your country. The king selected special warriors.'

'You mean knights? Like in tales of King Arthur?'

'You, Kuromori, are now a knight in my service. Do you know why you were sent here?'

Kenny nodded. 'Yeah, to use Amaterasu's sword to stop this Namazu thing before it crushes the West Coast with a monster quake. Do you know where it is?'

Inari stopped at the shrine. 'Genkuro warned you I would test you.'

'I thought you just did.'

'Only one with true wisdom can wield Kusanagi. Tell me, child, what is it that casts light but no shadow?'

'Huh?' Kenny's mind flashed through dozens of possibilities: the sun, a lamp, a bulb, a television, a torch . . . every light makes shadow. It was an impossible riddle. Then he looked at the shrine – and smiled.

'Flame,' he answered. 'A flame casts light, but it has no shadow.' He looked again at the shadows of the candles burning at the shrine.

Inari pressed her palms together. 'After Kuromori rescued the sword and felt its power, he knew it must be kept far away from the hands of men, for men would seek only to harness it for destruction. Since he was unable to hide it safely in the mortal world –'

'Grandad hid it in your world!' Kenny said.

'On my instruction, Kuromori left Kusanagi with Hachiman, the God of War. To retrieve the sword, you must find Hachiman and ask him to surrender it to you,' Inari said.

'And he'll do that?' Kenny asked.

'No. You will have to face him in combat and defeat him. Only then can you take the sword and wield it.'

'You've got to be kidding.'

'But beware. Like all gods, Hachiman can read your thoughts.'

Kenny shook his head. 'Nothing is ever easy, is it? So, where do I find him?'

Inari drew three letters in the air which glowed, spelling out: U S A.

'I have to go back to America? With only two days

left?' Kenny's sense of awe was fast being replaced by annoyance and disbelief.

'Time is short,' Inari agreed. 'You must travel quickly.' She began walking back towards the bridge.

'Wait. Can I ask a couple of questions?' Kenny said, knowing that his audience was over.

'You may ask,' Inari said.

'What's with this deadline? I mean, if these guys can control Namazu, what are they waiting for?'

'Everything has an appointed time, even vengeance. The attack is planned to mark the anniversary of something that happened long ago, by your counting.'

'OK. And how is it I can do . . . this?' Kenny concentrated for a second, channelling his *ki*, before holding up his hand which was now ablaze. 'Just by thinking about it.'

'You are not *Nihonjin* – not Japanese – and this means you are not bound by the same limitations,' Inari said.

'I don't get it,' Kenny admitted.

'Every person sets his own limits, decides what he can and cannot do. You are young and from a place which has different limits, where facing the impossible is viewed as a challenge, not an invitation to surrender.'

'You're saying I can do this because I don't know I shouldn't be able to do it?'

'I am saying that it is you, and no one else, who chooses what you can or cannot do.'

Inari stopped by the bridge.

Kenny persisted. 'The prophecy – your prophecy – says

if I succeed, someone I love will die. Who? Who will die?'

'Everything is spirit, Kuromori. Everything is connected, like cloud, river and sea. There is much bitterness and anger within you. This gives you strength, but it also makes you weak. Do not give in to your hate or it will consume and destroy you. That is the path taken by those we are trying to stop.'

'What else do I have?' Kenny said, his voice breaking. 'Everyone I've ever cared about, everyone I've ever loved has either been taken away from me, or – or they've walked out.'

'Your father did not have to leave you. By choosing to blame him, and in pushing him away, you made his choice easier.'

'No! How can you –? My-my mum died of cancer and my dad, he couldn't take it and he ran off. What was I supposed to do about that?'

'Kuromori, you accepted it and that acceptance makes you afraid to let anyone get close. You think by pushing everyone away you will not get hurt.'

Kenny could not meet Inari's penetrating gaze. 'Well, if you put it like that,' he muttered.

Inari smiled at him, her face radiating sadness and compassion. 'Kuromori, you are already hurt and you will never heal until you allow love back into your soul. Remember my words: love is many times stronger than hate. Those who love act without limits. You choose.'

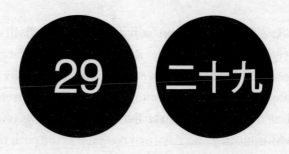

29 二十九

Kenny dragged his feet all the way back through the tunnel of *torii* gates, his heart heavy. He had come all this way to meet a goddess, no less, but instead of receiving answers about how to proceed, all he had got was more questions. He should have come out feeling invigorated and full of purpose; instead, he felt flat and dejected. He came to the end of the path and returned to the small shrine where the route had forked.

Kiyomi sat, leaning against a stone lantern, hugging her knees with her head resting on them. The sky was streaked lemon, orange and violet. A single star shimmered low on the horizon.

'Kiyomi,' Kenny said, kneeling beside her and touching her arm.

She looked up, blinking. 'Ken-*chan*? What time is it? Where have you been for so long?'

'I wasn't gone for long. Maybe an hour, tops.' Kenny looked at his watch; it was 18:58. 'Holy crap! No way!'

'Time passes differently for gods,' Kiyomi said, rising

to her feet. 'We have to go. You can tell me what happened while we walk.'

By the time they arrived at the *honden*, Kenny had finished recounting his meeting with Inari.

'How long were you staring at her?' Kiyomi asked. 'Or was it when you closed your eyes?'

'I don't know,' Kenny said, feeling defensive without knowing why. 'It felt like seconds.'

'Yeah, right. You were probably making goo-goo eyes at her for hours and didn't even realise.'

Kenny decided to let it drop. 'So, what now? We've got two days left and I have to go back to America. Is there an airport around here?'

They were making their way down the steps, exiting the largely deserted shrine.

'That doesn't make sense,' Kiyomi said. 'Why would Hachiman be in America? Tell me again, where did Inari say to find him?'

'She didn't say it. She wrote it: U, S and A in the air. USA, right? America.'

'But why didn't she tell you –? Ohhh . . . I get it.' She stopped on the stairs. 'It's not Yoo-Ess-Ay, you goof, it's Ooh-Sah.'

Kenny looked baffled – again.

'Usa. It's a city in Oita Prefecture, where the Usa Jingu is,' Kiyomi continued.

'What's the Usa Jingu?' Kenny asked.

'It's the main Hachiman shrine, just like this is the

main Inari one. Makes sense we'll find him there.' She started walking again.

'How far is it?'

'About four hundred kilometres west. We're going to need to take the *Shinkansen* again.' Kiyomi checked her watch. 'Come on, let's get some food and make plans.'

Half an hour later, they were in an *izakaya* – an informal Japanese restaurant – sitting on *tatami* mats around a low table. The waitress brought cold soft drinks, hot wet towels and a small bowl of soy beans, boiled in their pods.

Kiyomi ordered from a picture menu while Kenny split open a soy pod and nibbled on a green bean. It was sweet and nutty.

'I've ordered a mix of things,' Kiyomi said. 'You should like some of it.'

'I'm so hungry I could eat a bowl of *natto* with a raw sea urchin on top.' Kenny caught himself. 'You didn't order that, did you?'

Kiyomi smiled. 'No, but they can probably do it as a special for you.'

The *izakaya* wasn't busy. A group of businessmen in suits were playing drinking games at a large table and small huddles of friends were sharing plates of food.

'What happened with you?' Kenny asked. 'When you went up the other path. Did you see . . .?'

Kiyomi returned to studying the menu. 'I saw Inari too,' she said, without looking up. 'She was different from

222

how you described her. She looked like . . . my mother.'

'Oh,' Kenny said, squeezing on a soy pod. A bean popped out and fell into his drink where it bobbed and fizzed. 'She must appear differently to each person.'

'I suppose.'

Kenny fished the bean out. 'So, what did she say?'

Kiyomi shrugged. 'She said I have to help you, that you can't defeat Hachiman or Namazu by yourself.'

'Like, duh. Did she tell you how I'm supposed to beat this god in a duel, bearing in mind he's had thousands of years of practice and can read my mind?'

Kiyomi put down the menu. 'No, she didn't say anything about that. Just that I had to believe in you. Let go of the past. Set aside my hate.'

'Yeah? She told me the same thing.'

'I hate her,' Kiyomi said. 'Of all the forms to take, why choose my mother? Why can't she just leave –?'

The waitress returned with a tray of small plates and dishes. She set them on the table, bowed and left.

Kenny watched Kiyomi quietly fuming. 'Look, I know this isn't any of my business, and this isn't something you want to talk about, but maybe I can help if you tell me what happened with your mother,' Kenny suggested.

'Here, I'll fix you a sampler plate,' Kiyomi said, her chopsticks moving swiftly. 'Try the *yakitori* first. You'll like it.'

Kenny picked up a short bamboo skewer bearing small chunks of barbecued chicken in a sticky brown sauce.

He took a bite. 'Thank you. This is good.' He watched Kiyomi's face, looking for a sign that she might open up and let him in. 'So what happened with your mother?'

Kiyomi pushed her plate away and finished her drink. 'You first,' she said to Kenny.

'There's not much to tell,' he said. 'It started when I was three. Too young to know what leukaemia was. Or so I thought. Mum got sick. Dad . . . he ran away. Well, he was there, I suppose. He was probably just scared. Anyway, he stayed at work, wrote papers, just carried on like she was already dead, when she wasn't.'

Tears filled Kenny's eyes and brimmed over, tracing glistening lines down his cheeks. Kiyomi took Kenny's hand and squeezed it as he wiped them away.

'She hung on for three years. The treatment was awful. She had fair hair – that's where I get it from – but it fell out in handfuls. It was weird, visiting her in hospital. With a scarf over her head. She got thinner. So pale, her skin was like glass. And then, one day . . . while I was there . . . she died.' He stuffed the towel into his mouth and bit down on it to stifle the sob.

'In a better place now, everyone said. Like they know anything. The funeral was weird. It was sunny and warm, not cold and wet like it should have been. And Dad? He sort of fell apart afterwards . . . started drinking heavily and seeing other women. I went to stay with my grandad for a year. Then Dad got his life together and took us off to America, wanting a fresh start. Didn't take him long to ditch me though.'

Kenny blinked at Kiyomi through his tears, bringing her face into focus.

'I've never really told anyone that before,' he said. 'Sorry.'

'Don't be sorry,' Kiyomi said. 'I'm jealous. I wish I could cry. I wish my mum had died of cancer.'

'Then what –?'

'An *oni*,' Kiyomi said, her eyes narrowing and her mouth twisting into a snarl. 'Did you know their favourite snack is human flesh?'

Kenny shook his head, dreading what was coming next.

'Papa was away on business when the *oni* came. It was looking for him, sent to kill him by his enemies. When it found Mama at home . . .' She took a deep breath, straightening up. 'Let's just say there was a closed coffin at her funeral.'

Kenny took her hand. 'Kiyomi, I'm so sorry. Really, I . . .' There were no words left. Everything sounded so inadequate.

'It's worse than that,' Kiyomi said. 'I was there. Little me. Two years old, playing at home. I was the only one who could see the *oni*, since I have the Gift. I saw it and I screamed and I tried to warn Mama, but she couldn't see it and thought I was upset about something else so she didn't run and hide or call for help. I saw everything.'

Kenny shuddered. 'So that's why . . .?'

'On the train? Yeah. And it's why Papa made sure I

can take care of myself.' She leaned closer, her jaw set and a fierce look in her eyes. 'I'll make you a deal, Ken-*chan*.'

'Go on.'

'If I believe in you, truly believe in you, like Inari wants me to . . . Promise you won't let me down. That you'll do your bit - whatever the cost?'

Kenny squeezed her hand even harder. 'Deal. I promise you. Whatever it takes, I'll finish this.'

'Cross your heart?'

'And hope to die.'

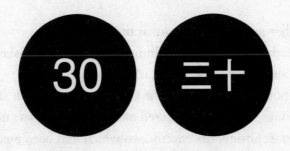

It was early afternoon when the two travellers stepped off the clunky red Nippo Line train at Usa Station. They had taken the bullet train to Kokura and changed to the coastal line for the final seventy-five kilometres. A ten-minute bus journey and a short walk brought them to a gigantic red *torii* gate, marking the outer boundary of the Hachiman Shrine.

Kenny stopped just before the gate and looked up at the towering lintels high above.

'Ready to do this?' Kiyomi asked.

'As ready as I'll ever be,' Kenny said. He took a deep breath, held it and stepped over the threshold.

The path ahead led to a picturesque footbridge across the Yorimo River. It arched gently upwards and was bordered by red handrails. A handful of worshippers made their way in both directions.

'It seems so peaceful,' Kenny said. 'Are you sure I'm going to have to fight this guy?'

For once, Kiyomi said nothing.

They came to a steep flight of stone steps, with

another immense *torii* gate at the top.

'Is this all meant to be intimidating?' Kenny asked, as he climbed the steps. 'If so, it's working.'

Another *torii* marked the entrance to the main shrine buildings. Kiyomi shuddered as they drew closer; unlike the Inari Shrine, the entrance to which had been guarded by twin fox statues, this *torii* had two huge black *oni*, each standing on a plinth on either side, with tusks bared in hideous snarls, and muscular arms holding a long pole with a curved blade at the end.

A family of four strolled past, without even pausing to take a picture.

'Yow, scary,' Kenny said. 'That makes a change from fox statues. Hey, how come no one else seems to be bothered by –'

'You, boy!' boomed one of the *oni*, its blood-red eyes glaring at Kenny. 'You are not welcome here. Begone or feel my wrath.'

Kiyomi stepped forward. '"Feel my wrath?" Is that the best you can do?' she scoffed.

The second *oni* jumped down from its stand, shaking the ground where it landed. It swung its *naginata* around and levelled the blade at Kiyomi's chest.

'We know who you are, little girl. No one enters our master's domain unless they first go through us.'

'Get lost,' Kiyomi said. 'Kuromori-*san* doesn't waste time on nobodies like you. He wants to speak to the head honcho, not the guys who clean the toilets.'

'You dare speak to us like that?' barked the first *oni*. Its face was so close to Kiyomi's that her hair rippled with each word.

'Tell your master that Kuromori-*san* has come to reclaim Kusanagi,' she said, unfazed and ignoring the foul breath. 'If he continues to hide behind you two overgrown gorillas, we'll have to assume he's afraid of the challenge.'

'*What?*'

'You heard me. Go tell him, and warn him not to keep us waiting.'

The two *oni* looked at each other, shrugged, and one stamped away towards the shrine buildings.

'You don't think you might be laying it on a bit thick there?' Kenny whispered to Kiyomi, nervously watching the *oni* blocking their way. 'I mean, what if they decided to fight?'

'*Oni* aren't that bright,' Kiyomi said. 'It's easy to bluff them.'

The first *oni* returned. 'My master will see you,' it said, with lips curling into a sneer. 'Follow me.'

It led the way under the *torii*, across a courtyard and up the steps to a magnificent *romon* tower gate, painted in red and white with a black roof. The gate opened into a covered corridor which ran along the outside of an inner sanctum. In the centre, behind a low hedge was the twin-roofed *honden*, home to Hachiman, the God of War.

The front doors slowly swung open by themselves and

229

a chill black fog spilled out, snaking round the visitors' ankles.

The *oni* bowed so low that his horns scraped the steps leading up to the entrance. 'Master, your guests have arrived.'

Kenny swallowed hard and willed his feet to climb the steps into the darkened interior. Kiyomi joined him and there was an echoing boom as the doors slammed shut behind them. To Kenny, it was the sound of a closing tomb.

'Kuromori,' a voice rumbled in the darkness, sounding like slabs of granite grinding together. 'I commanded thee never to return.'

'Uh, that was . . . a different Kuromori,' Kenny said, his voice sounding faint within the cavernous darkness.

'Come forward, child, that I may witness thee better,' the voice said.

Kenny took a step closer and felt the presence of another mind, probing into his.

'So my enemy's son has borne a son and the child now comes to claim his birthright,' the voice said. 'Thy grandfather bequeathed Kusanagi to me. It is mine.'

'My grandfather gave you the sword for safe keeping,' Kenny said. 'Not to keep.'

Hachiman's laugh was like rolling thunder. 'Possession is nine-tenths of the law. Art those not the words of thy people? The sword of Amaterasu is where it belongs: in the hands of a god.'

Kenny closed his eyes and focused his *ki*, picturing a bank of floodlights. A faint glow appeared within the *honden*; it intensified and spread to illuminate a huge hulking figure, towering over them. Hachiman, like his *oni*, was as black as obsidian. His eyes were cobalt-blue neon slits and muscles rippled across his powerful frame. He wore classical *samurai O-yoroi* armour which glowed silver, and his long hair was tied and folded in a traditional *chonmage* style.

Kenny recoiled from the terrifying sight. Hachiman was in every way the opposite of Inari. He swallowed hard and willed his knees to stop shaking. 'You know why I'm here.'

'And thou, child – dost thou know who I am?' Hachiman boomed.

'You're Hachiman, the God of War,' Kenny said.

'I am the God of Warriors, Kuromori. I am also the guardian of these lands. Whereas Inari casts her net wide and embraces all life everywhere, my loyalties lie only with my people.'

'I've come for the sword,' Kenny tried again.

'To what end, Kuromori? What possible use could a *gaijin* have for a weapon of such nobility and power?'

'I have to stop your pet, Namazu, before it kills millions of people.'

'Not people, Kuromori. *Gaijin*. Outsiders. Foreigners. Impure races. Their lives are worth nothing.'

'That doesn't mean you can just kill them. They've done nothing to you.'

'That is where thou art wrong, Kuromori. I understand war, but there is no honour to be gained in visiting further suffering upon the vanquished.'

'Look, I'm not here to argue the rights and wrongs of what happened seventy years ago. That was another generation, another age.'

A flicker of annoyance crossed Hachiman's features. 'A cowardly attack forced my people to surrender in shame,' he said. 'For the first time in history, my warriors were defeated. As their guardian, I too failed and had to witness countless humiliations as my punishment. This stain of dishonour can only be washed away with the blood of our enemies.'

'But that's all over,' Kenny said in exasperation. 'America helped Japan to rebuild. Our countries are friends now. Everyth–'

'Friends?' Hachiman spat. 'Thy people have no friends, only subjects to whom they dictate. Thou hast turned my people from warriors into sheep.'

'This isn't getting us anywhere.' Kenny sighed. 'I need the sword, this Kusanagi.'

Hachiman leaned closer. 'I will not yield the sword to thee or anyone else, Kuromori.'

'Then I challenge you to a duel. You versus me. One on one. Winner gets the sword.'

'Kenny, are you mad?' Kiyomi hissed.

'Silence, girl! Thou hast no part in this,' Hachiman said with a snarl. He fixed his glowing eyes on Kenny. 'Thou hast great courage for one so young, Kuromori. I accept thy challenge. We shall fight – to the death.'

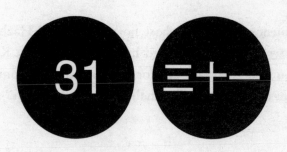

With one wave of Hachiman's massive arms, light flooded the interior of the *honden*. Medieval weapons of every type lined the walls. There were swords, shields, clubs, staves, polearms, axes, flails, whips, chains, daggers, knives, hammers, spears, darts, and countless others that Kenny could not name.

In the centre of the hall lay a large square platform of raised packed earth. A rope circle was half-buried in the clay, its diameter touching the edges of the square. Hachiman strode to the centre of the arena and made a sweeping gesture towards the armaments on the walls.

'Kuromori, choose thy weapon,' he said.

Kenny stepped up on to the platform and faced the god, trying to ignore his heart pounding like a jackhammer inside his chest. 'Let me get this straight,' Kenny said. 'As the challenger, I have the right to choose the weapons?'

'That is so,' Hachiman said. 'But I warn thee, Kuromori, I have mastery of every weapon within these walls.'

'And he can read your mind too,' Kiyomi whispered from the edge of the platform.

Kenny's gaze swept the room. Each time his eyes stopped on a particular weapon, he felt Hachiman's mind press against his, the god eager to know which weapon he would choose.

'OK,' Kenny said, after completing a full circle. 'I've made my choice.'

Hachiman cracked his knuckles in anticipation. 'And it is?'

Kenny put his hands behind his back. 'This.' He held up his pack of *MANDROID* trading cards.

'What? What trickery is this?' Hachiman demanded.

'It's a card game,' Kenny replied. 'A contest. A battle of skill. You said I could choose.'

Hachiman slammed a massive fist against the earth in frustration, splitting the mound and leaving a crater behind. His nostrils flared and his eyes burned brighter. 'Very well,' he breathed.

Kenny felt the god probe his mind again.

'I know the rules,' Hachiman said.

'One more thing,' Kenny said. 'To avoid any accusations of cheating, we can let my servant deal the cards.'

Kiyomi blinked in surprise.

'So be it,' Hachiman said. 'The girl will deal the cards.'

The god knelt down in the traditional *seiza* style, his calves under his thighs. Kenny sat cross-legged opposite. He wiped his sweaty hands on his jeans and fought the urge to be sick.

Kiyomi shuffled the cards, riffled them, made a

bridge and held the deck out for the cut.

'Just do what you did on the train,' Kenny whispered.

She dealt out seven cards each, put the deck down and withdrew. Kenny reached for his cards.

'Stop!' Hachiman commanded.

Kenny froze. Hachiman reached over and took Kenny's face-down cards, replacing them with his. Both players then picked up their cards and studied them.

'I win!' Hachiman declared, a triumphant leer on his face. He dropped a card. '*Power Boost*. Draw three cards,' he said, taking them from the deck.

Kenny's shoulders sagged.

Hachiman then placed his nine cards down, one after the other. '*Electrical Discharge*, lose three power points; *Napalm Blast*, lose five points of armour; *NATO Air Strike*, lose four armour points; *Orbital Satellite Strike*, lose four of each; *Ion Cannon*, lose six power points; *Laser Sword*, three more armour; *Cluster Bomb*, two points down; *Plasma Grenades*, lose three; and *Computer Virus*, drop two cards. Hah! Victory is mine.'

'Holy crap,' Kenny said, shooting an accusing glare in Kiyomi's direction. 'Was there a *Kitchen Sink* card you forgot to throw at me?' He tossed two cards on the discard pile, leaving him five to play.

'Thou art dead, Kuromori,' Hachiman rumbled. 'In every way. Thy armour is gone and thy power is depleted. Thy soul belongs to me.'

Kenny looked at his five cards and rearranged the

236

order in which he was holding them. 'You might be right,' he said, 'but then again . . .' He played a *Fusion Reactor* card. 'Three more cards back to me.' He drew the cards; now he had seven again. 'I'm going to deploy my *Forcefield Generator* to counter your napalm. That's five armour points back. If I combine my *Nanotech Bio-armour* with a trip to *Baikonur Cosmodrome* for a refit, I can regenerate another ten points of armour, right?'

'No,' Hachiman growled. 'What art thou doing?'

'A *System Reboot* should clear the virus; that's two cards back.' He took two more. 'And if I combine a *Power Glove* with a *Rocket Punch*, that should knock out your chest armour. Now an *Electromagnetic Pulse* to take down your on-board computer. If I discharge all my *Reserve Battery Pack* power and channel it into the *Plasma Cannon*, and with you a sitting duck . . .' Kenny did the maths. 'That means I blow your sorry ass to pieces.'

'*Yatta*!' Kiyomi screamed, leaping up and punching the air.

'What manner of treachery is this?' Hachiman roared, rising to his feet. 'Kuromori, thou hast cheated me in this contest.'

'No way!' Kenny said. '*I* didn't cheat. You'd know if I did.'

Hachiman's eyes glowed brighter and Kenny felt the god's mind push into his.

'Twas thee!' Hachiman said, jabbing an accusing finger at Kiyomi. 'Thou hast cheated.'

'I wasn't playing the game, remember?' Kiyomi said. 'You agreed it was you against Ken-*chan*. *He* beat you and *he* didn't cheat.'

Hachiman exploded into a tempestuous rage. Kenny threw himself to the ground, while Hachiman tore the weapons off the walls and hurled them down, stamping on them and smashing them to rubble with his fists.

'All these weapons!' he said, between blows. 'All useless against this child!' He straightened up. 'Kuromori, thou hast bested me this once. I accepted the terms of thy challenge; thus, I am honour-bound to accept the result, however deceitfully it was obtained. Pray that we never meet again.'

Kenny got to his feet and dusted himself down. He cleared his throat. 'I still need the sword.'

'Inari chose her champion well.' Hachiman held out his hand, palm upwards. The air burned a bright gold colour and an ancient, pitted, rusty blade shimmered into his hand.

'Take it,' Hachiman growled. 'Then go and never return.'

Kenny made it as far as the *torii* by the steep steps leading to the bridge, before he stopped and began shaking.

'Ken-*chan*, what's wrong?' Kiyomi asked, frowning.

'Just feeling a bit dizzy, that's all,' Kenny mumbled.

'Have a rest. It's probably just delayed shock.'

Kenny flopped down and leaned against one of the legs

of the *torii* while Kiyomi rubbed his back and shoulders.

'How's that?' she asked. 'Better?'

'Yeah, much better,' Kenny said, managing a weak smile.

'You were pretty awesome back there, you know?' Kiyomi said.

'It helped that you never admitted you'd cheated on the train. Since *I* didn't know, *he* couldn't know.' He looked at the rusted sword in his hand. 'Still, it's been a lot of trouble for this . . . piece of junk.' He tapped it on the ground. 'How do we even know if this is the real Sword of Heaven and not some fake that Hachiman dumped on us?'

Kiyomi shrugged. 'It has to be real. Hachiman wouldn't dishonour himself by breaking his word.'

Kenny scowled at the sword. 'There must be some way to tell if this is for real.'

'I know, why don't you try cutting something with it? If it breaks, it's a dud. If it's real, it should work.'

'OK. That's not a bad idea.'

Kenny picked himself up and went to a nearby maple tree. 'Ready?' he said to the watching Kiyomi. She gave a thumbs-up sign. Kenny swung the sword, aiming it at the twisted tree trunk. He applied very little force as he didn't wish to damage the tree or jar his wrist from the impact.

He needn't have worried: the sword passed through the thick trunk as easily as a stick through cobwebs.

'Oh my God!'

Kenny watched in helpless horror as the tree toppled over and crashed to the ground, branches crackling and splintering. He was still trying to understand what had happened when a sharp, wracking pain shot through his arm and a voice roared inside his head, saying, '*Who dares awaken Kusanagi from his slumber?*'

Kiyomi saw Kenny double up with pain and collapse on the ground. She ran over to him and did not see the huge shadow falling over her until it was too late.

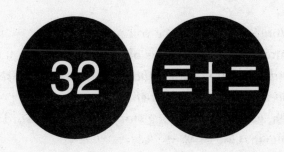

Kenny blinked, but saw no difference; all around him was a deep black void. Normally, he would expect to hear his own breathing, or the pulse within his ears, but even these were swallowed up by the darkness.

'*I say again: who dares disturb Kusanagi's slumbers?*' said the voice in Kenny's head. It was flat, emotionless and not human.

'Uh, that would be me,' Kenny said.

'*And who is "me"? Are you god or man?*'

'Definitely man. Well, near enough.'

'*A boy?*' The voice sounded vaguely amused.

'Yes. My name is Kenny Blackw – I mean, Kuromori. That's wh–'

'*Kuromori? Is that you?*'

'Yes. I mean, no. I'm a different Kuromori – from the one you might be thinking of. Depending if that's a good thing. Or not.'

'*Kuromori was a former master of mine. What are you to him?*'

'I'm his grandson, Kenny.'

'*How many years have you seen, child?*'

'Fifteen. I'm fifteen years old.'

'*Indeed? Tell me how a boy has come into possession of a weapon worthy of the gods.*'

'Oh, geez. That's a long story. I won the sword from Hachiman, God of War.'

There was a long pause before the voice spoke again. '*You, a mere boy of fifteen years, bested Hachiman in combat and claimed Kusanagi as your prize?*'

'I guess. It was a bit more complicated than that, but that's about right.'

'*Why?*'

'There's this dragon, you see, that causes earthquakes, and it's going to make an enormous one that'll kill millions of people if I don't stop it and I need the sword to do this.'

'*Namazu awakens?*'

'Yes, you know him?'

'*So, my old enemy stirs once more? And you, child, what other purpose do you have for the sword?*'

'Other purpose? None. I just want to get this done and go back to my life.'

'*You wish to possess the greatest weapon in these lands solely to save others? You have no desire to harness its power for your own ends?*'

'No, not really,' Kenny said.

There was another long pause before the voice spoke again. '*I sense you speak the truth, young Kuromori. You*

242

are most unusual. You have the heart of a warrior, the soul of a priest and the mind of a scholar. I have never had a master like that before. Very well, I will enter into your service and go with you. It will be . . . interesting. When you need me, you have but to call.'

Kenny remained baffled. 'Uh, thank you, I think. Do you mind if I ask a question? Who are you? Oh, and where am I?'

'I am Kusanagi, the Sword of Heaven, and you are asleep. I will awaken you – now.'

Kenny opened his eyes and saw an ant climbing a blade of grass in front of his nose. He was face down amid the wreckage of the maple tree. His hands were resting on the small of his back and his wrists stung from the cords tied round them. Kenny raised his head and saw from the coral-hued sky that the sun was setting. He rolled on to his side and a chill swept through him.

Kiyomi lay nearby, unconscious, next to the giant *torii*, the grass blackened around her and, everywhere, gouges in the ground, broken rocks and uprooted trees were evidence that a tremendous battle had taken place. Standing guard over her prone form was Taro, the huge red *oni* Kenny had met at the airport eight days earlier.

Sato was sitting beside Kenny, completing a *Sudoku* puzzle in a newspaper. He folded it, set it aside and repositioned his sunglasses.

'Mr Blackwood, you are awake,' he said. 'I trust you had a good sleep.'

Kenny fought to free his arms, but they would not move.

'Please, do not struggle,' Sato said. 'You may cause harm.'

'I'll cause harm all right,' Kenny said, his jaw clenched. He concentrated for a moment and the cord around his wrists charred and crumbled. He sprang to his feet.

Sato stood up and dusted off the seat of his expensive trousers. 'You did that without any *kata*,' he observed. 'Impressive. You have learned much in a short time.'

Kenny glared at Taro, standing over Kiyomi. 'Get away from her . . . and I'd better not find out you've touched one hair on her head or I'll –'

'Please, Mr Blackwo–'

'The name is Kuromori, and don't you forget it.'

'You are not in a position to make threats,' Sato said. 'Harashima-*san* is unharmed. I had to . . . quieten her, so that you and I could speak without interruption.'

'What do you want?'

Sato straightened his shirt cuffs. 'I want what I have always wanted: the sword, if you will. Kusanagi is a national treasure which belongs to the people of Japan. For far too long it has been hidden away. I want it back.'

'What makes you think I have it?' Kenny said.

'I have been watching you, Mr Blackwood.' Sato tapped his sunglasses. 'I saw the *oni* take you into Hachiman's *honden*. That you came out alive and carrying a sword tells me everything. Now, hand it to me, and no one will get hurt.'

'Over my dead body.' Kenny focused and called on Kusanagi as instructed. The sword shimmered into his hand, no longer rusted and pitted; instead, it was brand new, the blade shining as brightly as the rising sun.

Sato blinked. 'If you insist.' He drew in the air with his right hand and pointed at Kenny with his left. The air sizzled and a bolt of lightning streaked towards the boy.

The sword leapt in Kenny's hand and twisted to meet the lightning. The crackling energy deflected away at an angle and struck a stone lantern, shattering it into tiny fragments which pattered on the ground like rain.

'Whoa!' Kenny said, his hand tingling. He looked past the blade, at Sato. 'No way am I giving you this sword.'

'Just like your grandfather,' Sato said. 'It would seem that stealing runs in the family.' He gestured and sent a ball of blazing fire hurtling in Kenny's direction.

'I'm not stealing it,' Kenny said. The sword swept downwards, slicing the fireball in two and sending the halves fizzling into the fallen maple tree. 'I'm using it to help people. Do you have any idea what's going to happen?'

'My orders are to retrieve the sword and to return it for safe keeping,' Sato said, considering his next attack.

'Return it to who? Safe keeping for who? Who asked you to do this?'

'That is none of your concern, Mr Blackwood.'

Kenny's eyes widened. 'You don't know, do you? They haven't told you.'

'Told me what?' Sato asked, tendrils of energy rippling over his hands.

'Let me guess: you have until tomorrow to find the sword, or else. Is that right?'

Sato gave nothing away, but Kenny watched Taro's head whip round.

'Have you ever wondered why, after seventy-odd years, they suddenly have a deadline to find the sword?' Kenny continued. 'It's because they need it out of the way. Before tomorrow.'

'Why tomorrow?' Taro growled. 'What's happening?'

'Don't fall for the boy's tricks,' Sato snapped.

'Tomorrow, the bunch of evil tossers you work for are going to use the dragon Namazu to kill millions of people in America.'

'That . . . is . . . not . . . possible . . .' Sato said, his voice little more than a whisper. The coruscating energy in his hands died away.

Kiyomi groaned and stirred. 'Ken-*chan*?' she said. She saw Taro towering above and scrabbled back, her feet kicking at the earth. 'Get away from me, you freak, before I rip –'

'Kiyomi, no!' Kenny called.

Sato turned towards Kiyomi, his face pinched. 'Please, Harashima-*san*, for once, do not let anger cloud your judgement. Reason can only be heard in the absence of noise.'

'You see?' Kenny said. 'That's why my grandfather sent me here, and it's why they sent you only now to find the sword. They're using you.'

'Give me the sword,' Sato said, 'and I will keep it safe.'

'No chance,' Kenny said. 'Kusanagi and I have a job to do. You can help us or you can have the deaths of millions on your conscience. That's the choice.'

'I have my orders,' Sato said, uttering the words without conviction.

'Then you are on your own,' Taro declared, taking a step back. He held out a huge hand to Kiyomi. She hesitated, before taking it and he helped her up.

'Just say that we got away,' Kenny said to Sato. 'After tomorrow, none of this will matter any more.'

Sato exchanged a look with Taro; an understanding seemed to pass between them.

'Mr Blackwood . . .' Sato began. 'Ken-*san*, I know that . . . since the sword has accepted you as its master, I can neither take it from you, nor prevent you from leaving with it. At the same time, I have my orders . . .'

'So does your friend here, but he's willing to ignore them.'

'Sir,' Taro said, 'the prophecy . . . the heir of Kuromori has claimed the sword as his birthright. We cannot stand in the way of the gods.'

'I don't want to fight you, sir,' Kenny said to Sato. 'You're not the enemy.'

Sato nodded. 'I . . . thank you, Kuromori-*san*, for not forcing a decision upon me. I will give you twenty-four hours to get away. If what you say is true, the search will be ended by then. If not . . . I will find you.' He bowed and turned to Kiyomi. 'Kiyomi-*chan*,' he said, and bowed to her too. 'We are now, as you say, quits.'

Kiyomi smiled. '*Ojisan*,' she said and bowed deeply. 'I'll tell Papa that you're well.'

'Ken-*san*,' Sato said. 'Akamatsu. That's who I work for. Good luck. I believe in you.'

'Be careful,' Taro added.

'One more thing,' Sato said to Kenny. 'They have your father.'

'No!' Kenny doubled over, as if punched in the gut. 'No. Not my dad as well.'

'I am sorry,' Sato said. 'My orders were to detain him. I should have realised they would use him against you.'

Kenny glared at Sato. 'How? What are they planning? Where is he?'

'I do not know, but my guess is they will trade his life for the sword.'

Kenny watched Sato and Taro disappear down the stone steps, before asking Kiyomi, 'What was all that about, with the bowing and message for your father?'

Kiyomi sighed. 'Didn't anyone tell you? Sato-*san* is my father's younger brother. He's my uncle.'

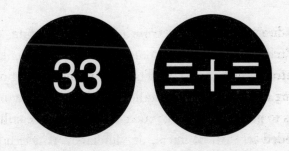

'Ken-*chan*, where is the sword?' Kiyomi asked as she and Kenny hurried across the footbridge and away from the Hachiman Shrine.

'I'm not sure,' Kenny replied. 'This might sound dumb, but I think it's . . . inside me.'

She paused, frowned, then shrugged. 'OK. So we've got the sword, we've got you, and we've got half a day left. All we need now is to get you to Namazu before he does his stuff.'

'You've forgotten something,' Kenny said. 'We have to rescue my dad.'

Kiyomi rested a hand on Kenny's arm. 'Ken-*chan*, of course, but first we have a deadline . . .'

'That could be too late!'

'It will be too late for fifty million people if you stray off course now,' said Kiyomi. 'The prophecy –'

'Stuff the prophecy!' Kenny jerked his arm away and his jaw tightened. 'Don't go there. Just don't. I'm not having this prophecy crap, not if it means losing my dad.'

'Kenny,' Kiyomi said, softly, 'I understand, OK?'

'Where is Namazu?' Kenny asked, still bristling.

'We don't know. That's something that Papa, Genkuro-*sensei* and your grandfather have all been working on.'

'How? My grandad's on the other side of the world.'

'Yes, but he's still in touch with Inari. He still has his network of contacts, in England, America, the government, here, in the *yokai* world. He's still able to connect pieces that we can't even see.'

'Well, that's just great. All this and we don't even know where the monster is?'

They had reached the now-empty car park. Stars flickered overhead like distant candles and orange street lamps lined Route 10, leading back to the city of Usa.

Kiyomi went straight to a telephone booth to call home.

'I thought you said communications were risky,' Kenny said, squeezing into the cramped booth beside her. 'That they could be tracked.'

'Yeah, but it's a bit late now. We're out in the open and the poop hits the fan in a few hours.' She listened to the purr of the phone ringing before Oyama picked up the receiver. Kiyomi spoke quickly with him and then her father, in Japanese.

Kenny stepped out of the booth and whistled tunelessly to himself, hands in pockets. He looked around the deserted car park and began pacing, counting the minutes. It was a warm night, but without warning a chill suddenly washed over him, like a refrigerator door opening. The chirping of frogs and crickets stopped and an eerie quiet fell. The street lights grew dim.

Kiyomi swore and tapped the telephone receiver. 'Hello? Hello? Stupid thing.' She hung it up. 'Weird. Line went dead. I'll have to . . .' Her eyes grew wide as she looked past Kenny and she grabbed his hand. 'Uh-oh. We have company.'

All around, from every direction, ghostly figures in flowing white robes were converging on them. The spectres floated, slowly and silently, coming closer and closer. As they drew near, Kenny and Kiyomi could make out long, unkempt hair, sunken eyes and hollow cheeks.

'*Yurei*,' Kiyomi said. 'Hundreds of them.'

The ghosts flooded into the car park and formed a swirling circle around the perimeter.

'We're surrounded,' Kenny said.

More and more *yurei* gathered, pressing closer, hands outstretched.

'Tell me quickly,' Kenny said. 'These things are harmless, right?'

'It depends on which stories you read,' Kiyomi said, a note of panic creeping into her voice, as the ghosts approached. They were almost within touching distance.

'What's the worst case?' Kenny's eyes swept the parking bays, looking for any gap.

'Their touch stops your heart, they rip out your soul or tear your limbs off.'

'Better keep them away, then.' Kenny focused inwards, finding the quiet place where he had spoken to Kusanagi, and called it forth. The sword shimmered into his hand and he swung it at the nearest *yurei*, whose wizened hand had almost reached Kiyomi.

To Kenny's surprise, the sword affected the spirit as if it had physical form. The *katana* blade sliced it in two and the *yurei* shrieked before melting into the air.

The other *yurei* shrank back at the sight of the sword. It bucked in Kenny's hand and swung towards the nearest spectres as if drawn by a powerful magnet.

'*Kuromoriii,*' one of the *yurei* wailed. '*Give uss peeeace.*'

'Me?' Kenny said, holding on to the sword as tightly as he could. 'You're the ones causing trouble.'

'*Send uss on our wayy or give uss our revenge,*' it said. '*Release uss.*'

'Revenge? What revenge? And how can *I* free you?'

A ripple of agitation pulsed through the ethereal horde. '*Revenge againsst those who sstarved us to death . . . those who left uss to die in the cold . . . those who sstole away our treasures.*'

The sword was straining to reach the *yurei*. Kenny's feet slid in the dirt as the blade dragged him forward.

'Kiyomi! What do I do?' Kenny called, his arms trembling with the strain. 'It's trying to . . . get at these things.'

'Maybe you should let it!' Kiyomi cried. 'See what it wants to do.'

'Are you nuts? What if it flies off and doesn't come

back? This thing's got a mind of its own.'

'Which means it might have a plan, which is more than we do.'

Kenny's fingers were tiring and his grip on the hilt was loosening. 'OK . . .' Kenny said. 'Kusanagi, do your stuff, whatever it is.' He let go.

The sword hung in the air and glowed, its brightness rising to a blinding intensity. Kenny shielded his eyes but, through his fingers, he saw the blade begin to sweep around in a circle, swirling faster and faster. Energy crackled and the nearest *yurei* were sucked towards the whirling centre of the vortex, where they vanished like bubbles of foam down a drain. Hundreds of wailing *yurei* were dragged screaming towards the sword and funnelled away. The shrieking ended, the light died and the car park was empty. The sword dropped to the ground.

'Where have they gone?' Kenny whispered.

Kiyomi stared at Kusanagi in horror. 'Oh my, I never knew,' she said, her hand covering her mouth. 'No wonder the *yokai* fear it.'

'Never knew what?' Kenny asked.

'The sword. It's a doorway to *Yomi*.'

'And what's *Yomi*?'

'You'd call it Hell.'

Kenny sat on a bench by Route 10, watching the sparse traffic go by. Two hours had passed since the *yurei* had been banished and Kiyomi had insisted they wait for her father to send some help. She huddled down under a street light, her foot tapping and teeth grinding quietly, while he tried to make sense of everything that had happened.

He had reached the point where disorientation was starting to feel normal and nothing could surprise him any more. Even the thought of facing a dragon within the next few hours left him feeling strangely calm. He knew it wouldn't last.

The beep of a car horn made him jump and a black Toyota sedan pulled up and eased into the car park. The driver stepped out and bowed to Kiyomi as she made her way over. He wore a black suit, patent leather shoes and his hair in tight Afro-style curls. He opened the rear door and Kiyomi ushered Kenny inside before joining him.

Kiyomi exchanged a few words with the driver and he handed her a thin dossier and a mobile phone. She leafed through the folder, skimming the contents quickly, while the car pulled away and sped towards town.

'Kenny, this is Yoshida,' she said, nodding towards the driver, who waved a three-fingered hand in Kenny's direction. 'He works for my father, as a local . . . representative. We need to get back to Tokyo as soon as possible. Yoshida's going to drive us as far as he can, probably to Nagoya, and we can catch the *Shinkansen* from there.'

'And how long's the journey from here to Nagoya?' Kenny asked, dreading the answer.

'Maybe nine and a half hours.'

'And this thing's supposed to happen at one? That doesn't give us much time to get back.'

Kiyomi sighed. 'I know. Got any better ideas?'

'Start by telling me who's behind this. Who are we up against? Sato gave you a name.'

Kiyomi nodded and handed Kenny the folder. 'Tsuneo Akamatsu, CEO of Akamatsu Heavy Industries.'

Kenny flicked through the dossier, which was written in Japanese, and stopped at a glossy monochrome photograph of a distinguished-looking, elderly Japanese man. 'He's a businessman?'

'Yeah. Papa's been keeping an eye on him for years, as he does with lots of the old-school sympathisers. He emailed me this. As far as we can tell, Akamatsu gave himself over to Hachiman years ago. In return, Hachiman rewarded him with wealth and power. He's built up a vast business empire, fuelled by lots of government contracts, especially military ones.'

'Great. But we still don't know where Namazu is hiding.'

Kiyomi held up the phone. 'People are working on it. As soon as they know, we'll know. Papa's got everyone ready to move.'

'But what if they figure it out too late? Will I still have to face Namazu?'

'Ken-*chan*, what do you think?'

Kenny perched on the seat edge. 'I think we've come an awful long way and gone through a lot of crap to find this sword. I think I've had enough of these guys pushing us around. I think that, even if we're too late and they smash the West Coast, they won't be satisfied and they'll look for a new target. I think, whatever happens, they need to be stopped, whatever the cost.'

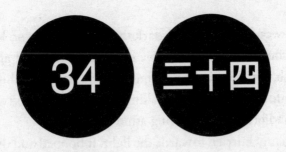

34 三十四

Kenny dozed off on the back seat. The combination of exhaustion, the warmth of the car and the gentle rocking of the suspension lulled him into a fitful sleep.

When he next opened his eyes, Kenny found himself in a thick pine forest. Bright sunshine played in dappled pools around him. A squirrel scurried away, but there was nothing but greenery all around; thick ferns covered the forest floor and the trunks of firs marched as straight as soldiers around him.

Kenny looked for a path, but found no sign of one. Having no compass, or sight of the sun to navigate by, he studied the tree trunks. Green moss and grey lichens grew on one half. That would be the side exposed to the rain, Kenny decided. If he kept moving in that direction, he would at least avoid going in circles. He set off, feet crunching through the ferns and squelching in the mulch.

The shadows deepened and the light dimmed. It seemed to Kenny that he had walked for hours, but the landscape was unchanging. He remained stranded in the forest.

Eventually, it grew so dark that Kenny could no longer see where he was going. He stopped and leaned against a tree, his stomach gnawing with hunger and his legs aching. He was about to slump down when he saw it: a bluish light, softly glowing amid the trees.

Kenny hurried towards the light. It bobbed and dipped before dancing away from him. He stumbled after it, ignoring the branches whipping at his face, as he used its radiance to find his way through the tangle of fallen branches, ferns and hollows.

The light finally stopped and hovered, as if waiting for Kenny to catch up. Breathless and panting, he drew closer and saw an enormous *torii* in front of him, standing in the forest. Kenny stepped under the gate and found his feet on a narrow bamboo bridge arching over a lake, its surface as still and clear as a mirror, reflecting the star-filled sky. Small paper lanterns hung on the bridge, lighting the way. Ahead, Kenny could make out the silhouetted black hump of an island.

When Kenny reached the craggy island, he saw that it was teeming with small brown deer, with white spots across their backs like fallen snowflakes. The deer huddled together, nervous at Kenny's approach.

As soon as he stepped off the bridge, the island lurched and shook, throwing Kenny to the ground. The deer bolted as one and dived into the lake, their heads bobbing as their hooves churned the water. The island began to sink. Kenny dived for the footbridge and held on to it as the island disappeared into the lake. Moments later, the island surged upwards again and began to transform. Its lower section fell away and Kenny saw rows of gigantic teeth before the dragon's head fell upon the swimming deer and swallowed them whole.

Then it turned towards him.

Kenny awoke with a jolt and reached up to massage his neck, which was stiff from sleeping with his head against the car window. Kiyomi was asleep, still clutching the phone in her hand. Kenny watched her. She looked calm, peaceful for a change, with no sign of the underlying hurt and pain that he knew she usually hid from the world.

The driver, Yoshida, noticed Kenny stirring in his rearview mirror. '*Ohayo gozaimasu*,' he said.

'Yeah. Morning,' Kenny managed, stretching his arms. He looked out of the window and saw the eastern sky streaked with bars of gold. He immediately checked his watch. It was 06:04. He groaned inwardly and fought down a wave of nausea. Six hours, fifty-six minutes left to prevent a disaster.

The phone rang. Kiyomi was instantly awake. '*Moshi moshi*,' she said into the phone. She listened intently before lowering it.

'Ken-*chan*, there are three possible locations where Namazu may be hidden,' she said. 'Genkuro-*sensei* thinks

259

it could be Numazu in Shizuoka. Your grandfather suggests somewhere under Tokyo. My father thinks Kashima.'

Kenny chewed on a fingernail. 'That's not really helping us,' he said. 'How did they come up with those places?'

Kiyomi spoke quickly into the phone. Kenny waited, trying not to count the seconds ticking by.

'Genkuro-*sensei* says Numazu has historical links with Namazu. Papa has been looking at Akamatsu's businesses and found quarrying activity in Kashima. Your grandfather has calculated earthquake epicentre patterns, the Ansei Edo ones, in particular. They want to know if any of those seem right to you.'

'Me?' Kenny said. 'Can't they decide among themselves?'

'You're the chosen one of Inari!' Kiyomi snapped. 'You're supposed to have some divine insight here.'

'OK, sorry. Let me think for a sec.' Kenny closed his eyes and kneaded his temples, trying to find some inspiration. He chewed his lip and shook his head. 'Try Tokyo. That's where we're headed anyway.'

'Are you sure?' Kiyomi fixed him with her gaze, looking for conviction in his eyes.

Kenny looked away. 'No, I'm not, but you wanted an answer.'

Kiyomi sighed and spoke into the phone. 'It's done,' she said, ending the call. 'Papa is going to send some men to search the sewer system.'

'Why the sewer?' Kenny asked.

260

'It has to be somewhere deep underground, wet and dark. Like in your dream.'

'Oh, yeah. That.' Kenny felt a gnawing sense of dread, which made his chest ache. The clock was running down and he still had no idea if they were on the right track or what he should be doing.

The driver Yoshida watched him from the rear-view mirror and began talking again. '*Amerika-jin, desu ka?*' he asked Kenny.

'Yoshida's asking if you're from America,' Kiyomi said, her fingers drumming against the window.

'Er, yeah. But before that, I lived in England,' Kenny said.

'Ah, EPL,' Yoshida said, his face breaking into a smile. '*Puremiariigu sakka, ne?*'

Kenny looked to Kiyomi for a translation.

'What? He's speaking English, you know,' she grumbled. 'Premier League soccer. He's a fan.'

'Oh, really?' Kenny said. It seemed a strange time to talk about football, but he welcomed the distraction. 'What's your team?'

'*Manchestah Yunaitedo*,' Yoshida said, changing lane to overtake a cement truck.

Kenny pulled a face.

'*Anata wa?*' Yoshida said.

'Me? Newcastle United. Same as my grandad,' Kenny added.

'Ah, *Kebin Keegan. Aran Sheerah.*'

'Yeah, that's right, though now I'm in America I watch Portland Timbers, in the MLS.'

Yoshida said something to Kiyomi. 'He's asking if you've seen any J League soccer. If you have a favourite Japanese team,' Kiyomi said, her voice flat and uninterested.

'No,' Kenny said. 'How about you? Can you recommend one?'

'*Antorazu*,' Yoshida said, with pride. '*Riigu championzu, desu.*'

'Who?' Kenny said to Kiyomi. 'I got the 'league champions' bit, but missed the first part.' He chewed his fingernail again.

'Antlers, he said.'

'*Antlers*? That's a weird name for a team,' Kenny said.

'Not really,' Kiyomi said. 'You have Sheffield Wednesday and Aston Villa. What's that about?'

Yoshida said something else and gestured for Kiyomi to explain. She sighed. 'He says they're called "Antlers" because Kashima is famous for its deer.'

'Deer?' Kenny sat up.

'Yeah, they even have a pair of antlers on the club badge.'

Kenny's stomach seemed to somersault. 'Quick – what does Kashima mean? What are the *kanji*?'

Kiyomi shrugged. '*Ka* is from *shika*, meaning "deer" and *shima* is "island".'

'It means "deer island"?' Kenny said in disbelief. 'No

freaking way. Yoshida, stop the car! Kiyomi, get your dad on the phone – now!'

'This is the second time you've had a dream and not told me about it, you idiot!' Kiyomi railed at Kenny. 'This is important stuff.'

Kenny shrugged in apology. 'I'm sorry, OK? It didn't seem relevant. It just seemed weird to me.'

Yoshida had pulled the car over on to the hard shoulder of the Sanyo Expressway, while Kenny and Kiyomi stretched their legs and pored over the map.

'How far's Kashima from here?' Kenny asked.

'About five hundred kilometres,' Kiyomi replied. 'There's no way we can get there in time.'

'What about *Shinkansen*?' Kenny tried.

'We'll be there mid-afternoon, if we're lucky. Still too late.'

Kenny kicked one of the car tyres in frustration. 'There has to be a way,' he said, half to himself. 'There has to be.'

Yoshida wound the window down and spoke to Kiyomi.

'Come on,' she said to Kenny. 'We have to get moving before the highway patrol spots us and asks why we've stopped.'

Kenny climbed into the car – and froze. Yoshida had taken advantage of the break to have some breakfast. An open *bento* box was on the seat beside him and he was munching a cucumber stick.

The sight triggered something in Kenny's memory. He grinned and said, 'Kiyomi, I know this is going to sound crazy, but you have to trust me. I've got an idea and it just might work.'

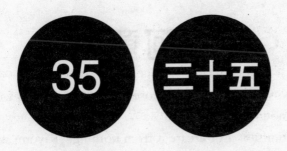

The black sedan left the Sanyo Expressway at the turn-off for the city of Miki, joined Route 175 briefly and made a right turn towards Torimachi. It passed a secluded Sumiyoshi Shrine, took the next right and stopped by a murky green pond, with housing on all sides.

Kenny jumped out of the car and knelt by the water's edge. Kiyomi joined him. 'Are you serious?' she said.

'Remember what Inari told me?' Kenny said. 'Everything is connected. She specifically told me cloud, river and sea. She chose me because I think differently, right? I don't know that certain things can't be done.'

'Like what you're going to do now? Ken-*chan*, it's never been done –'

'Which doesn't mean it *can't* be done,' Kenny said. He showed her the *tanuki* whistle. 'Look, this is tuned in to Poyo somehow and the *kanji* underneath? That says *tanuki*, right? It's the same principle. Now, go ahead.'

Kiyomi rolled her eyes and drew two *kanji* characters in the dirt with her finger:

河童

'Now if we focus on those characters, maybe we can summon it,' Kenny said.

'Summon it or create it from nothing?' Kiyomi said.

'We'll both just do our best, right?'

From a nearby house, an elderly lady opened her front door to let a cat out. The cat took one look at Yoshida sitting in the driver's seat, yowled and bolted in the opposite direction. The door slammed and the old lady hurried to close the blinds.

Kenny tried to remember what Genkuro had taught him. He cleared his mind, focused his will, drew on his *ki* and pictured his target clearly.

'It's not working,' Kiyomi said.

'Shh. Keep trying,' Kenny muttered, concentrating hard. *Come on*, he told himself. *You can do this. You just have to believe it.*

The surface of the pond shivered and rippled as if disturbed by something moving beneath. Two bulging eyes peeped up and a voice whined, '*Nandayo?*'

Kiyomi took a step backwards as a familiar face from the Imperial Palace moat pond climbed out of the water. 'Oh my God. It worked.'

'Wow,' Kenny said. 'It did. Here, I've brought you a present,' he said to the *kappa*, holding up a cucumber stick.

The creature grabbed for the cucumber. Kenny held

it high, out of reach, and the *kappa* jumped and hopped from webbed foot to webbed foot, its hand outstretched.

'Give it me,' it wailed.

'Not so fast,' Kenny said. 'You owe me a favour.'

The *kappa* stopped and turned its frog-like gaze on the boy. 'What favour?'

'I need you to take me and her to Kashima, as fast as you can,' Kenny said. 'Do it and I promise you a crate of cucumbers afterwards. Can you do this?'

The *kappa* eyed him with a mixture of curiosity and hostility. 'Cannot do,' it croaked. 'Forbidden.'

'Can't or won't?'

The *kappa* remained stubbornly silent.

'Suit yourself,' Kenny said, 'because there's a world of difference between can't do and won't do.' He opened his mouth as if to start munching on the cucumber.

'No, wait!' screeched the *kappa*. 'Maybe there is way.'

'I'm listening,' Kenny said, waggling the cucumber.

'Secret ways. Old paths. These take you.'

'And they come out where?'

'Kashima Jingu. Pond.'

Kenny looked at Kiyomi. 'Close enough,' she said. She pulled out the phone and dialled her father's number.

'How long will it take?' Kenny asked the creature.

It held a webbed hand up against the sky and spread the fingers. 'In time it takes sun to go from here' – it wiggled its thumb – 'to here.' It shook its little finger.

Kenny calculated that it was about an hour.

Kiyomi finished the call. 'It's all arranged,' she said. 'Papa's on the move. He and his men will be at the quarry and will meet us there. If we're late, they'll have to go without us.'

'OK, we ready to do this?' Kenny asked.

Kiyomi nodded, biting her lip. Kenny could understand her reluctance to enter the murky water alongside the *kappa*.

'Let's just say goodbye to Yoshida first,' Kiyomi said. 'We'd never have got – Hey, where'd he go?'

The driver's door hung open and the boot was popped.

Kenny sprinted over to the car. He looked inside and saw an empty suit of clothing on the driver's seat. Puzzled, he went to the boot and lifted the lid. He jumped back at the sight of an unconscious man lying inside, his hands and feet tied with nylon cord. It was definitely Yoshida.

Kiyomi hurried over and laid one hand on the man's forehead, the other tracing symbols in the air. 'I'd say he's been out for maybe twelve hours,' she said.

'Twelve hours?' Kenny said. 'Wait, if this is Yoshida, then who's been driving us all this time?'

'I'd say him,' Kiyomi said, pointing.

Kenny looked in the direction she was indicating and could just make out a brown fox scurrying north towards the wooded hills. It looked back and waved three tails.

'Inari's way of keeping us on track,' Kenny said. 'Divine guidance. Foxes are her messengers, right?'

*

268

Kenny held Kiyomi's hand and the two of them waded into the pond. The *kappa* blinked its double eyelids and held out a hand to each.

'Must not let go,' it said.

'No problem,' Kenny said, pulling out a length of nylon cord from his pocket. He used it to tie first Kiyomi's and then his own wrist to the *kappa*'s. 'Let's go.'

Taking a deep breath, Kenny plunged his head below the surface of the water. At first, he could see nothing but green murk and silt, but the *kappa* waved a hand and the water cleared as quickly as a film of oil dispelled by a drop of soap liquid. Kenny was now able to see a glowing circle beneath the water, about two metres across. Its edges were a flickering greenish-gold and the water inside was a different, bluer colour than the pond water.

The *kappa* led the way towards the circle and into the darker water within. As he entered the circle, Kenny felt an incredible suction force, like a whirlpool pulling at him, and he, Kiyomi and the *kappa* shot down a long funnel of water, hurtling at an incredible speed. Kenny looked at the endless tunnel stretching before him and imagined that this must be what it was like for a surfer inside a barrel wave.

His lungs burned and he closed his eyes, remembering again what Genkuro had taught him about channelling his *ki* to control elements and transform matter. He imagined an air bubble. When he opened his eyes again, Kenny saw the quicksilver membrane of an air pocket around his head and breathed freely. He looked for Kiyomi and was relieved to see that she had done the same.

Without warning, the tunnel came to an end and the three travellers slowed to a stop as they hit still water. The dark ruins of an ancient city lay below them. The *kappa* paddled a short distance and Kenny made out another glowing portal ahead. They entered and were once again sucked into a whirling tunnel, thrust forward by the powerful current like bullets down a rifle barrel.

They shot out of yet another swirling vortex, rolled to a stop in the still green water and the *kappa* swam upwards, towing Kiyomi and Kenny behind.

'Done,' it said, as soon as their heads broke the surface. 'Here, Kashima Jingu. Now pay me. Crate of *kyuri*. Now.'

Kenny untied the cords and rubbed his wrist. He and Kiyomi climbed out of the murky pond and lay on the mud, waiting for their stomachs to settle. Kenny felt as if he was still whooshing along a tube of water.

'I'm lucky I didn't eat,' he groaned. 'Otherwise . . .'

'That was like the world's worst funfair ride,' Kiyomi agreed.

The *kappa* stamped its foot and shrieked, 'Feed me!'

Kenny struggled on to all fours and looked around.

'Poyo!' Kiyomi cried in delight as the fat *tanuki* barrelled into her. 'Oh, how I've missed you.'

Kenny looked up and saw Oyama approaching, a

large plastic crate in his huge hands. He set it down by Kenny and opened the lid. It was crammed with *kyuri* – knobbly Japanese cucumbers. The *kappa* did a dance of joy and threw itself into the crate.

Oyama pulled Kenny to his feet.

'*Domo arigato*, Oyama-*san*,' Kenny managed.

The big man almost smiled before grabbing him in a huge bear hug. Kenny's feet dangled loosely before Oyama set him down and wiped the corner of his eye.

Kiyomi was all business. 'We have to move. Did you bring everything?'

Oyama bowed in response and led the way along a concrete path, under a huge granite *torii* and on to the road where a black van was parked. He opened the rear doors, pulled out a steel ramp and stood back to reveal a sleek black motorcycle in the back.

Kiyomi smiled grimly. 'It's show time.'

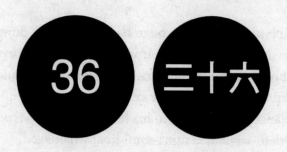

36 三十六

Kiyomi stepped into the van, went to a steel chest in the back and opened the combination lock. She reached inside and pulled out backpacks, cases, holdalls, bundles, boxes and duffel bags. Kenny watched her work her way through the luggage.

'Here.' Kiyomi tossed him a black jumpsuit. 'Dry clothing. That should fit you.'

She peeled off her wet outer clothes and slipped into a black one-piece. She then pulled on a belt with many small pouches, two shoulder holsters into which she placed automatic pistols, another belt with *shuriken* clipped to it and strapped a *katana* on to her back.

'Please don't tell me you're going to need all that,' Kenny said.

'I hope not, but I'm going prepared,' Kiyomi said, stuffing several one-kilogram blocks of C-4 plastic explosive into a backpack, along with hand grenades and detonators.

'So, what's the plan?' Kenny said, zipping his soggy pack of trading cards into a leg pouch.

'Five years ago, Akamatsu Heavy Industries bought a quarry about thirty kilometres north-west of here. Papa became suspicious because there wasn't much granite in the area and the quarry seemed to produce very little to sell. He sent some men in as workers and they reported back that the quarry was a front for a mine.'

'A mine? Digging for what?' Kenny asked.

'Copper, supposedly. Once you confirmed that this was Namazu's resting place, Papa gathered as many men as he could and they're ready to hit the site. Genkuro-*sensei* is with them. They're waiting for us. You ready?'

She pulled on her motorcycle helmet with its mirrored visor and straddled the bike.

'As ready as I'll ever be,' Kenny muttered to himself. He climbed on behind Kiyomi, wrapped his hands round her waist and the bike slipped silently down the ramp.

Kenny had no idea what the motorcycle's maximum speed was, but he was pretty sure that Kiyomi had exceeded it. He was grateful that he was sitting behind her and didn't have a direct view of the lorries and cars they blitzed past.

Kiyomi slowed and pulled off Route 185, heading along a narrow gravel path that led into woodland. She checked the integrated GPS system and homed in on the coordinates her father had given her.

The motorcycle pulled into a clearing and skidded to a stop beside two flatbed trucks with canopies over the back. Kiyomi jumped off the bike and ran along a trail to

273

the edge of a rocky overhang, closely followed by Kenny.

'Kiyomi-*chan*, over here,' Harashima called and held up a hand. He was lying in long grass, completely hidden. Kiyomi ducked down and crawled to join him.

Her father had a pair of powerful binoculars trained on the large quarry site which sprawled below them, a grey gouge in the green face of the earth. A high fence encircled the site, topped with coils of razor wire. Lookout towers gave it the appearance of a prison camp. Huge heavy trucks and bulldozers lay idle and the quarry was still.

Half an hour remained until the West Coast was obliterated. Kenny wiped sweat from his forehead and took slow, deep breaths to calm his racing pulse.

The quarry gates opened and a pair of black limousines entered, gliding as smoothly and silently as sharks. They drove down the sloping road which curved round the terraced rock walls and stopped outside some Portakabins that served as the site offices.

'There's Akamatsu,' Harashima said, looking through the binoculars.

'Who's that with him?' Kenny said, squinting at the distant specks.

Harashima said nothing and handed him the glasses. Kenny looked and stifled a gasp.

'Who is it?' Kiyomi asked.

'My dad.' Kenny lowered the binoculars. His mouth was suddenly dry and his heart was pounding. 'They're holding him prisoner, like Sato said. They want to swap him for the sword.'

Kiyomi grabbed the binoculars and looked. 'I make it four armed guards. They're heading to that open-cage elevator. You can see it, under that headframe structure.'

'That must lead down to the chamber where Namazu sleeps,' Harashima said.

'So that's our way in,' Kiyomi said. 'If Kenny and I can reach the lift, we can get to Namazu.'

'First things first,' Harashima said. 'Akamatsu has a lot of security down there. He isn't taking any chances.'

'How many men have you got, sir?' Kenny asked.

'Twenty-two. They're all good men and I trust them. Genkuro-*sensei* is waiting on the other side of the quarry.'

'And how many goons does Akamatsu have?'

'At least a hundred, and that's only counting the human ones.'

'We're going to need a diversion,' Kiyomi said. 'Leave that to me.'

Four security guards shared the cramped cabin which lay inside the quarry gates. Highlights of the summer *sumo* tournament blared from a portable television set and a pot of coffee simmered on a hotplate. One of the guards yawned and sauntered outside. He fumbled a cigarette stub from his jacket pocket and hunted for a lighter.

A low rumble made him turn round and he stared, the cigarette dangling from his lip, as a five-tonne truck rounded the corner and hurtled towards the entrance. The driver leapt out just before the truck ploughed through the gate and careened down the slope, roaring past the security checkpoint.

The other three guards tumbled out of the cabin in time to see the truck bear down the ramp and smash into the quarry offices, before exploding into a huge fireball, sending flaming pieces of debris soaring high into the air.

The *arooo-gah*, *arooo-gah* of klaxons shattered the stunned silence, and a second truck clattered over the remains of the front gate, scattering the dazed guards. It trundled down the quarry road, closely followed by a black motorcycle with two riders.

Guards in the nearest watchtowers opened fire with heavy machine guns and bullets strafed the dirt road around the truck.

The vehicle slowed to a stop by the burning wreckage of the cabins, and armed men, dressed in black with faces covered, leapt out from the back and ran for cover behind parked bulldozers, heavy machinery, oil drums and portable toilets.

A guttural roar shook the air and two of the men flew backwards. A terrifying green *oni* melted into view, a thick metal rod in its hands. Three more club-wielding *oni* showed themselves amid the men and lashed out, scattering Harashima's men like tenpins.

Kiyomi throttled hard on the motorcycle, gunned the engine and sped towards the nearest *oni*.

'Kenny! Down!' she yelled and, drawing the *katana* from its scabbard, she ducked low, zoomed the bike between the unsuspecting *oni*'s legs and sliced upwards with the sword as she passed. The *oni* howled in pain and fell to the floor, its hands clasped over its groin.

Seeing this, the other three *oni* turned to face the new threat. Kiyomi skidded to a stop, the back of the bike fishtailing in a half-circle.

'Me know you, little girl!' one of the *oni* barked. 'You give me this.' He lifted his head to show a nasty-looking scar across his throat.

'Time to finish the job,' Kiyomi said, dismounting, *katana* in hand.

Kenny stood next to her, straightening his back, puffing out his chest and standing with his legs apart, trying to look as impressive as possible.

'What's the plan?' he whispered. 'There's three of them and two of us. We're outnumbered.'

'Not any more,' said a high, clear voice from behind Kenny.

'Genkuro!' Kenny cried. 'Am I glad to see you!'

The old man bowed. 'And I you, little ones. Now, however, is not the time for conversation.'

'No, it's time for kicking *oni* ass,' Kiyomi said, her teeth clenched and nostrils flaring.

'Remember, you must control your anger before it –'

'Too late,' Kenny said, watching Kiyomi charge the nearest *oni*.

With a roar, the monster swung its iron club down at her head. Kiyomi sidestepped, waited for the club to slam into the ground and swung her *katana*. The *oni* stared in disbelief as its hands fell away, still holding the club. With deadly efficiency, Kiyomi stepped behind the creature and slashed its Achilles tendons. With a scream of pain, the *oni* collapsed to the ground, waving the stumps of its arms. Kiyomi finished it with a single blow.

The other two *oni* rushed towards her. Genkuro closed the gap in a heartbeat, caught one of the ogres by the foot and twisted, sending it flying over Kenny's head to crash into the truck.

The remaining *oni* stopped to size up the frail-looking old man. Genkuro bowed to the creature and then adopted a fighting stance. The monster grunted and smashed at him with its club. Genkuro's left hand flashed upwards and he parried the blow, blocking the huge metal beam with his bare hand. With his right, he landed a chop on the *oni*'s wrist.

Kenny winced at the sound of bone snapping and stared as a ripple went up the *oni*'s arm. The staccato sound of crackling bone continued as the shock wave travelled to the monster's shoulder, along its ribcage and down its spine. The *oni* flopped to the ground, its body reduced to a large bag of skin, as its pulverised skeleton could no longer support it.

A low growl made Kenny turn and he saw the last *oni* disentangle itself from the wreckage of the truck and lunge towards him. At his command, Kusanagi shimmered into Kenny's hands and he felt a surge of energy rush through him. He leapt into the air, soaring six metres straight up and out of reach. The charging *oni* rumbled beneath him and, as Kenny came down again, the sword whipped through the air.

The *oni*'s body crashed to the earth in a cloud of dust, moments before its head bounced to a stop in front of an impressed-looking Harashima.

'*Sugoi!*' he said, with obvious delight. 'Just like your grandfather.'

A spray of bullets chewed up the ground, sending Harashima and his remaining men scrambling for cover.

An armoured jeep, with a heavy machine gun pintle-mounted in the back roared towards them.

'No!' Kenny shouted and stepped into its path.

The tail gunner lined the boy up in his crosshairs and squeezed the trigger, sending a hail of bullets in Kenny's direction.

The sword in Kenny's hands moved so fast it was like a shimmering steel curtain. Sparks flew and bullets ricocheted away. The jeep bore down on the boy to crush him but, once again, the sword moved to protect its master; Kenny threw himself to one side, rolled and rose to one knee as the jeep sped past him. The sword sliced low along the length of the chassis, cutting through steel like it was tissue paper: the front tyre exploded; the pole supporting the gun fell in two; and the rear tyre blew. The jeep slewed wide, flipped and rolled.

Kenny stared in horror at the carnage around him and at the sword in his hands. He felt exhilarated, high on adrenalin, yet sick to his stomach.

'Ken-*chan*, you must go!' Harashima shouted, pointing at the lift cage. Kiyomi and Genkuro were inside, holding the gate open for him.

Kenny looked around and saw scores of armed security guards closing in. 'But sir, you'll need help out here,' he said.

'We'll hold them as long as we can. Our lives are not important. What matters is you stopping Namazu. Now, go!'

'But sir –'

'No. No buts. Go!' Harashima slipped the safety off his sub-machine gun and ducked down behind an oil drum. 'If Kiyomi can leave me to take care of myself, then so can you. Now hurry!'

Kenny sprinted for the lift as the sound of gunfire exploded all around him. He dived into the cage and Kiyomi slammed shut the retractable grille while Genkuro hit the down button. With a mechanical whine, the lift shuddered and dropped into the black depths of the earth.

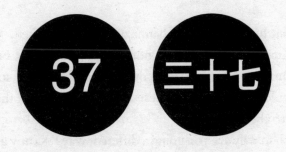

'Kiyomi, it's not too late to stop this thing and take it back up,' Kenny said, raising his voice above the rattling of the lift, which clattered and shook on its way down. 'There's still time if you want to go and help your dad.' His finger hovered over the lift controls.

'No. He made me promise the same thing as you: to finish this, whatever the cost,' she said, a look of fierce determination blazing in her eyes. 'There's no going back – for either of us.'

Sheer rock walls slid upwards past the cage. A flashing amber light fixed to the roof provided glimpses of the shaft as they descended. The clattering of the lift echoed round the enclosed space and the temperature dropped sharply.

The lift slowed and bumped to a stop. Kiyomi hauled open the gate and stepped out into a staging area. Tunnels led off to the left and right.

'Which way do we go?' Kenny asked.

'I will go this way,' Genkuro said, pointing left. 'You go the other.'

'But how do we find Namazu?' Kenny insisted.

'Kuromori-*san*, this is not a real mine. This breach was made for one purpose only: to find Namazu so that he could be controlled. There are few tunnels and they all lead to the same place.'

'Then why are you going a different way?' Kenny asked.

'I am going to find your father,' Genkuro said, 'so they cannot use him against you. You must find Namazu.'

'Come on,' Kiyomi said, tugging Kenny's sleeve. 'We've got thirteen minutes left.'

'Wait. One last thing,' Kenny said to Genkuro. 'Am I ready? To do this?'

Genkuro tilted his head to one side and studied Kenny closely. 'No,' he said, 'you are not, but why does that matter?'

'Why aren't I ready?' Kenny said, throwing out his hands in exasperation. 'I got your stupid sword, didn't I?'

'Because you are still angry and bitter. You must master your hate before your hate –'

'– masters me. I know, I get it,' Kenny said, pulling his sleeve free from Kiyomi's grasp. 'Go. Have fun. Say hi to my dad when you see him.'

Genkuro bowed. For once he didn't smile. He turned and disappeared off into the left-hand tunnel.

'What the hell was that about?' Kiyomi said. 'Genkuro-*sensei* was only trying to help you, you know.'

'Yeah, yeah. Take his side, as usual.'

'Urgh!' Kiyomi slammed a fist against the rock wall,

then composed herself once more. 'You're such a dick sometimes,' she said, before turning on her heel and stomping down the other tunnel.

Kenny hesitated, then ran to catch up. 'I'm sorry,' he called. 'I don't know why I –'

'Shhhh!' Kiyomi hissed. 'Why not just phone them and tell them we're coming?'

'Sorry,' Kenny whispered.

The tunnel was cold, with rough-hewn rock walls. Weak electric lights fizzed at five-metre intervals and cables snaked along the walls. A strange, musky smell permeated the tunnel, and grew stronger the deeper they went.

'Ew. Is that what Namazu smells like?' Kenny asked, wrinkling his nose.

'No,' Kiyomi said. 'It's something else, more like –'

A low growl reverberated through the darkness. Kiyomi drew her *katana* and crouched low. Kenny summoned his sword.

A clicking sound came from ahead and a shadow blotted out the light. Kenny saw a long spindly leg, with a dagger-like claw at the end. It was followed by another and another. The creature scuttled into view. It had the black, hairy, bulbous body of an enormous spider, but the head and horns of a bull.

'An *ushi-oni*,' Kiyomi said, raising her sword.

'That's an *oni*?' Kenny said. 'How come it looks like a cross between a cow and a spider?'

The *ushi-oni* stopped, staying out of reach of the

swords, and bellowed again at the intruders.

'We haven't got time for this,' Kenny muttered. 'How do we get past this – *ummf*!'

He never finished the question. The *ushi-oni* had twisted its body, aimed its spinnerets and spewed a fountain of thick sticky silk at Kenny's face. Kenny slashed and clawed blindly at the webbing, but his fingers became entangled. When he realised he couldn't breathe, panic started to creep in.

Kiyomi rushed to help him, but the *ushi-oni*'s bulk slid across her path. It skittered forward on four hind legs with its front legs held up to strike. It slashed and speared at Kiyomi. She parried and blocked, twisting aside, while the claws flew in from every direction.

'Kenny!' she cried as the monster forced her back, until her heels touched the rock wall.

Kenny saw lights flash before his sealed eyes and felt light-headed: he was blacking out. *No! This isn't about you any more! Your dad needs you, Kiyomi needs you, millions of lives are depending on you.* Genkuro's calm words came back to him and, with one last effort, he ignored the alarms ringing in his head and sought out the quiet centre, where his *ki* was located.

'Kenny!' Kiyomi screamed again, her *katana* flashing and the *clack-clack-clack* of her parrying filled the tunnel. The *ushi-oni* was too fast for her and it had too many weapons; as soon as she fended off one thrust, another two were launched, and with both hands holding the sword she was unable to trace any *kanji* in the air.

She deflected an incoming spider leg, ducking as it slammed into the wall above her head, but the follow-up strike punched through her left shoulder. Kiyomi gasped in pain and a second claw ripped through her right calf. The *ushi-oni* had her pinned to the wall like a mounted insect and opened its jaws to reveal rows of long pointed fangs.

Kenny summoned fire and then pressed his flaming hand to his face. The thick webbing melted away like candyfloss and he opened his gummed eyes in time to see Kiyomi's sword fall from her hand and her body go limp. The *ushi-oni* opened its jaws even wider and reached out to close them on Kiyomi's head.

'Nooo!' Kusanagi materialised back into Kenny's hand and, with all his strength, he struck at the creature's hind legs. The sword sliced through the tough, armoured exoskeleton, cutting the limbs in half. In that same instant, Kiyomi punched her right fist into the monster's gaping maw, driving her arm in as deep as her shoulder, and snapped her arm back before the teeth could close on it.

With two of its back legs gone, the *ushi-oni* squealed and toppled to one side, its belly crashing against the rock floor and legs flailing wildly. It pulled its claws free from Kiyomi and scuttled round to face Kenny.

It lashed out with its forelegs, thrusting them like spears to rain down on the boy. Kenny's sword danced in a sweeping arc and pieces of spider leg clattered to the floor. With only two intact legs remaining, the *ushi-oni* struggled to retreat, pushing its six stumps against the ground. And then it exploded, a fireball erupting from its bloated abdomen, splattering juices throughout the tunnel and sending chunks of carapace ricocheting off the wall.

Kenny ran to Kiyomi. Her leg and shoulder were wet and sticky. He touched the cloth of her jumpsuit and his hand came back stained red. She smiled through the pain and raised her left hand to show Kenny the ringed pin of a hand grenade around her finger.

'Told you – *oni* aren't very bright,' she whispered.

'Come on, we've got to get you some help,' Kenny said.

'No, Ken-*chan*,' she gasped. 'There's no time left. You must hurry.' She shrugged off her backpack, letting it hit the floor.

'I'm not leaving you,' Kenny said. 'You're not going to die down here in this pit.'

'I've had worse.' Kiyomi leaned back against the wall and pulled herself up on to her good leg. 'See? I'm . . . fine.'

She tore the right sleeve off of her jumpsuit and tied it above her wounded calf to slow the bleeding. Leaning on her *katana* for support, she hobbled to Kenny and handed him the rucksack.

'Seven minutes to save America,' she said. 'All you have to do is stop Namazu. Easy.'

Kenny looked at her face and decided not to argue. He nodded, pulled on the pack and led the way.

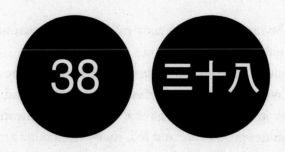

38 三十八

The tunnel dipped sharply downwards and snaked around. Every time Kenny slowed to wait for Kiyomi, she railed at him and insisted he hurry ahead.

He rounded a turn and saw that the passage ended, opening on to a dimly lit space. Kenny stopped, feeling dank, cold air seep into the tunnel, and listened, hearing men's voices echoing ahead. He crept forward and stepped out on to a high, narrow gantry which ran along the circumference of an enormous natural cavern, so large that it could have housed an aircraft carrier. Halogen lights burned all around, casting eerie shadows against the rock walls. Thousands of stalactites hung like jagged teeth reaching down to threaten a skyscraper city of stalagmites.

Far ahead, to the left, Kenny could see the glass windows of an observation platform reflecting the lights. Men were moving around outside and their voices carried into the gloom.

Kiyomi hobbled up to Kenny, peered over the handrail and gasped. She nudged him with her elbow and pointed into the cavern depths. Kenny followed the direction and squinted downwards.

At first, he could discern nothing unusual. The rock floor was dark, wet and strewn with rubble. And then he saw it: the breathing gave it away. A long swathe of stalagmites gently rose and fell, each cycle taking around twenty seconds. Kenny's eyes traced the contours of the movement and he made out a narrow raised section of floor the length of ten football pitches laid end to end.

'That's Namazu?' he said to Kiyomi, his voice a horrified whisper.

She nodded, tracing the creature's outline in the air with her finger. 'Shoulder, back, hind leg, tail all the way down there, back up, leg, body . . . the head's that way.' She pointed in the direction of the observation deck. 'I told you he was big.'

'And I'm supposed to stop that thing – with a *sword*?' Kenny said. 'Is this even going to get through its skin?'

'You've got three minutes to think of something,' Kiyomi said. She leaned back against the rock wall and grimaced, waiting for a spasm of pain to pass.

'You're hurt,' Kenny said. 'I can't leave you.'

'You have to!' Kiyomi shot back. 'It's your job to stop Namazu, remember? Not mine. Now *go*.' She pushed him away.

'All right,' Kenny said. 'I . . . I'll do what I can.'

He turned and sprinted down the metal walkway, his trainers pounding on the grillage, sending tremors reverberating along the scaffold. He looked down and saw that he was running in parallel with Namazu's body, approaching the creature's left shoulder. He had never imagined that the dragon would be so enormous. Seeing it now, this seemed obvious – how else could it shift entire land masses? – but his mind still rebelled against the concept.

As Kenny neared the observation platform, the guards standing outside began pointing and shouting at him. They slipped automatic weapons off their shoulders and levelled them. At his command, Kusanagi, the Sword of Heaven, shimmered into Kenny's hand and leapt into the air as a storm of bullets slammed into his path.

A low subsonic rumble filled the cavern as soon as the sword appeared and a cracking sound echoed as the rock floor began to split apart. Kenny held on to the sword while it bucked and twisted, swatting bullets aside and sending them zinging all around to punch tiny craters into the rock. Stalagmites snapped and rivers of dust poured off the sides of the now rising floor.

Kenny's fingers stung from the vibrations of the bullets along the sword and his ears rang from the echoes of the staccato symphony. The shooting stopped. Kenny lowered the sword and saw the guards backing away from him.

The low rumble shifted to a growing roar. It was like a huge ancient engine was warming up and changing gears.

Kenny looked down and saw why Namazu had been

so difficult to see before: thousands of years of sleeping at the bottom of the cavern had meant that dust, rock falls, limestone deposits and the drip-drip of mineralised water had all accumulated on and around the great beast, blanketing it on the cave floor. Now that Namazu was awakening, all of this detritus was breaking loose to reveal scales as black and shiny as polished obsidian.

An enormous five-toed claw reached up for a foothold and shook the ground as it slammed down. A row of spines, each as thick and tall as a pine tree, reared up along the dragon's back and its massive serpentine body slowly uncoiled.

Kenny watched, in awe, as the dragon's head lifted. It looked like a weird fusion of other animals: the head was equine in shape with long pointed horns that swept backwards; catfish-style whiskers hung down around the mouth which was edged with sharp, feline teeth. Its eyes burned amber with black vertical slits for pupils.

The sword in Kenny's hand radiated a blinding white light. Namazu turned its gigantic head towards it and roared in defiance. The sound filled the immense cavern and echoed back like a freight train in a tunnel. Kenny lowered his head to shield his eyes, and would have run were it not for the sword rooting him in place. He tried to let go but his hands were fused to the hilt.

Namazu opened its gaping jaws to reveal a pink expanse the size of an Olympic swimming pool. The sword dragged Kenny forward, slamming him against the handrail. It was as if Kusanagi wanted to launch itself down the dragon's throat with Kenny as a passenger.

'No,' Kenny growled through clenched teeth, struggling to hold back the sword. 'I control you . . . not the other way round.' The sword pulled him upwards and Kenny found his feet slipping on the handrail, trying to balance himself.

'Namazu! *Yamero!*' a man's voice rang out in a commanding tone.

The dragon froze.

'Not now. You have work to do first. Then you will kill the boy – slowly,' the man said.

Namazu closed its mouth and dropped to lie on the cave floor once more. The light from Kusanagi dimmed and it released its grip on Kenny. He immediately fell backwards, landing in a heap on the walkway. Picking himself up, Kenny saw an older Japanese man standing in silhouette before the observation platform. A younger man in a white lab coat stood beside him, holding a laptop computer.

'You are Kuromori, yes? The child of prophecy? The knight come to slay the dragon?' the older man said to Kenny.

'And you're Akamatsu,' Kenny said, moving towards him, one step at a time.

Akamatsu gestured to his assistant and the man resumed his tapping on the computer. As he did so, the dragon changed its position on the cavern floor.

'Stop right where you are, Kuromori-*san*, and do not have any ideas about breaking the laptop,' Akamatsu said. 'As you just saw, it is the only thing stopping Namazu from eating you.'

The scientist moved away and took up a position on the other side of the platform, where he continued his typing.

Kenny stopped and looked down at Namazu again. The dragon was placing its claws into cave-like hollows in the floor and rearing its back to push up against huge stalactites.

Kenny stared. 'You're controlling Namazu? How?'

'This cave is like a heavenly machine, that only Namazu can operate,' Akamatsu said. 'All of the earth's fault lines converge here. The hanging rocks are like the pillars of the world and the holes in the floor are like pedals. This is how Namazu shakes the earth.'

'But how can anyone control a dragon?' Kenny repeated, his mind churning.

Akamatsu looked at his watch. 'We are a little late because of you, but no matter. I have waited seventy years to see the Americans suffer. A few minutes more won't kill me.'

The dragon thrust its fists down into the pits and strained upwards against the roof.

'What do you know of direct neural interfaces?' Akamatsu said, looking at Kenny with undisguised malice.

'Until now, I'd never heard of them,' Kenny replied.

A cracking sound came from above and dust fell in showers as Namazu pushed. A low rumble sounded, deep in the bowels of the earth.

'My company is a world leader in this technology,' Akamatsu continued. 'You put electrodes into the brain. Apply electrical stimuli and you control motor skills. This is difficult to do in people – they usually die, which is an expensive waste – but many experiments were done on animals. Using these, we created a program to control Namazu.'

'You hotwired his brain?' Kenny said.

Akamatsu smiled. 'Yes.'

Namazu twisted and Kenny heard another low rumble, like distant thunder.

Akamatsu checked the time again. 'We still have a few minutes. The chain reaction is beginning. Each new shock amplifies the previous one. They will build in power until the earth splits under California.'

Kenny's eyes darted from Akamatsu to Namazu. 'But why? Why are you doing this? It can't just be because Hachiman –'

'Do not speak his name, child! You are not worthy.' The smile was gone.

'But why? Why kill millions of people who haven't done anything to harm –'

'That is where you are wrong, boy. You may know my name, but you do not know me.' Akamatsu paused and drew himself up. 'My father was Shigeru Akamatsu, a humble market trader, but a good man and a devoted father.'

'So what went wrong?'

Akamatsu's laugh was more like a bark. 'After the war, there was much hardship in the cities. Millions were homeless. My people lived like dogs, fighting for scraps and sheltering in bomb craters. You cannot imagine such degradation.'

'No, probably not,' Kenny agreed.

'Thousands died from exposure and starvation, left to rot in the streets, while the invaders lived like kings. My father tried to help. He brought food from the countryside and sold it to feed the people, but the Americans shot him and killed him. War profiteering, they called it. Black marketing. But they didn't stop Americans from selling their own goods. They took my father away and killed him to protect their own profits.'

The dragon twisted again and thrust at the floor and ceiling. Another deep tremor rolled beneath the earth.

'Look, I'm really sorry, but that's seventy years ago,' Kenny pleaded. 'It's over. The world is different now.'

'Not for me!' Akamatsu said. 'The Americans still live like kings, growing fat while millions starve. Nothing has changed. They still wage wars and leave broken countries behind. But I will have my revenge. My family's honour demands it.'

'How is killing all those people going to change

anything? It won't bring your father back.'

'No, but it will teach the Americans what it is like to suffer, to lose everything, to live in ruins. And the best part, my master stroke, is that they will beg me to help them and pay me handsomely in return.'

'But how? You're in Japan and they're over –'

'Foolish child! I have been planning this for years. My companies have been buying up emergency relief supplies – generators, tents, blankets, fuel, water purifiers, dried foods, medicines, everything – and stockpiling them so that when the earthquake crushes the West Coast, I will be ready to step in and provide all the help needed, for a price, of course. Perfect poetic justice.'

'You're utterly insane,' Kenny said. 'That's not revenge, that's greed, pure and simple. You know I can't let you do this.'

'You have no choice. I lost my father as a child and so will you, unless you hand me the sword now. If you do, you have my word, upon my family's honour, that I will let you and your father live.'

Kenny's guts wrenched in turmoil. His father's life versus millions of others. It wasn't a choice. Genkuro had gone to help and Kenny knew that his own path was fixed. He would have to trust his *sensei*, that was a choice.

'No deal, you whack-job. The sword stays with me. You want it? Come and get it.'

'Very well. We both know you cannot stop me, you pathetic child.'

Kenny cast around, desperately searching for anything he could use. The laptop was too far away. If he destroyed it, it would unleash the dragon. If he did nothing, a massive earthquake would strike America, killing fifty million people and destroying everything he knew. Akamatsu was right: there was nothing he could do.

And that was when a crazy idea popped into Kenny's head. 'We'll see about that,' he said.

He climbed up on to the handrail, spread his arms and threw himself off, plummeting towards the rocky cave floor far below.

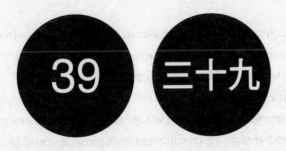

Kenny screwed his eyes shut, concentrating on everything Genkuro had taught him about controlling the element of air, and tried not to think about the stalagmites waiting below to impale him.

The wind rushing past his face changed in strength and direction. Kenny opened his eyes and saw the rock floor falling away as a powerful gust checked his fall and carried him across to land with a thump on Namazu's curved back. *It worked!*

'What are you doing?' Akamatsu screamed down at him.

Kenny scrambled to his feet and, using the row of spines along Namazu's back for a guide, he sprinted up towards its head.

Namazu twisted again and rippled its serpentine body, sending another shock wave into the ground. Kenny slipped on the smooth scales and fell on to his backside. His hands and feet scrambled for a grip on the slick surface and he felt himself sliding off, towards the hundred metre drop to the ground. He rolled on to his stomach and, taking the sword in both hands, drove it downwards, into the dragon's side. The blade sank in, up to the guard and halted his slide.

Time was fast running out. Kenny pulled the sword free, hauled himself back up and pelted the last two hundred metres to reach Namazu's great horned head.

Akamatsu was bellowing orders in Japanese to his few remaining men but Kenny ignored him, held on to a horn for support and levelled Kusanagi for a strike to the top of Namazu's head, as Poyo had shown him.

'Wait!' Akamatsu bellowed. 'Whatever you're doing, it will not work.'

'Let's find out,' Kenny said. 'You said if I destroyed the laptop, Namazu would eat me. So, what's going to happen when I destroy all the electrodes you've put in his brain?'

Kenny took the look of dawning horror on Akamatsu's face as his answer.

'*Sayonara*,' he said, raising the sword.

'Kill him!' Akamatsu shouted at the guards. They grabbed their handguns and took aim at Kenny. 'Now!'

Kenny shut his eyes, braced himself for the gunfire and drove the sword down into Namazu's brain.

Akamatsu's head flew backwards, a *shuriken* glinting between his eyes. Four gunshots exploded like firecrackers in the dark and the startled guards all dropped to the deck. The last shot punched a hole through the laptop and felled the technician holding it.

Kiyomi dropped the smouldering pistol and collapsed, landing heavily on the walkway.

'Kiyomi!' Kenny called out, but she gave no answer.

He stopped and looked at his feet, a deepening sense of dread gnawing at his insides. A low vibration made the scaly surface tremble beneath him, steadily building in power. 'Oh, crap,' Kenny whispered, looking around for somewhere – anywhere – to run.

The rumbling sound continued to grow louder until it resounded throughout the cavern. Namazu's head shot upwards, sending Kenny's stomach down into his shoes. The gigantic jaws opened to release an ear-splitting roar of pure rage which shook the air.

Kenny sprawled in a hollow on top of the dragon's huge head, its curved muzzle stretching before him. He pulled the sword free from the creature's skull and it glowed brightly once more.

Namazu bellowed again and shook its head violently, flinging it from side to side. Kenny screamed as his feet flew out from under him and he fell, his arms and legs flailing into space. The dragon's jaws flashed towards him. Kenny twisted in mid-air and the teeth snapped shut, centimetres from his head. Kusanagi lashed out, slicing through one of the barbels dangling from the dragon's chin. It howled and wiped the wound with a massive claw.

As the rock floor rushed closer, Kenny concentrated as hard as he could, summoning the wind to slow his fall.

A powerful updraught caught him, pushed back and he tumbled to a stop at the bottom of the cavern. Namazu, towering high above, swung its head round, searching for its enemy.

The sword glowed brighter than ever in Kenny's hands. 'No! Not now, you stupid thing,' he growled through gritted teeth, struggling to control the weapon. The sword waved itself through the air, as if trying to attract the dragon's attention.

It worked. A house-sized fist soared through the air, blotting out the light. '*Chikara!*' Kenny shouted, drawing the shape he had seen Kiyomi use on the subway train and, pushing off from a stalagmite, he flung himself aside. The shock wave buffeted him as the dragon's claw smashed into the ground with all the force of a meteor impact. Kenny barely had time to cough among the dust and falling debris before Kusanagi spun him to his feet and sank itself into one of Namazu's fingers.

'Whose side are you on?' Kenny shouted at the sword.

Namazu raised its claw to examine the metal splinter. The sword remained firmly embedded and, since Kenny's hands were unable to release their grip on the handle, he dangled helplessly, watching row upon row of scales slide past at dizzying speed and the floor plummeting below him. An amber eye the size of a tennis court came into view and Kenny saw himself reflected in the black slit of the dragon's pupil.

It sniffed at him, then reached out with its enormous

tongue to scrape him off. Kenny had had enough. He brought both feet up to rest on either side of the sword, leaned back and strained, using his legs as leverage. The huge purple tongue curled towards him.

All of a sudden, Kusanagi came loose and Kenny stood up so quickly that he lost his footing and fell, tumbling backwards through the air, to land on the wet, spongy surface of Namazu's tongue. The shadow of the dragon's upper jaw fell over him as it whipped its tongue back into its mouth. Kenny saw the massive teeth approaching, rolled on to his chest, raised the sword high and plunged it into the monster's tongue.

Namazu roared in pain; the edges of the tongue rose up to form a chute and a blast of fetid wind and saliva ejected Kenny high into the air as the dragon spat him out across the cavern.

Kenny spread his arms and focused. He saw the lights of the observation platform glinting ahead and spun, aiming himself in its direction. At the last moment, before impact, he transformed his body into metal. He smashed through the front window in a hail of laminated safety glass, crashed off a table and rolled to the floor. Metal gave way to flesh as he scrambled to his feet, grateful to still be alive.

The dragon roared and twisted in a half-circle, seeking its quarry. It stamped at the ground and lashed at the rock walls with its rippling tail, scoring deep gouges into the sides. Dust showered from the ceiling.

Kenny crept out on to the gantry while Namazu had its back to him and looked around, searching for inspiration. The cavern floor was a bed of rubble, the stalagmites ground to dust under the dragon's circling weight. Vertical cracks and fissures ran up the walls and across the ceiling, converging overhead like a giant spiderweb.

An idea flashed into Kenny's mind. He slipped off the backpack and reached inside, adjusting the contents before running to the edge of the steelwork. His feet clanged off the walkway and Namazu homed in on the sound, undulating towards him like a giant eel. Kenny lunged at a rocky outcrop, found a grip and hauled himself upwards.

Seeing this, Namazu sped up and threw its massive shoulder into the rock wall. The cavern shuddered, cracks deepened along the walls and rocks fell from the ceiling. Kenny drove his sword deep into the rock and hung on with all his might as Namazu slammed into the wall again and again. The dragon then reached into the observation room, swiping a great claw through the interior, and peered inside.

Kenny began climbing again. He found hand and footholds, pulling himself up as quickly as he dared, keeping to the shadows and the recesses formed by the stalactites.

Below, Namazu reared up on its hind legs, stretched its neck as far as it could and searched for him, sniffing the dank air. Kenny's arms and legs felt like jelly, but he knew he mustn't stop. He kept climbing.

A crunching, scuffling sound made Kenny look down. His heart missed a beat when he saw Namazu's claws digging into the rock, finding sturdy holds. The dragon began to climb after him.

Kenny closed his eyes, slowed his breathing and summoned his *ki*. With a crackling sound, tiny pebbles rained down off the cavern wall and thousands of fine roots appeared, pushing their way out of the rock and interweaving to form a coarse mesh. They grew round Namazu's claws and the dragon stopped to sniff at them. It then ripped its hands free and began climbing again. Kenny waited until the dragon had its belly against the roots before changing them into fire.

The wall ignited, sending a sheet of flame around the startled Namazu. It screeched, jumped back from the blaze and fell, landing on its back with an earth-shaking crash. Kenny looked down, summoned Kusanagi to hand and slashed at a nearby stalactite. The sword sliced through the rock and the huge stone dagger plunged downwards.

'Heads up!' Kenny shouted.

Namazu raised its head just as the stalactite bore down, spearing into its left eye. With a deafening howl of agony, the dragon thrashed against the ground, trying to dislodge the stone shard.

Kenny made his way higher up the ceiling, hanging upside down from the network of roots. He was exhausted, but forced himself to make one last effort. He hooked his feet into the roots, freed his arms and slipped off the backpack. Holding it in one hand, he thrust Kusanagi into the rock with the other, carving out a narrow hole. He crammed the rucksack into the opening, counted to three, and let go, falling into a gust that swept him away.

The C-4 plastic explosive ripped through the rock ceiling and the resulting shock wave blasted along the many fractures, shattering the stone slabs that had supported each other for millennia. While Kenny floated downwards, as softly as a feather, he almost felt sorry for the dragon, writhing far below, unaware of the thousands of tonnes of rock that were free-falling towards it.

Namazu looked up; its one good eye widened before the avalanche of rock thundered down upon its head and shoulders, burying it alive.

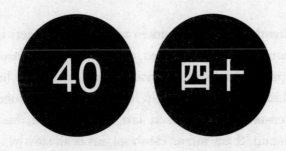

Kenny drifted down, settling near Kiyomi's fallen body, which lay crumpled on the walkway leading to the observation deck. His heart sank and he knelt beside her, lifting her bloodied face from the metal grillage, gently pulling against the stickiness and smoothing the imprinted grid lines.

Congealed blood stiffened her clothes and she lay cold and limp in his arms. Kenny listened for a heartbeat but there was no sound. He pressed his face against hers and hot, stinging tears ran down his cheeks.

'Kuromori-*san*! You did it. You did it!'

Kenny looked up, wiping his eyes to clear them. Sato was standing on the platform, surveying the damage. Taro moved behind him, stepping over bodies.

'It's Kiyomi,' Kenny said, his voice sounding strange and distant to his ears. 'She's . . . she needs help . . .'

Sato broke into a run and came to crouch beside Kenny, a stricken look on his face.

'Please,' he said, motioning for Kenny to release his grip on Kiyomi's shoulders. Kenny watched the government man gently lay his niece down and trace characters in the air around her. Sato frowned, jaw clenched, and furiously drew more shapes of increasing complexity. Taro leaned over him, watching carefully, his fingers twisting together.

'Ken-*san*,' Sato said, at last, leaning back, his eyes welling up. 'I am sorry.' He shook his head slowly.

'No,' Kenny said, his voice breaking.

'She lost too much blood.'

'No! I don't – I won't accept tha–'

A man's voice came from behind him. 'Kenny? Is that –?'

Kenny stumbled to his feet. 'Dad?'

Charles Blackwood closed the gap and threw his arms round his son, squeezing him tightly. 'Kenny, I thought I'd never see you again,' he said, blinking away tears. 'Thank God you're safe.'

Genkuro slipped past and knelt beside Kiyomi's body. He sighed heavily. 'And so the prophecy is fulfilled,' he said. '*One he loves must also die.*'

Kenny broke away from his father and faced the aged *sensei*. 'You could've helped,' he said, distraught. 'Where were you?'

'Kenny, please,' Charles said. 'This man just saved my life. They . . . they were going to shoot me. And he . . . What is going on?'

'Kuromori-*san*,' Genkuro said, 'Kiyomi-*san* is at peace and Namazu's threat is no more. We should go now.'

'No,' Kenny repeated. 'It's not – This can't be . . .

Not after everything we went through.' His eyes filled up once more.

'Taro, carry her,' Sato said. 'Come, Ken-*san*. Please, do not dishonour her memory this way. Kiyomi is gone. You must accept this. You have no choice.'

'There's always a choice,' Kenny said, turning to Genkuro, his eyes blazing. 'Isn't that what you said to me? Isn't that what Inari said too?'

'That was a very different matter,' Genkuro said, his gaze fixed on the ground. 'Kiyomi-*san* is gone. Her spirit has left her body.'

Kenny shook his head. 'No, she can't be. This isn't fair. How can we come through all this and share so much, only for . . .?' He wiped his nose on his sleeve. 'Wait.' Kenny fixed his eyes on Genkuro. 'You said her spirit, her *ki*, is gone, right?'

'Yes, that is so.'

'Then . . . what if I gave her some of my *ki*, you know, like a transplant or a transfusion? Would that –?'

'Ken-*san*, I know you are hurting,' Genkuro said. 'You and Kiyomi-*san* were close, but, in spite of your pain, you must accept she is gone.'

'No. I watched my mother die.' Kenny flashed a defiant look at his father. 'I'm not going to lose someone else I care about. Not without a fight. There has to be a way.'

'Ken-*san*, you cannot give life,' Genkuro said, his voice becoming harder. 'Only the gods can do that.'

Kenny's eyes widened. 'Wait, I can try. I want to try. I

can do things that you can't. You said it yourself, when I made water without drawing a letter.'

'You cannot create spirit,' Sato said, spacing out each word. 'You can only shape it with your will.'

'What if I gave her my spirit? Would that work?'

'This is madness,' Sato said, spreading his hands.

'But would it work?' Kenny insisted.

'It might,' Taro said, 'but only at the cost of your life. It would need all of your *ki*.'

Sato glared at the *oni*.

'I'm willing to do that,' Kenny said, drawing a deep breath.

'No!' Sato, Genkuro and Charles said in unison.

'Kuromori-*san*, your life is too important to treat so lightly,' Genkuro said. 'You –'

'Take mine,' Taro said softly.

'I'm sorry?' Kenny said, staring at him. 'What did you . . .?'

'Please, use my *ki*,' Taro repeated. 'My people have already taken so much from this child: her mother, her childhood, her happiness. It is only right.'

'Taro, no,' Sato said, horrified. 'Old friend, don't do this. Please.'

Taro ignored him. 'Kuromori-*san*, there is a way, if you use the sword. Kusanagi is a portal to *Yomi*. It crosses the two worlds of the living and the unliving.'

'Kuromori-*san*, this is impossible,' Sato warned. 'No one has ever done this.'

'It is forbidden,' Genkuro added, firmly.

'Strike me down with the sword,' Taro continued, not taking his eyes off Kenny. 'Allow it to hold my *ki* and then let it enter the girl. Do you understand me?'

Kenny nodded. His mouth was dry, his face felt hot and his hands were clammy.

'Taro! Don't do this,' Sato said.

'And Kuromori-*san*, be sure to tell her that not all *oni* are bad.' Taro dropped to his knees and tore open his shirt, exposing his brick-red chest.

Kenny's heart was pounding and he felt sick. 'Kusanagi,' he said to the sword that materialised into his hand, 'are you ready to help me do this?' He approached the kneeling *oni*, pressed the point of the sword against Taro's chest and tried to stop his hand from shaking. He had dispatched monsters in the heat of battle, when it was kill-or-be-killed, but this was different. Taro was no monster, in spite of appearances, and to kill him in cold blood . . .

'I – I can't . . .' Kenny whispered, his lips trembling.

'I can,' Taro said. He grabbed the handle of the sword and thrust it into his own heart.

A silvery blue mist flickered up from the *oni*'s chest and entered the sword blade, setting it aglow with the same ethereal colour. Kenny pulled the *katana* free, pushed past the grim-faced Sato and touched the metal against Kiyomi's body. The ghostly flame bled out of the sword and melted into the girl's chest.

Taro slumped sideways and Kenny flopped back on the floor, drained of all strength.

Sato attended to Taro, searching for a pulse, while Genkuro knelt beside Kiyomi. 'What you have done is very foolish and very dangerous,' he said, glaring at Kenny. 'This is not good –'

Kiyomi coughed. Kenny was at her side in an instant. She coughed again, her eyelids flickered open and she convulsed before drawing in a huge lungful of air.

Kenny helped her to sit up and she touched a hand to his wet cheek, letting his tears trickle down her wrist.

'Ken-*chan*, I've just had the weirdest dream,' she said.

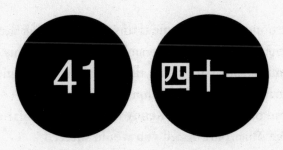

The following day, a memorial service was held. Taro's ashes were buried in a corner of Harashima's compound, and a headstone was laid as the centrepiece of a modest shrine.

A small group of mourners was present to pay their respects: on one side were Harashima, Oyama, Sato and Genkuro; on the other were Kenny, Charles, Kiyomi and Poyo.

'When my beloved wife Mayumi was taken from me, twelve years ago,' Harashima said, 'I would never have imagined that an *oni* would give his life to save my daughter.' He smiled at Kiyomi. 'I allowed hatred to rule my heart for so long, but it turns out I was wrong. I have learned much these past few days.'

Sato nodded but said nothing.

When the short ceremony was over, the mourners made their way back through the lush gardens towards the house. Kenny caught up with Genkuro.

'*Sensei*,' Kenny said. '*Sensei*, please. I know you're hacked off with me over what happened yesterday. Why didn't you try and stop me if this was such a big deal?'

Genkuro slowed and a smile broke across his face. 'Kuromori-*san*, part of me thought that you would fail and that nothing would happen.'

'And the other part?' Kenny prompted.

'The other part hoped you would succeed.'

'Oh, I see. I get it. Sort of.'

'You have another question,' Genkuro said, waiting.

'Yeah. Uh, what do I do with the sword now? Do I have to give it back to . . . anyone?'

Genkuro sighed. 'No, Kuromori-*san*, you do not. Kusanagi chose you to serve as his master and you won him in combat. Besides, if I am right, this is only the beginning and there will be much work for you and Kusanagi to do.'

'Why is it I don't like the sound of that?' Kenny said, with a frown.

'Perhaps because you have finally found some wisdom?'

Sato clapped a hand on Kenny's shoulder. 'Kuromori-*san*,' he said, 'tell me something.'

'Sure,' Kenny replied.

'When you had Namazu pinned, you do realise you could have stabbed the sword into its brain, and channelled your *ki* down the blade to destroy its central nervous system? That would have killed it. Why did you do it in such a difficult manner?'

'Now you tell me!' Kenny laughed.

Sunset painted orange pastels on the walls of Kenny's room as he rolled up his last T-shirt and stuffed it into his backpack. Once his toothbrush was packed away, the last sign of the room's occupant would be removed and it would be as if he had never stayed there.

His chest felt like a weight had been dropped inside. He took out his *tanuki* whistle and set it, standing upright, on the low table.

Knuckles rapped on the *shoji* door.

'Come in,' Kenny said, without looking up.

Kenny's father slid the door open. 'Harashima said I would find you here.' Charles stepped into the room, beamed at his son and reached out for a hug.

Kenny sat back on the *tatami* mat, crossed his legs and folded his arms.

Charles lowered his hands. 'Kenny . . . son . . . I just want to tell you that your grandfather is really proud of you, of what you've done.'

'You spoke to Grandad?'

'I did. As you can imagine, we had a lot to discuss.' Charles stood across from Kenny, the table between them. 'May I?' Charles dipped a knee, about to sit.

'Go on then.'

Charles sat in the traditional *seiza* style, legs tucked underneath. 'Did you know the Japanese have eight million gods?'

'You're kidding me.' Kenny's eyes were wide, in a mixture of shock and surprise.

'*Yaoyorozu-no-kami* is what they call it. I should have realised a few could be real.'

'It's more than a few, Dad.'

'So I see.' Charles clasped his hands together and rested them on his lap. He dropped his eyes, avoiding his son's glare.

Kenny looked down too. A ray of sunlight sparkled off his father's hand, and Kenny saw that the old wedding ring was back in place.

'Kenny, I know you're angry with me,' Charles continued, 'and you have every reason to be. I've . . . not been the best fath–'

'Hah! You can say that again!'

'All right. I've been a very poor role model for you, and –'

'Dad, you're the bloody invisible man!' Kenny exploded. 'You know, it would've been easier for me if you'd been dead!'

Charles winced.

'No, really,' Kenny said. 'Because at least then I wouldn't have had to put up with people asking why you weren't there at graduation, or football matches, or award ceremonies, or any of that crap. You were never there when I needed you. You never saw me learn to ride a bike, never picked me up when I skinned my knee, never saw me score my first goal – all the other dads were there, but not you! You even forgot my birthday.'

Charles blinked to clear his filling eyes.

'What was the point in having a kid if you didn't want to be a dad? Was I a mistake? An accident? An embarrassment to you?' Tears ran down Kenny's cheeks, blurring his father's face.

'No, Kenny, it was nothing like that.'

'Then why did you run half way around the world to get rid of me? Why do you hate me?'

'Kenny, you know I don't hate you. You're my son and . . . and . . . '

'And *what*?'

'And I love you,' Charles whispered. He held his arms out. 'Please, Kenny, don't push me away. Don't become me . . . '

Kenny kicked the table aside and flung himself at his father, burying his head against the man's chest.

'Down in that cave,' Charles whispered, running a hand through the boy's hair, 'when I thought I was going to die, my only thought was that I wouldn't see you again; I wouldn't see my son grow up to be a man. I've missed so much already. I don't want to miss any more.'

Later that evening, Kenny and Kiyomi sat side by side on the steps of the *dojo*, counting fireflies and watching the sky fill with stars.

'So, what did your father say?' Kiyomi said.

'What, about me staying here?' Kenny said. 'We're working on it. First he's got to sort out papers, find me a school. Then we need to have a really long talk with my grandad. There are a lot of blanks to fill in. We'll see where we are after that.'

'Oh,' Kiyomi said, looking away. 'Sounds heavy.'

'Not as heavy as the last ten days.'

The distant sounds of Toyko traffic carried on the soft breeze.

'Did you hear?' Kiyomi said. 'On the news yesterday, a minor earthquake hit the West Coast of America. Scientists are baffled by the seismic profile, because it was building in intensity and then suddenly fell away.'

'Really?' Kenny said, keeping a straight face. 'Well, stranger things have happened, I guess.'

'Yeah, like my uncle showing up to save Papa's backside yesterday.'

'And you falling for a geek.'

Kiyomi smiled. 'Who said I was falling for you?'

'Who said I was a geek?'

They looked at each other and exploded into laughter.

On the other side of the *dojo*, Poyo's ears twitched and he grinned, drawing a heart shape in the dirt with his claw.

Glossary

akaname (*ack-a-nah-meh*) – filth-licker; a demon with a very long tongue

Amerika-jin, desu ka? (*America-jean-dess-kah?*) – are you American?

anata wa? (*ah-nah-tah-wah?*) – and you?

anime (*an-ee-meh*) – film and television animation

bashi (*bah-shee*) – bridge

bento (*ben-toh*) – lunch packed in a box

bo (*boh*) – long staff used in martial arts, about 1.8m long

bonsai (*bon-sigh*) – artificially dwarfed tree

bosozoku (*boh-soh-zoh-koo*) – biker gang

-chan – term of affection appended to a name

chankonabe (*chan-koh-nah-beh*) – a hearty soup

chanoyu (*cha-noy-yoo*) – traditional Japanese tea ceremony

chikara (*chee-kah-rah*) – power

chonmage (*chon-mah-geh*) – a traditional Japanese male hairstyle

daikon (*die-kon*) – type of large white radish
dameh da (*dah-meh-dah*) – it's no good
dojo (*doh-joh*) – training area for martial arts
domo arigato (*doh-moh-ah-ree-gah-toh*) – thank you

ema (*emma*) – small wooden plaque on which Shinto worshippers write prayers or wishes
enoki (*eh-noh-kee*) – type of thin, white, long-stemmed mushroom

futomaki (*foo-toh-ma-kee*) – long thick roll of sushi
futon (*foo-ton*) – a thin padded mattress

gai-haiden (*guy-high-den*) – Shinto outer hall of worship
gaijin (*guy-jean*) – foreigner, outsider
gambatte (*gam-bah-teh-neh*) – do your best; good luck
gi (*ghee*) – a martial arts training uniform

haiden (*high-den*) – Shinto hall of worship
henna gaijin (*hen-nah-guy-jean*) – a strange foreigner; one who adopts Japanese ways
hira-shuriken (*hee-rah-shoo-ree-ken*) – a flat, metal throwing star
honden (*hon-den*) – Shinto main shrine; place where holy object resides
honto, da! (*hon-toh-dah*) – yes, really; so it is; that's right!

ike! (*ee-keh*) – go!

irrashaimase! (*ee-rah-shy-mah-say*) – welcome!

itadakimasu (*eat-a-dakky-mass*) – bon appétit; enjoy your meal

izakaya (*ee-zah-kai-yah*) – an informal Japanese restaurant

jo (*joh*) – a wooden staff, about 1.2 metres long, used in some Japanese martial arts

jubun da (*joo-boon-dah*) – that's enough

kame! (*kah-meh*) – bite!

kamishimo (*kammy-shee-moh*) – traditional Japanese outfit comprised of a *kimono*, loose pleated trousers and a sleeveless jacket

kanji (*kan-jee*) – a system of Japanese writing using Chinese characters

kappa (*kap-pah*) – water demon

kata (*kah-tah*) – a system of repetitive training exercises to master complex choreographed patterns of movement

katana (*kah-tah-nah*) – a long single-edged *samurai* sword

kendo (*ken-doh*) – a form of fencing with two-handed bamboo swords

ki (*kee*) – energy, spirit, life force

ki demo kurutta ka? (*kee-demoh-koo-roo-takka*) – are you out of your mind?

kitsune (*kee-tsoo-neh*) – a fox

koanchosa-cho (*koh-an-cho-sah-cho*) – Japanese Secret Service

koi (*koy*) – ornamental carp

kuro (*koo-roh*) – black

kyokenbyo (*kee-yoh-ken-bee-yoh*) – rabies

kyuri (*kee-yoo-ree*) – slim knobbly cucumber

madoshi (*mah-doh-shee*) – sorcerer

manga (*man-gah*) – Japanese comic books

miso (*mee-soh*) – seasoning paste made from fermented soya beans, barley or rice

mori (*mor-ee*) – wood; forest

moshi moshi (*moh-shee-moh-shee*) – hello when answering the phone

naginata (*nag-ee-nah-tah*) – a long, bladed weapon, like a polearm

nandaro? (*nan-dah-roh*) – what do you want?

nandayo? (*nan-dah-yoh*) – what the heck is it now?

natto (*nah-toh*) – fermented soya beans

ne? – question-forming suffix, like 'eh?'

Nihonjin (*nee-hon-jean*) – Japanese person

nukekubi (*noo-keh-koo-bee*) – a type of vampire with a detachable flying head

numa (*noo-mah*) – swamp

nure-onna (*noo-reh-on-nah*) – a half woman, half snake hybrid creature

ohayo gozaimasu (*oh-high-yo-goz-eye-mass*) – good morning

ojiisan (*oh-jeee-san*) – grandfather

ojisan (*oh-jee-san*) – uncle

okubyomono (*oh-koo-bee-yoh-mon-oh*) – coward

oni (*oh-nee*) – demon, devil, ogre or troll

otaku (*oh-tah-koo*) – ultra nerd; huge geek

otoji (*oh-toh-jee*) – uncle

otosan (*oh-toh-san*) – father

o-yoroi (*oh-yoh-roy-ee*) – traditional *samurai* heavy armour

Puremiariigu sakka (*poo-reh-mee-ah-ree-goo-sak-kah*) – Premier League Soccer

romon (*roh-mon*) – roofed gate

ryokan (*ree-yoh-kan*) – traditional Japanese inn

-sama (*sah-mah*) – term of great respect appended to a name

Samurai (*sah-moo-rye*) – a member of the Japanese warrior class

-san – term of respect appended to a name

sashimi (*sah-she-mee*) – bite-sized pieces of raw fish eaten with soy sauce or horseradish

sayonara (*sigh-oh-nah-rah*) – goodbye

seiza (*say-zah*) – traditional formal way of sitting; like kneeling with buttocks resting on heels

senbazaru (*sen-bah-zah-roo*) – one thousand origami paper cranes held on a string

sensei (*sen-say*) – teacher; master

sento (*sen-toh*) – public bathhouse

shacho (*sha-choh*) – company president

shiitake (*shee-tah-keh*) – type of flat, dark mushroom

shika (*shee-kah*) – deer

shima (*shee-mah*) – island

Shinkansen (*shin-kan-sen*) – bullet train

Shinto (*shin-toh*) – the 'way of the gods'; native Japanese religion

shoganai (*shoh-gah-nigh*) – it can't be helped

shoji (*shoh-jee*) – sliding paper screen door

shuriken (*shoo-ree-ken*) – concealed bladed weapon; metal throwing star

subarashii (*soo-bah-rah-shee*) – wonderful; fantastic

sudoku (*soo-doh-koo*) – a number-placement puzzle

sugoi (*soo-goy*) – great; amazing

sumo (*soo-moh*) – Japanese heavyweight wrestling

sushi (*soo-shee*) – small balls or rolls of rice with vegetables, egg or raw seafood

taiko (*tye-koh*) – barrel-shaped drum

take (*tah-keh*) – bamboo

tanto (*tan-toh*) – short sword, between 15 and 30 cm long

tanuki (*tah-noo-kee*) – Japanese raccoon dog

tatami (*tah-tah-mee*) – rush-covered straw mat

tofu (*toh-foo*) – soya bean curd

torii (*taw-ree*) – traditional Japanese shrine gate

uni (*oo-nee*) – sea urchin

ushi-oni (*oo-shee-oh-nee*) – a monster with the head of a bull and the body of a spider or crab

uwa! (*oo-wah*) – exclamation of surprise, like "wow!"

yakitori (*yah-kee-taw-ree*) – chicken pieces grilled on a skewer with a sweet sauce

yakuza (*yah-koo-zah*) – Japanese gangster

yamero! (*yah-meh-roh*) – stop what you're doing!

yaoyorozu-no-kami (*yow-yoh-roh-zoo-noh-kah-mee*) – eight million gods

yatta! (*yah-tah*) – I did it; yes!

yin yang – Chinese philosophical concept of opposite forces acting in harmony

yokai (*yoh-kigh*) – supernatural creature such as *oni* and *nure-onna*

Yomi (*yoh-mee*) – the underworld; land of the dead; Hell

yurei (*yoo-ray*) – ghost, spirit of the dead

Coming soon

THE SHIELD OF KUROMORI

Sneak preview...

The motorcycle blazed through the mangled iron gates, into the Observatory. The entrance to the main building was partly screened by a roundabout, which was planted with a stand of palm trees encircled by tall sculpted bushes.

Kiyomi wrenched the handlebars to the left, skidding to avoid the obstacle.

'There they go!' Kenny said, pointing at the van, which was disappearing behind a plum-coloured building on the right.

'Where are they going?' Kiyomi wondered aloud, cranking the throttle. 'This doesn't make any sense.'

They hurtled past a small car park and rounded the same three-storey building. Ahead, at the end of a short avenue, was a white, circular structure, with a metal-panelled dome roof.

The delivery truck screeched to a stop beside a staircase leading into the observatory, and the rear doors were flung open by a pair of huge, hulking figures.

'Two *oni*,' Kiyomi growled, eyes narrowing. 'Let's –'

A blinding flash of light cut her short. Kenny barely had time to flinch before a searing wall of hot air slammed them both off the bike, as a section of the nearest building erupted with a deafening roar.

The evening sky wheeled crazily overhead and tree branches tore at Kenny's clothing as the blast flung him high into the air. He crashed down on to a small shrub and slowly rolled to his feet, his ears ringing. Printed pages fluttered around, many edged with orange flames.

'Kenny!' Kiyomi was already up and heaving her motorbike to a standing position. She pointed at the fractured building. 'People are trapped in there. You go and help them. I'll deal with the *oni*.' She swung a leg over the bike.

Kenny opened his mouth to protest, but Kiyomi cut him off.

'Don't argue. You're better at that stuff. I can handle two *oni*.' She sped away, towards the domed building, zigzagging her way round the chunks of rubble strewn across the road.

'*Tasukete*! *Tasukete kure*!' a woman was shrieking, her voice barely audible above the jangle of fire alarms.

The cry came from above and, looking up, Kenny made out two fists, pounding against a cracked window pane on the top floor, leaving red smears on the glass. An orange glow flickered from behind her, while plumes of oily black smoke belched from fissures in the creaking, sagging roof.

Kenny took a deep breath, backed up a few paces and then sprinted towards the burning building. As soon as he hit the kerb, he bent his knees and leapt into the air, his brow furrowed in concentration. A sudden, powerful gust of wind thrust him upwards and he landed on the window sill, some eight metres above the ground.

'Get back!' Kenny warned the woman, summoning

Kusanagi, the Sword of Heaven. The blade shimmered into his hand and Kenny swept it around the frame, slicing through the glass as easily as if it were cling film. The panes collapsed inward and Kenny dived into the building. The Japanese woman stared at him in disbelief.

'Come on!' Kenny shouted above the alarms and the crackle of fire. 'We've got to get out of here before the roof caves in.'

'Go? Where?' the woman said, her eyes darting around.

Kenny ran to the door and recoiled as the intense heat from the burning corridor forced him back. The building groaned like a huge wounded beast and Kenny felt the floor shift beneath him.

'The window! Now!' he yelled, throwing his arm round the woman to propel her forwards, but it was too late.

With an angry bellow, a section of floor yawned open, collapsing under Kenny's feet. He tumbled downwards, into the smoking ruins of the room below, followed by half of the roof.

Having safely parked her bike, Kiyomi was now creeping along the dark passageway leading into the observatory. Guttural voices echoed within the musty dome ahead, at first indistinct, then gradually becoming clearer.

'*Urg-ra n'guh-n-hak ra-rar ng gah*-with this stupid thing?'

'How would I know?' the other *oni* replied. 'I've learned not to ask too many questions. Give me that pole. Not that one; the one behind you. It should be numbered.'

Kiyomi heard the hollow clank of metal against metal.

'Is this even going to work?' the first *oni* said. 'How heavy is this thing, anyway?'

'Seventeen tonnes, more or less.'

'And the frame is going to take that?'

'It only needs to hold till we cut the mounting.'

'Where are the others? They're late. What's keeping –? Wait . . .' The *oni* let out two loud snorts.

'What is it?'

'I thought I smelled a human in here.'

Kiyomi froze, pressing herself against the wall.

The *oni* sniffed again. 'Huh. It's gone now.'

"You're just smelling your own backside. Where's the cable?'

Amid the clank of metal and the grunting of *oni*, Kiyomi crept closer to the end of the passage thatled from the front stairs. The ogres had entered through a ground level access and were in the equatorial room, the huge circular chamber that lay beneath the twenty metre high dome.

The room itself was dominated by an enormous, cream-coloured, double-barrelled telescope, twelve metres long and almost a metre wide. It sat at a 45-degree angle on a complex mounting system of wheels, gears, pulleys and levers, all poised on a single, massive, white-painted column of solid steel.

Wooden beams radiated from the centre of the ceiling like the ribs of a giant umbrella, arching high overhead to form a vaulted roof, connected by thousands of interlocking planks. It had been built in 1929, by shipbuilders who had used their knowledge of ship's hulls to construct the dome.

'Careful, careful . . . Got it!'

Kiyomi craned her neck to observe the two *oni* working on the floor below. One was brick-red with a single horn growing from his forehead; the other was sky-blue with a chipped tusk. Red was supporting a steel tube A-frame, while Blue positioned the legs against the concrete outer wall. Scaffolding poles and heavy steel cables spilled out of canvas bags by their feet. Both *oni* wore silvery overalls.

'Hurry it up. Five minutes left to complete the hoist,' said Red, propping the scaffold against another A-frame to form two sides of a pyramid, its apex above the telescope mounting.

'They'd better be here soon with the cutting gear,' Blue grumbled, bolting the sections together.

Double doors crashed open behind Kiyomi, making her jump. She whirled and saw two burly shadows filling the doorway: more *oni*.

'The party don't start till I walk in,' boomed the one in front. 'You can hit the music now.'

Kiyomi swore under her breath; two *oni* were a challenge, four were deadly – and she was caught in the middle.

To be continued . . .